A STOUT DEATH

The Bethany R. Judge Series
By Thomas J. Miller

An Oktoberfest Death
A Stout Death

A STOUT DEATH

A Bethany R. Judge Mystery

THOMAS J. MILLER

Target Gravity Press

A STOUT DEATH
A BETHANY R. JUDGE MYSTERY

ISBN: 979-8-9858299-0-7

For more information, contact thomasjmillerauthor@gmail.com

Cover by Olivia Sandlin

Target Gravity Press

For my son, Owen

CHAPTER 1

EDWARD ROTH

He never slept well at this altitude. Six summers of doing this annual economic conference and it never got better for him.

But why should it? He was a born and bred east coaster. His body and mind simply felt better near sea level. And, to him, that was what mattered most. Functioning at his best in the nation's epicenters of power, in cities like Washington D.C. and New York. Not in this tourist town. Today, though, he had to be at the top of his game.

He was the second child of William and Ester Roth, mostly forgotten as a kid. He blamed his siblings for that sad truth. First, there was the athletic older brother, always cool and popular. Then there was the younger brother, always seeking attention by getting himself in trouble.

And then there was him. The middle child. His parents had named him Edward David, as if on a whim, agreeing on his moniker only as they had left the hospital. The act had seemed inconsequential, muddied by the exhaustion of labor and birth and the newness of their second child. But, just like that, the boringness of his name had set him on a nondescript path. No sports. No adventures. Only academic pursuits. He had spent his life surrounded by friends whose hands were stained by ink and newspaper print but had never touched a football.

Edward stretched, breathing deeply, pulling the morning and the workday into his consciousness. He opened the hotel room curtain. Squinting, his eyes slowly adjusted to the rush of brilliant, late summer sunshine. Across the valley, climbing into Jackson Hole's pristine blue sky, loomed the Grand Teton. Neighboring peaks filled out the mountain range. Edward had learned their names over the years. Mount Owen and Teewinot Mountain, Mount Moran, the Middle and South Teton. Edward stopped and frowned. He should know more of them by now. Perhaps it was the altitude muddying his mind, or maybe his memory was starting to fade. Age was catching up to him faster than he preferred to admit. High school seemed like only yesterday, a blink of the eye from his first day of freshman year until now. The years had just sailed past. How was that possible? It was some strange trick of the mind. But also a relief in so many ways. High school had been the four worst years of his life. No football trophies. No beautiful cheerleader girlfriend. No student council presidency. None of the things his older brother had done for himself.

Even Edward's mom had expressed hope that high school would be her second son's opportunity to blossom. She had purchased him the nicest clothes she could afford, even begging Edward not to grow before the first day of school. Preferably longer. She had even paid for a nice cut that feathered Edward's hair, parted down the center. It was the look the most handsome boys were wearing at the time.

But all that effort was for nothing. From the first day of high school until the last, he was taunted for his zit-covered face. Teased for the erections that popped up spontaneously in class. Tormented for his gangly body and skinny arms.

He had graduated valedictorian and marched off to Harvard with a full academic scholarship. But his success had felt hollow, somehow not sparking the same excitement of a last-minute touchdown pass or the kiss of a beautiful girl. Edward's parents had been happy with the financial rewards, certainly, but far too focused by that time on their youngest son, who started drinking when he was thirteen and was arrested for shoplifting at fourteen.

Edward had done his best to shrug off the injustice. *Stay focused on the future*, he would recite to himself, not knowing how that future might unfold. He had wanted an education that would help him understand and make sense of the world. Something that would enhance his developing mind. Something beyond the rote memorization techniques he had mastered. Something that would provide him insight into the vagaries of humankind and the world they had created.

Edward rubbed his eyes, feeling the edges of weariness begging him back to bed. He needed a cup of coffee and a trip to the gym. It was an odd combination, he knew. First pasting his tongue with the bitter thickness of coffee, then hitting the elliptical machine. But he had read the suggestion in a book once. The trainer of a celebrity claimed it would kick start the mind. But, more importantly, the metabolism.

Edward had made it his morning routine. And it seemed to work. At just under six feet tall, Edward weighed 175 pounds. Not exactly the best BMI score, he knew, but worlds apart from the obese majority that filled his profession. Hell, even his once upon a time football-stud-of-a-brother had grown fat in his older years. Everyone these days looked like balls of dough. Edward was committed to fighting against that societal tide, knowing each day's effort was part of that battle.

He stared out his hotel room window, pondering the permanence of the mountains before him. "The march of time is relentless," he said to himself. "How do we control change?" That had been the central question of his academic pursuits. And then, ultimately, his dissertation and now his career. Controlling change. Managing the economy. Creating consistency in a human world that is ever shifting and always chaotic. Just the idea felt unthinkable, overwhelming. How could a system be created to control the forces of the global economy when it was impossible to control the actions and behaviors of any single individual?

But Edward had designed the theory. He wrote it and defended it and earned his Ph.D. He had built his career upon concepts of his creation, his star always on the rise. He had climbed the ranks of Washington D.C.'s most influential economic think tank. He was a fixture on the major business news stations. Edward was a well-recognized talking head, polarizing yet composed. And this year, the D.C. rumor mill suggested that Edward topped the list to become the president's next Director of the National Economic Council. It was just a waiting game. Edward could be patient for that. Just like the mountains.

Edward dialed room service and ordered a pot of freshly brewed coffee. He might need more than one cup this morning, and a few extra minutes at the gym to wake his body and turn on his brain. It was going to be a long day. Everyone was feeling the stress of the occasion. The major business news stations and social media were all wondering if the famous economist, Edward Roth, would fall in line with the president. Would he recommend cutting interest rates?

To some extent, it felt like a foregone conclusion. The world economy was in tatters after the explosion in Berlin. Those right-wing Germans had done more than just damage the environment. What kind of bomb had that been anyway?

Nobody knew and Edward doubted that anyone ever would. Some things were destined to remain forever a secret.

But with investors and consumers scared, other major economies were pushing their interest rates to zero. In many cases, even to negative rates. Cheap money would catch everyone's attention, Edward knew. Borrow and buy. That was the prescription for the world economy from everyone else in his profession.

But that was the rest of the world. America was a different story. Consumers already were buying whatever toys and trinkets they wanted. Home builders and home buyers were in equally high supply. The U.S. stock market kept climbing. Travel was up and unemployment was down.

Yes, if ever there was the perfect definition of a Cinderella economy, this was it. How it was possible, even Edward struggled to answer, not with so much chaos engulfing the rest of the world. But that hardly mattered. He would save that analysis for another day. The truth of the situation was just that. The truth.

"Hell," he muttered under his breath, "consumer spending makes up sixty-eight percent of the fucking U.S. economy. If they are fat and happy, why hit the accelerator?"

But that was the president's wish. "I want some of that action," he declared in a speech, referencing the negative interest rates in Europe. "We can't compete with our interest rates so high. They need to come down."

The president's unprecedented comments sparked a frenzy on Wall Street, in markets around the globe, and in the news offices on every continent. Never had a sitting president actively criticized the Federal Reserve. Never had the leader of the country attempted to influence the Fed Chairman's efforts to guide the economy.

"Punch the fucking gas and watch inflation take off," Edward said, feeling his anxiety rise. He eyed the coffee machine in the cubby under the desk. Could he tolerate the packaged stuff that came with the room? He quickly dismissed the thought. Not only was it stale coffee, but the risk of some disgusting contamination in the machine made his stomach turn. Who knew how they serviced those things. God could only guess what some disrespectful vandals might have decided to deposit into the water reservoir.

Did the president even understand economics? There was a strong chance he did not. His tendency was to follow his gut, not the advice of experts. Not careful contemplation and proven research. The Federal Reserve existed to guide the growth of the United States economy, manage target employment rates, and keep prices stable. Cutting rates now risked disequilibrium. It would make the money supply too loose and encourage rampant consumption. That would drive up inflation, ultimately costing jobs and hurting the economy in the longer run. Edward knew that those were simple facts.

And they were also things that were taught in basic micro and macroeconomics courses. Even high school students knew this stuff. They were theories that had stood the test of time. For crying out loud, the Fed had jacked up interest rates before to fight double digit inflation in the United States. How do you crush ten percent inflation? Raise interest rates to twenty percent. Cut back on demand. Temper expectations that prices will continue to rise. Eventually, the economy will recalibrate.

"And it did," Edward said, nodding, agreeing with himself. Sure, the result was an American recession, but the remedy had set the stage for the ongoing expansion. Things kept going good for America because the Fed did the basic economic blocking and tackling, never mind the occasional hiccups that happened along the way.

Suddenly impatient, Edward dropped to the floor and started to crank out sixty push-ups. His goal was to reach one hundred without stopping, an admirable target for a guy that had never touched a weight in high school. He had barely understood fitness all the way through college, and only realized the benefits of staying healthy about ten years ago. That sort of epiphany happens when you can't climb a flight of stairs without gasping for breath.

He became fixated on the push-up idea in the weeks leading up to this trip. It started at an annual rib cookoff in Cleveland, Ohio. There had been so many delicious types of ribs, enough gluttony to almost make him consider adding a few points to his BMI and being happy about it. But, instead, he had just nibbled and strolled, taking in the sights and the occasional flavor, the beautiful backdrop of the Cleveland skyline completing the canvas of his experience.

He had heard some music and drifted in that direction, where suddenly it was less about the food and more about games and fun and experiences. Edward had noticed one booth—a United States Marine recruiting team—and was pleased to see them encouraging each passerby to participate in a Marine Corps challenge. Most tried the pull-up bar, and one stunning civilian lady met the Marine Corps minimum on her first effort. Her boyfriend or husband, perhaps wisely knowing he would not perform as well, opted instead to challenge a young Marine to a push-up contest. It was a close competition, until about sixty push-ups. That was when the civilian slowed, then flagged, and then collapsed to the ground. But the Marine still had plenty left in his tank. Edward ran the calculation in his head and guessed one hundred was a good number. If his body could pump out that many push-ups, he might just be able to defeat a Marine in a similar challenge. Wouldn't that be ironic?

Edward counted. Fifty-nine. Sixty. Then he pressed to the top of the move and jumped, pulling his feet beneath him in one swift, athletic action. That was his favorite part, the grand finale. Once he could accomplish that, he knew he was ready to advance to the next step, adding an additional ten push-ups to the morning. It took about a week for each progression, to feel strong enough at that final rep to believe the thrust would propel his body into a tight crouch, his feet firmly planted on the floor. Tomorrow, his goal was seventy repetitions.

Edward felt energized now, his muscles crying with the burn of lactic acid, his breath quick and labored, his heart pumping from the cardiovascular exertion. He sometimes wondered what might have been in high school, what kind of person he would have become had he discovered this latent athletic talent in his youth. Perhaps burnt out, fat, and complaining about life, like his older brother. Perhaps scraping by on low wage jobs, still saying he was *fighting the man*, like his younger brother. Edward sniffed at that last thought. Shit, he was one of the most well-respected economists on earth. Just look it up online or in the dictionary and Edward's face would be there. He was the definition of *The Man*.

The morning was getting away from him. The first meetings would start in a few hours. It would be bad form to be late. Edward really needed that coffee so he could hit the gym, then the shower. That was his routine. A stupid one, he knew, but things had to go in order. Coffee first, then the gym. Perhaps a little obsessive compulsive, but the predictability had served him well over the years.

He checked the clock. He would call the front desk again in a few minutes if room service had not arrived. This was a time to pause, to reflect on the day to come. His surprise announcement. Patience was key to staying calm. Like the mountains.

Happening just once-per-year, the Jackson Hole Economic Symposium carried the significance of being one of the most important central bank conferences in the world. It started in 1978, sponsored by the Kansas City Federal Reserve, and was first held in Jackson Hole in 1981. The running joke was that those midwestern flatlanders wanted to find a more majestic setting for a working vacation.

There was hardly a place better for that than in the shadow of the Grand Teton, home of the Snake River and some of the best fly fishing in the nation. Jackson was next door to the National Elk Refuge, founded by Congress in 1912 on 1,000 acres of public land and expanded with an additional 1,760 acres purchased along Flat Creek. It was now a sanctuary for one of the largest elk herds on the planet.

Edward smiled. Some conference attendees liked the fact that Jackson was barely a two-hour drive from Old Faithful Geyser in Yellowstone National Park, but Edward appreciated that the conference coincided with fly fishing season on the Lower Flat Creek, right in the heart of the Elk Refuge. Opening day was August 1st. There were some beautiful rainbow and brown trout in those waters. Edward would hire a guide this year, that was for sure. It was a challenging stream—the fish were damn smart—and Edward had never caught a fish on Flat Creek over all his years of trying. He was tired of getting shut out.

There were about 120 people in attendance at this year's conference. The event was limited to a group from specific industries related to the topic under discussion. Select media was also invited. The world markets were watching. Edward could almost hear his talking head colleagues on the morning business shows saying his name, speculating about what news might come from the Symposium, and cautioning how the stock and currency markets might gyrate as a result.

Edward felt his pulse quicken slightly as he imagined what was to come on this first day. So many people were guessing about his position, but nobody really knew, did they? No, Edward had been keeping his opinions to himself lately. Perhaps that should have been a tip-off to the pundits out there. When Edward Roth goes silent, be prepared for something big.

Like so many recent Symposiums, they were back to the tried-and-true topic of monetary policy. How were central banks around the world managing their money supply? Where were interest rates currently, and where were they heading? What would this do to the established economies and to the emerging markets?

Edward had heard all the opinions and speeches over the years. Still, nothing had changed. In fact, they had only gotten worse since the explosion in Berlin. To stimulate spending and growth, struggling countries were keeping their interest rates near zero. Consumers, corporations, and investors had become addicted to cheap money. Almost like crack. And now there was no clear way to break the cycle of dependence. Every time a central bank tried to raise interest rates the tipping point eventually came when investment ceased, spending slipped, and the economy tipped toward recession.

A series of images flashed through Edward's mind. September 11, 2001. It was the day when everything had changed. Planes flying into buildings. New York's World Trade Center collapsing. The country had felt so falsely secure, emboldened by its own sense of superiority on the world stage. But in the aftermath of the attacks, invisible tendrils of anxiety had crept into the veins of the collective consciousness, fed by the fears of central bankers who wanted nothing more than to keep their economies strong and their consumers spending.

And none, Edward thought, were more guilty than America's Federal Reserve Bank. Fight inflation? That was barely an afterthought anymore. Keep the money cheap, basically free. Borrow and buy. Pay it back later. Treat mortgages like Halloween candy, damn the consequences. Keep feeding the addiction. Low interest rates were the world's heroin needle, buried in the arm of the global economic ecosystem. There was no way to pull it out.

Edward sniffed audibly, deriding the thought. He wasn't just anyone. He was Edward Roth. Edward David Roth. He had earned his Economics Ph.D. Fought for and defended his most controversial ideas. Built his career at one of the nation's most powerful think tanks. Professed economic policy on national and international television. So much power. So much opportunity. These things, he swore to himself, he would not squander.

Yet he sometimes wondered how it all came to be, and how what was rumored about his career might occur. Was it a request of the sitting Fed Chairman? Or perhaps an idiosyncrasy of the current president, who seemed to prefer a revolving door of advisors rather than a permanent team? Had nobody in the White House or Congress studied his pedigree, read his dissertation, considered his past speeches or votes to formulate an outlook on how Edward might pontificate from a lofty position?

Edward shook his head. At this point, it really did not matter. Here he sat, and wherever he went, there he was. The same Edward David Roth that rose from the ashes of high school obscurity. The same person that eclipsed all his classmates at the nation's foremost university. The same economics expert now in line to become one of the most powerful men in the world.

Edward's room telephone suddenly rang. He grabbed the handset, startled by the cacophony. "This is Edward," he said, annoyance creeping into his voice. The weight of the day was beginning to descend upon him, the enormity of what he would set into motion looming larger than the Teton Range.

"Good morning, Mr. Roth," said the voice. "We are confirming your room service order. Just coffee, correct?"

"Confirming my order? Yes, of course, just the coffee."

"Our apologies, Mr. Roth. We have some new staff members, and this was somehow overlooked. We are brewing fresh coffee for you now."

That was something to look forward to, Edward supposed. Fresh coffee was certainly better than the burnt down crap they served in some of the East Coast hotels he visited. That one in Baltimore, it was the worst, even though the concierge was one of the nicest guys he had ever met. He had really gone out of his way to make sure Edward was comfortable in the city, had all the information he needed to enjoy his stay and get where he needed to be, and had even put a bottle of wine with a plate of cheese and crackers in Edward's room as an end of the workday surprise.

But the coffee had been horrible. Try as he might, that was the main thing he remembered whenever he thought about that trip.

Edward supposed that if he were married, if he had a wife to watch and critique his behaviors, she would have found a reason long ago to judge his coffee addiction. He built his day's routine around cups of the thick, black liquid. If he were honest with himself, Edward would have to admit it had gotten to the point of being obsessive compulsive. Could his fictitious wife ever understand his coffee love affair?

Edward suppressed a smile, knowing these musings were part of his caffeine cravings. He could create magnificent descriptions of economics and how it related to the human condition. He could compose brilliant concepts that argued the necessity of normalizing the expectations of American and global consumers. He could publish or read his writings and come across as a refined, stately man.

But to bare his soul about coffee? He would fail at that.

Edward knew he was being ridiculous. His coffee infatuation had started so innocuously. Just a cup here or there during college. He could remember the little coffee shop near campus, with its beat-up old couches and chairs and the all-you-can-drink blend of inexpensive Arabica. He smiled at the memory. One dollar got you all the coffee you could stomach. Talk about inflation. Edward doubted he could find a deal like that near any college these days.

Nope, thanks to the power of capitalism, American taste buds had taken a decisive turn to the carnal pleasure of dark roasted, specialty coffees. Truth be told, the country was all the better for it. And not just in the quality of the products they could now enjoy. Coffee was an important avenue of consumer spending, a mere drop in the lifeblood of the economy but invaluable, nonetheless. The entire industry was worth nearly two million jobs and $74 billion dollars to the American gross domestic product, or 1.6 percent. Not too shabby for a bitter drink with questionable health benefits.

Of course, nobody could understand his personal devotion, and it wasn't even about the caffeine buzz. Admittedly, that helped, sure. Edward could confess that. And there was no denying that he was addicted to caffeine. But was that such a bad thing? He wondered about that—usually on the days when he drank more than one pot of coffee. He did not want to compromise his personal health. In the end, the medical research seemed inconclusive, so Edward had picked the side that argued coffee's positive marginal utility. After all, the beverage had served him well up until now.

He looked out the window, imagining now the Boston skyline, not the peaks of the Teton Range, thinking back years earlier when he was preparing to defend his dissertation. Staring out the window back then, his nerves frazzled and his mind in a whirl, Edward could hardly imagine the impending hours of scrutiny, of question and answer, of debate and defend, that stood between him and his Ph.D. He had been naked in his hotel room, thirty stories above Boston, a slick sheen of nervous sweat covering his skin. Edward had kept playing scenarios in his head, attempting to visualize success, trying to light a path in his mind that would lead to the shining moment of congratulatory handshakes and a new title behind his name.

It was at that moment that someone had knocked lightly on that Boston hotel room door. “Room service,” a female voice had said. Edward had slipped on a robe and hastily opened the door.

“I didn’t order room service,” he had said, a nervous tremor in his voice.

The woman had looked at her platter, at the coffee pot and mug, at the sweeteners and cream. She had furrowed her brow, confused. “I am certain they said room 3015,” she had said, her accent light, perhaps Polish.

“You know what?” Edward had said. “I’ll take it. I didn’t order it, but I’ll take it.” He had reached for the platter, his hand softly brushing hers. She had smiled and, in that moment, reminded Edward of an angel.

“I’ll let them know not to charge your room,” she had said. And with that, she was gone.

A believer in serendipity, Edward had set the tray on the desk near the window, pouring the steaming coffee into the mug. The aroma of the dark liquid had filled the room with voluptuous suggestions of chocolate. He had tried a sip, cringing at the heat that bit his lips, pausing as the bitterness enveloped his tongue, then opened into a sweet acidity that tempted another taste. The black coffee had been perfect. He had decided there was no reason to kill it with sugar or sweetener or even cream.

Edward had turned on the radio beside the bed. A Boston station came to life, the deep and resonant voice of a deejay talking about a band from Ireland and their newest hit. The music had started. Edward had never heard the track before.

He had sipped his coffee more quickly, nearly emptying the cup, the music subtle and seeping into his skin. Edward had let his body sway, first right and then left, feeling the sound and then the lyrics. Soon he had dropped his robe and was naked again, dancing in front of the window, hundreds of feet above the streets of Boston. By the end of the song, he had known he would crush his dissertation defense.

Edward's cell phone buzzed, pulling him from his reverie. He shook his head, angered with his lack of discipline. He was in Jackson Hole. That was what mattered now, not the distant past. He could not afford to get lost in his thoughts. Not on a day like today.

He crossed the room to retrieve his phone, fearing that work was already intruding upon the morning. His entire routine was getting out of order. This could signal a bad day. Edward frowned, wondering if perhaps he should close the curtain and pull the room back into darkness. Maybe try for a quick nap. That would reset things. Get him back on track.

Edward grabbed his phone, the screen still bright from a recently arrived text message. The sender was not on his contact list. He did not recognize the number. This was not so unusual. Congresswomen, congressmen, and senators often sent Edward anonymous messages from random numbers. Who was he kidding? They probably had their underlings do the dirty work using burner phones. The messages were typically just subtle suggestions intended to sway his thinking. But nothing that might cause their name to be leaked to the media. It was a clever strategy. Edward enjoyed the game. It was fun trying to guess the person behind the texts.

"You must know many citizens will suffer from your plan," the message read. "Mine especially. We are a fragile economy. Our sources for growth are limited. Will you really be so stout as to move your announcement forward?"

Edward smiled. He could narrow this down quickly to a handful of suspects. What parts of the country were most fragile? Sections of Appalachia. Parts of the South. Areas in the Mountain West. Any regions in America that had been in recession for a long time, never finding their way into the twenty-first century. Or those parts of the nation with limited industry. It would not be hard to puzzle this one together.

There was a knock on his door. "Room service," a woman's voice said. For a moment, Edward felt himself transported back to Boston. He smiled. Perhaps today would work out for him after all.

He was typing his response on the phone's touchscreen as he opened the door. The woman waiting outside was somewhere around middle age, with long blonde hair and almond-shaped green eyes. She stood at the door, her hands holding a silver tray. On it, a red and gold ceramic coffee pot and a large coffee mug promised Edward the caffeine boost his body was craving.

"Please, come in," Edward said, slightly distracted. "Set it on the table. Would you mind pouring me a cup while I finish this?"

The lady obeyed, moving languidly across the room. She prepared and poured the coffee as if she had no next assignment. As if, perhaps, she expected a tip. Edward paused with his clumsy phone typing. His economist's mind was annoyed. There was a time in American history when tipping was really despised. Why didn't that stick? In 1897 the New York Times had called it the *vilest of imported vices* and, in 1915, six states had abolished tipping. Those laudable efforts were repealed in 1926.

Yes, repeals such as that proved that leadership could create change. He might not like that example, but it provided evidence that there was no reason to hold to the status quo. Edward understood the path he was choosing. This would not be easy. There would be fights. There would be arguments. He would be skewered in the press.

Edward continued typing his response into his phone, writing: "I appreciate your message and take note of your concerns. I appreciate also that you see me as strong of character. But more than that, I have done the research. I have created the models. There will be some pain, but we will all benefit in the end. So, to answer your question, yes, I will remain 'stout' and deliver on my beliefs."

Edward re-read his text. He knew it was long but didn't care. If the response somehow got leaked, he wanted an accurate representation of his position. Satisfied after a moment, he pressed send. Placing his phone on the desk, he lifted his coffee for a first sip.

The room service attendant stood there stupidly. She didn't even put out her hand. Edward could appreciate that, at least. He wondered about the etiquette at that moment. Should he fumble in his wallet for a dollar or two? Should he tell the lovely lady to put a tip on his room charge? Should he just thank her and then direct her to the door? Damn these stupid tipping expectations! Should not everyone just be treated as professionals?

Edward heard a subtle *ping*, the unmistakably modern sound of an incoming message. He looked at his phone. The screen was still dark. His next thought was that the stupid room service lady wasn't hurting for money, not if she had enough cash to afford her cell phone service. He had the urge to remind her about how things had been before the advent of the cellular network, then decided she could care less about the ramblings of a man that was probably a decade her senior. Why would she want to listen to stories about how he had grown up with a single wall phone in the kitchen and always worrying about long distance charges? Perhaps she had experienced something similar and was more than willing to pay the price to eliminate the problems that technology had solved. And, he had to admit, there was no denying that connecting the entire world had been another boon for the global economy. Certainly, he could appreciate that.

The room service attendant was reading something on her phone now, a quizzical look on her face. She studied it, her eyes squinting like she was farsighted. After several long moments, she looked up at Edward.

"Senator Young sends his greetings," the lady said.

Edward had started to take a sip of coffee but stopped, lowering the cup from his lips. He cocked his head, surprised. "Senator Young?" he asked. "Of Utah?"

Edward's mind raced to process the sudden turn of events. He did not notice the room attendant's left hand rising toward him, nor did he discern the matte-black, silenced pistol that she was holding. There was a brief sound of bursting air and the quickest sensation of pain in Edward's head. Blood exploded behind him, splattering the walls. Edward lurched back from the bullet's impact, struggling for a moment to keep his balance, then collapsed, a puddle of red already forming around his lifeless corpse.

CHAPTER 2

JACKSON HOLE

Bethany Judge stood on the southwest corner of Jackson Town Square. She gawked at the massive elk antler archway that rose above her, a unique monument to the animals that had long occupied this part of Wyoming. Bethany had not yet seen a live elk, but it was certainly on her bucket list for this trip.

A mother beside Bethany stared down at her phone, reading from the small screen and then explaining to her son. "It says here that there is an arch like this at each corner of the square," she said. "Local Boy Scouts collect the antlers from the Elk Refuge to be used for repairs. Remember the Elk Refuge? We drove past there just a few minutes ago. And listen to this! Each arch lasts about fifty years before it needs to be completely rebuilt. Can you believe that?"

The young son sighed, obviously bored, probably suffering from video game detoxification. Bethany smiled. It would do the kid some good. She knew the benefit of a fresh start, of changing scenery, and at that exact moment she felt a sense of freedom to drift into the square, into a simpler time when the world was far different than today, far different than the things that had brought her to this beautiful place.

Bethany looked over her shoulder at the buildings behind her. "Nice looking bar," she said involuntarily, not realizing the words had slipped out.

"Ooh, that's a tourist favorite," the mother beside her said, jumping into Bethany's musings. "I was reading about it on the internet last night when we were at the hotel in West Yellowstone. It's been around since the 1930's. All the famous people have been there. Presidents. Celebrities. How cool is that? Of course, with our young son here I don't know if we'll be going inside or not. You have to be twenty-one, I'm told."

Bethany looked down at the boy, forcing a grin. Not being able to pop into a bar for a beer was reason enough not to have kids. She had worked far too long in life, both as a police officer and now as a beer expert, to let young children dictate her activities for the day.

"That's unfortunate," Bethany said, lying. "I imagine I'll have to visit there some evening."

"Well, do have fun," the mother said, drawing up closer to Bethany, lowering her voice to a whisper. "Just be careful, you know. If you drink. We're at a high altitude here. Everything I read says that you must be smart about it. It says that dehydration is a big problem for visitors and that you should drink lots of water. Oh, and that alcohol will sneak up on you faster."

"Thank you for that," Bethany said, "except I don't drink alcohol. I drink beer. And sometimes wine and spirits. But mostly beer." She turned to leave. "I hope you folks have a wonderful stay."

Bethany crossed East Broadway Avenue, staying on South Cache Street, walking in the direction of the formidable mountain that towered before her. She guessed it was the town ski hill, probably a local favorite, and imagined that soon it would be filled with the sounds of skis and snowboards schussing on packed powder.

But not yet. It was mid-September, and the Wyoming air was brisk but not yet cold enough for natural snow or the production of the man-made stuff. Bethany could see black dots on the hillside, hikers climbing the steep terrain, making their way up to the mountain summit.

I might need to get some shoes for that, Bethany thought. *Get some exercise. Kill some time.* She continued walking, shaking her head at the poor taste of that thought. *Kill some time? C'mon, Bethany!*

As much as she might want to call this a vacation, it was anything but that. She blamed the Buffalo Daily, her stupid hometown newspaper, and the damn headline she had been unable to ignore. "ECONOMIST EDWARD ROTH MURDERED," it had screamed in bold, black letters. Reading those words, Bethany had felt the faint tickle of memory back to September 2001 – back to the days after 9/11 and the World Trade Center collapse – and had suppressed the sense of dread. Nothing good ever came out of tragedies that poked at the national psyche.

Bethany had purchased the newspaper and paired it up with two vanilla creme donuts. Morning sweets were not her typical style—not since retiring from the police department, anyway—but neither was buying the local paper. The former she had surrendered to her love of beer, selecting that single source for most of her carbohydrate intake. The latter had fallen out of vogue decades earlier, first with the launch of the internet and then the invention of laptops, tablets, and especially mobile phones. News was everywhere, all the time. Who wanted the day-old, stale stuff? Donuts and newspapers had that in common anyway.

Or maybe it was more complicated than that. Donut shops had survived the low-carb diet crazes and were contributing to another wave of American obesity. Newspapers were managing to maintain a media foothold. Maybe it was a nostalgia thing that kept them both around.

Bethany had held the newspaper in her hands, enjoying the unique feeling of the newsprint on her fingers, wondering if the sensation was why some of the wisest and wealthiest investors had thrown their money behind the industry in the last decades. She then devoured the article about Edward Roth's murder while nibbling on the donuts, enjoying the rush of sugar and the reminder of all those days in her cop car, of all those hours spent with colleagues that became friends and eventually felt like family. Retiring from the force had been the hardest thing she had ever done, but she had needed the new life she planned to build—a life about beer, about traveling for beer, about judging beer produced in America and around the world.

Somehow, though, she kept getting dragged into drama.

She had read the headline again and again, mostly because the rest of the article was vague, lacking immediate details, signaling to Bethany's ex-police officer mind that nothing certain was known about the crime. The investigation remained wide open. Local authorities were pleading for calm and regional leaders were deflecting the crisis, claiming a random act of violence.

Bethany liked that idea at first. Why not? Wealthy and successful people were often murder targets. Smart criminals knew what to do. Case the behavior of their marks. Decide when to make the move. Do it quickly and decisively. Strike fast and hard.

But Bethany doubted that money and merchandise were the motive in the murder of Edward Roth, and she knew the newspapers would not tell that part of the story. Not yet. Not while the cops were still sorting out the details. But her imagination—and her police officer intuition—screamed questions in the recesses of her mind. Was it the person, Edward Roth? She barely knew the name, though it was clear he was somebody special. Was it the place, Jackson Hole? She doubted it. She vaguely knew its reputation. A great place for a vacation. Not too far from Yellowstone. An adventure into the great outdoors.

Exactly the type of trip her ex-husband would have always refused.

No, there was just that one line in the Buffalo Daily article, the one that most readers probably ignored, but exactly the one that had sent shivers down her spine:

"Federal Marshals are working with Utah state officials and have reached out to leaders of the Mormon Church to support the investigation."

Bethany had thought about those words, her eyes locked into a one-thousand-mile stare, seeing nothing as her mind had just continued processing, taking its sweet-old time, churning through the possibilities, contemplating the words she had just read. *Utah. Mormon.*

And then the icy question that bit her extremities: *Amanda Lang?*

When that name had risen into her thoughts, Bethany remembered the postcard she had received after arriving home from Munich. Now tattered at the edges, it was smudged and worn from Bethany reading and re-reading the words. The postcard had suggested an ominous tone, a taunting reminder that what Amanda had started in Munich was not yet complete. There was a surprise waiting, a next step in Amanda Lang's plans.

But the nature of Edward Roth's murder did not seem like the logical continuation of whatever Amanda might have planned and, with it, Bethany had struggled to trust her intuition. Killing an economist at the Jackson Hole Economic Symposium? Even one that, according to the newspaper, was on the short list for a White House role? How did that fit into the events that happened in Munich, or what had occurred in Berlin, at the German Parliament? The effects of that explosion and the mysterious compounds released from the blast were still being studied. Experts believed the human and ecological impact would eclipse that of Chernobyl in the coming years.

"A shame, the water over there and everything," Amanda Lang had written on the postcard. *"You'll just have to drink more beer! Why don't you come on out and visit sometime? If you thought that was good, you'll love this."*

That afternoon, the newspaper story still rattling in her mind, Bethany had booked her flight to Jackson Hole. She would get to Utah, Wyoming's neighboring state, after a little investigating of her own.

Bethany stopped and looked around, getting her bearings. She found that, while lost in thought, she had wandered aimlessly and now stood outside the United States Post Office. She gave it a nod of appreciation, surprised for a moment that regular mail delivery could succeed in a Wyoming mountain community. *Neither rain, nor sleet, nor snow*, Bethany thought. *And certainly not the secluded town of Jackson, Wyoming will stop the U.S. mail.*

That was the moment when Bethany smelled it. Sweet and unmistakable, the aroma of roasted grain and boiling sugar wafted over her like an invisible, heavenly cloud. Bethany's heart hammered in her chest, her senses telling her that a brewery was near and that they were in the middle of a brew day. She increased her pace, pressing toward the odor's source, her thoughts reinforcing her anticipation. *It's sort of like when you smell a skunk. If you get a little whiff, you know it isn't close.*

But if you get a massive noseful, you know the critter is nearby. Bethany grunted, knowing she had learned about skunks the hard way, having trapped her fair share while working as an officer of the law. Make one mistake and pay the price. Outside of a bite, getting sprayed was always the major risk.

But a brewery carried little risk, only reward, and a moment later Bethany saw a tan building. Steam rose from a roof chimney. She nearly shrieked with joy. Her mouth began to water, anticipating the first taste of malt and hops. She wondered briefly if they were a lager or ale brewery, but after a moment decided it did not matter. The only question worth asking was about the quality of their product. Bethany beelined toward the entrance, determined to be that judge.

She walked past the brewpub's windows and, glancing to her right, caught a glimpse inside the building. Tall ceilings, inviting. She turned the corner, seeing a tan grain silo emblazoned with the brewery's distinctive green and white logo. *So, this is the brewery my beer nose discovered,* Bethany thought. She tapped her nose, wanting to laugh out loud. It was almost without fault, this *beer nose* of hers. It had become a sixth sense of sorts, leading her to good breweries and brewpubs ever since she became certified as a beer expert. Even when she wasn't thinking about beer—like moments earlier—her beer nose would magically detect places worth visiting. And then she would just stumble upon them.

"Tools of the trade," Bethany said under her breath.

Bethany opened the brewpub's door, allowing the swirling aromas of grain and hops and wood-fired pizza to fill her nostrils. She inhaled deeply. This was the best of all sensations, that moment of tasting with only the sense of smell, breathing in deeply to hit the olfactory bulbs, then exhaling through her nose to cross those smell receptors once more. The entire process enhanced her imagination of the way the beers would dance across her palate, of pondering the subtleties that awaited her when she sipped the first pint.

The brewery was cavernous and industrial. Built upon an old brick foundation, it was modern in every way. Large windows welcomed the mountain sunshine. Sound echoed through the space, giving the room a sense of fullness even when mostly empty, like now. About a dozen people sat at dining tables or at the bar. Most were eating pizzas or sandwiches prepared in the restaurant kitchen. Others just sat at the bar, sipping on pints, reading something or another on their phones or laptops.

The brewhouse was directly in front of her, a stately entrance piece. Clad in copper, it was clean and nicely polished, an homage to the hard work of the brewing team to keep the system looking as good as the beer they brewed. Bethany smiled. A well-cared-for brewery was always a good omen. She felt saliva building under her tongue at the thought of what was to come.

Bethany looked up to the second floor. Fermenters and brite beer tanks lined the area at the top of the stairs. Stainless steel serving tanks sat behind glass walls, above the restaurant floor, obviously well chilled. Bethany noted another set of serving tanks at ground level, equally well-cared for. She nodded in approval. This place had it going on.

Bethany walked to the bar, pulled out an empty stool, and took a seat. The blonde-haired woman sitting beside her shot a quick glance, taking note of Bethany's clothes. The look in her eyes made it clear to Bethany that she needed to find a different wardrobe if she wanted to look like she belonged in this mountain town.

"What's good?" Bethany asked, trying to take the edge off first impressions. To her, of course, everything looked good. The Pale Ale. The Pilsner. Those sounded like the perfect kind of beers to relieve the burdens of travel. Light, crisp, and predictable. And without too much alcohol to cloud her mind.

"I'd have told you to get the Stout," the lady beside her said. "Except it's not on tap right now. It's like a really dark beer. Better in the winter."

Bethany nodded, feigning some ignorance. "Of course," she said. "I'm not a fan of dark beers and warm weather."

The bartender approached, handing Bethany a menu.

"Nothing to eat right now," Bethany said. "But I'll start with a pint of the Pilsner."

"Good choice," the bartender said.

"That Stout has been a big award winner," the lady beside her continued. "From back when they started the brewery. About the time when I first moved here."

"Then I'd think they'd keep it on tap all the time," Bethany said.

"You might, except I think it sells better as a seasonal beer. It has won at least three gold medals at the Great American Beer Festival. And two silver medals. Maybe more than that, for all I know."

The bartender placed the Pilsner in front of Bethany. The golden liquid shimmered from the traces of afternoon sunlight streaming through the tall brewery windows. Thin lines of carbon dioxide bubbles rose steadily from the base of the glass, collecting at the top of the beer, forming a deliciously white head of foam. Bethany lifted the glass, feeling the coldness against her hand. She drifted her nose across the top of the beer, sniffing deeply, allowing the aromas to register in her mind.

She raised her eyebrows, then lowered the glass for another look, surprised. Pilsners might be boring to most fans of craft beers, but Bethany knew them as the true test of a brewery's capabilities. If there was a flaw, there was no way to hide it in a beer like this. And by Bethany's nose, this Pilsner was flawless.

"Don't like the way it smells?" the woman beside her asked.

"On the contrary," Bethany said, "this beer has an amazing nose. Perfect for the style. I can't tell you how many Pilsners are ruined with DMS or diacetyl."

"DMS? Diace...what?"

Bethany laughed, taking a small sip. "Sorry. I get carried away. I'm actually a certified beer expert. And when I find something special, I tend to get excited." She paused. "And I've been rude. My name is Bethany. Bethany Judge."

The woman's eyebrows rose, and she smiled, suddenly interested. "Heather Johnson," she said. "A beer expert, huh? Never heard of that before, but I guess it makes sense. Everyone is worked up and excited about craft beer these days. You were keeping that undercover or something? Doing a little secret shopping, maybe?"

"Oh, no. Nothing like that. I wasn't trying to be secretive. I'm here for something entirely different and, as luck would have it, I stumbled upon this place. And now I'm practically in awe. What a gem of a brewery! I can't wait to try the other beers."

Bethany took another drink, this one much longer, the golden liquid draining into her mouth. She swallowed, suppressed a mild belch, and smiled.

"And if the Pilsner can be chugged, I like it even better. Good for the younger crowd. A way to keep the cash flow flowing. We need to keep these breweries financially healthy!"

Heather sat back, remembering. "Let's see," she said. "I've been in Jackson Hole almost thirty years. And this brewery was here then, but pretty new if I remember correctly." She waved at the bartender, yelling, "Hey, Mike, when did this place first open?"

"The day you moved to town!" he yelled back, flashing a thumbs-up.

"Safe to say they're financially healthy if they've survived this long," Heather said, smiling at Mike's inside joke. "And so, what's this about DMS and the other thing you mentioned?"

"Just some flaws that you might find in beers," Bethany said. "You learn about that stuff when you do the certification program. Once you know them, you can pretty much catch any off-flavors in beers. And light Pilsners like this, well, they tend to suffer from flaws the most. Part of it is the brewing process. Part of it is the malt content and delicacy of the style."

Heather grabbed Bethany's glass and took a sniff. "So, what would it smell like? Or taste like?"

"Well, it's hard to teach you since I'm not finding any flaws in this beer. But DMS stands for Dimethyl Sulfide. It smells like cooked corn. You find that in beers that aren't boiled long enough or have other production issues. Some beers can hide it, but light Pilsners can't. So, to find a clean Pilsner is a good indication that the rest of the beers are equally good, perhaps even better."

"And the other thing you said? Die—something?"

"Diacetyl. That's a buttery taste especially common to lagers. Yeast strain has a lot to do with controlling that off-flavor, but so do other major factors like managing fermentation temperature and proper sanitation techniques."

Heather grabbed her half-full beer and raised it up. "Well then, cheers to great beer in Jackson Hole," she said. "I didn't know we had it that good."

Bethany touched the base of her nearly empty glass against Heather's, looking her new acquaintance in the eye. That was a custom she had picked up in Germany, during her ill-fated trip to Munich. It had seemed odd at the time, holding the gaze of your drinking companion every time you raised a glass for a toast. But, for some reason, it now felt natural. Like something she was obliged to do out of respect for the other person.

"Cheers," Bethany said, finishing her pint. She waved down the bartender. "Hey, Mike, I'll take a Pale Ale this time. And whatever my friend Heather is drinking, one for her, too."

Moments later, Mike served two perfectly poured beers. "A Pale Ale for you," he said, sliding the glass to Bethany. "And an ESB for Heather."

Heather nodded thanks. "It's my go-to during the fall," she said. "One of the beers that has been around since I first moved to town. It's predictably good, but even better as a bridge between summer and winter."

"Sounds like you have a future as a beer judge," Bethany said, laughing and toasting her new friend once more. As their glasses touched, a hollow pang of sorrow flashed through Bethany's mind. She could hardly think of the words *beer judge* without recalling Munich, without remembering Herta Stocker and her cute little play on words. *"Bethany R. Judge,"* Herta had said. *"Does anyone call you Bee? My little Bee R Judge? Beer Judge."*

Bethany closed her mind to the memory. It was too painful, too clear, and part of the reason she was in Jackson Hole right now.

"So," Heather said suddenly, sensing Bethany's turn of mood, "if you're not here on a secret beer mission, what brings you to the most beautiful place on the planet?"

Slowly, Bethany pulled out her phone and punched in her four-digit PIN. The screen opened, brightly lit, the background photo showing Bethany holding the certificate that designated her status as a beer expert. She tapped the icon for an internet browser, waited for it to open, then quickly typed a search request. She selected a result, then turned the phone to Heather for her to read.

"I'm sure you've heard about this," Bethany said.

Heather squinted her eyes, trying to focus, the first indicator of advancing age. "'Murder at Jackson Hole Economic Symposium,'" she read aloud from the headline. "Yep. Pretty big news around here. You can imagine why."

"Pretty big news around the country," Bethany said.

Heather took a gulp of her beer, then paused to pull her long blonde hair over her left shoulder. She stroked it a moment, working out any tangles. Her face looked puzzled. "Are you here to report on it? Doing some research or something? I mean, the FBI and the cops have been around here like crazy. What's another person going to do? Especially a beer expert?"

Bethany cringed a little at the unintentional slight. She couldn't blame Heather for the comment, for not knowing her professional background beyond what she had already shared. But it still stung a little. Bethany knew the caliber of cop that she used to be, and sometimes she still felt the job coursing in her veins. As much as she was glad to have ditched the career, she did not want to forget that she had once been a police officer.

"I was a cop, actually," she said. "In a previous existence. In Buffalo."

"Wyoming?"

Bethany shook her head, slightly annoyed with the question. "You're giving me a hard time, right? Is there really a Buffalo, Wyoming?"

Heather lifted her phone and typed quickly, then showed the screen to Bethany. "Nineteenth largest city in the state of Wyoming," she said. "With a population just under five thousand."

Bethany shook her head again, this time suppressing a laugh. "There's more people in the Village of East Aurora. That's a suburb of Buffalo, New York. And there's a couple of nice little brewpubs in East Aurora, by the way. In case you ever find yourself there, be sure to check them out. They make some really solid beers."

Heather spun on her stool and slid her cell phone into her purse. "I don't want to be rude," she said. "And phones have a way of making people not focus on what's in front of them." She turned back to Bethany, taking a few moments to carefully study her face and physique. Finally appearing satisfied, Heather cocked her head and looked squarely into Bethany's eyes. "Then you are telling me you were a cop in Buffalo, New York?"

"That's right," Bethany said, nodding but feeling slightly apprehensive. "And sorry I got snappy. A woman I met once acted like she didn't even know there was a city named Buffalo in the state of New York. Can you believe that? She asked the same question as you did. Buffalo, Wyoming? I mean, what the hell? Buffalo, New York was once an important city! You know that, right?"

Heather shrugged. "Does it really matter anymore? I'm originally from New Jersey. I'm here now. You're here now. And I'm getting the vibe that you left there for good reasons."

"I'm a retired cop now, by my choice. Being a beer expert," Bethany said, pausing to raise her hands and make air quotes, "and becoming 'Beer Judge' is a second career of sorts."

"So, then you're here as a cop? Is there a Buffalo connection to this whole thing?"

Bethany shook her head. "As a cop, not at all. And outside of me, no, I don't think this has anything to do with Buffalo."

"Outside of you?" Heather asked.

"Just following a hunch. An experience I had when I was in Europe not too long ago. In Munich, actually. And I'm sure you heard about the explosion in Berlin. And now the aftereffects?"

"Of course! Shit, that was awful. Who hasn't? I mean," Heather said, taking a long pull on her beer, "you think this is related?"

Bethany lifted her glass and took a drink, stopping to admire the beer as she swallowed. She pointed to the glass. "And that is an amazing Pale Ale. This place is winning my heart." She placed the glass on the bar. "Honestly, I don't know. I'm following my gut. There are some threads from Munich and Berlin that just might connect to here."

"Well, you know," Heather said, "my mom always said to trust your intuition. She was a born and bred New Jersey girl and it was one of those things she lived by. If she felt nervous about something happening on the school bus, we stayed home that day. If she had the feeling we might have trouble traveling to the grocery store, we didn't go until the feeling passed. Stuff like that. Later in life, I told her it was all unnecessary, that all her concerns were for nothing. Because nothing ever happened. We lived a boring life. And you know what she said? That was because she had always listened to that little voice inside her head and never put us in harm's way. Who can argue against that, right? Disprove something that never happened?"

Bethany again lifted her beer. "To your mother," she said. "She sounds like a wonderful woman. I like her already." They clinked glasses and both took a sip. "Yeah, so that's it. I'm on the path to something a bit different, I guess. I'll leave the big investigation to the experts."

Suddenly Heather sat up straight, realizing something. She held up her index finger. "Hold on," she said. "One sec." She twisted around, pulling her purse off the chair back. She placed it on her lap and dug feverishly, again producing her cell phone after a few quiet curses under her breath. She tapped the screen, bringing the phone back to life, and entered something in the search engine.

"Come on," she whispered, moving her right hand as if encouraging the machine to work faster. "The damn thing is running slow. Ah, here it comes." She punched one of the search results and waited again. A few moments later, she pushed the phone toward Bethany's face.

"Ever hear of this?" she asked.

Bethany read the screen, browsing the story as Heather spoke.

"It happened shortly after I moved to Jackson," Heather said. "The president liked to vacation out here. Did it twice, in fact. A friend of mine even had the opportunity to shake hands with the president and his wife. It was at some sort of private art showing out near the Elk Refuge, toward the airport. Nothing deep, you know, my friend was just a food server but pretty cool regardless. He got a photo of himself with the president.

"But that part doesn't really matter, sorry. What's important, the part that you're reading about, is still one of the great unsolved mysteries of Jackson Hole. Maybe this new situation will eclipse it, we'll see, but this was big news back in the day. Just not much internet to spread the news, you know, so it kind of got lost in time."

Bethany quickly read the story headline and browsed the first few sentences. "A U.S. Air Force plane that accompanied the president crashed into a mountain when departing Jackson?" she asked.

"That's right," Heather said. "Everyone on board was killed."

Bethany touched the screen, catching the main points as she scrolled through the story. "It says here eight crew members and a Secret Service agent."

"That's right. And the president had left Jackson by helicopter just a few hours earlier. I guess the plane that went down was carrying presidential vehicles and other equipment."

"Ok," Bethany said, still reading. "But so what? It says it was an accident. That the crew failed to monitor the terrain around Jackson Hole airport."

"Now just think about that for a second," Heather said. "They reported that, great. And military officials confirmed it, wonderful. But come on! Everyone in Jackson knows that was a crock of shit. Those were professional pilots. Military pilots! A crew of eight! Do you really think eight professional, military pilots would have screwed up their pre-flight and in-flight protocols and simply flown into a mountain? If the internet existed back then like it does today, the conspiracy theories would have been everywhere. Remember that airline situation a bunch of years back when the co-pilot locked the cabin after the captain walked out to use the restroom? And then crashed the plane into the mountains? Would you call that an accident?"

A rush of wind swept through the brewpub, pulling Bethany's attention from the conversation. She turned her head toward the door, squinting against the light that poured in through the brewery's large windows. A young family of three stood in the doorway, all smiles and excitement. Their son pulled on his mother's dress. "Pizza!" he said over and over, his pudgy face lit with expectation. The father swept up the boy in his arms, pointing his wife to a table in the middle of the restaurant. Moments later, they were seated and perusing their menus.

"That reminds me..." Heather said thoughtfully, pausing to contemplate. "Holy shit, I haven't thought about this in years." She scooted her stool away from the bar, grabbing Bethany's arm.

"What is it?" asked Bethany.

"I need to show you something," Heather said, excitement rising in her voice. "Grab your beer. Hey Mike, keep our spots. We'll be right back."

They walked to the brewpub's front door and stopped. Heather turned slightly so that they faced the base of the stairs that ran up to the second level. Bethany glanced over at the brewhouse to her right, then up to the fermentation room and serving tanks, admiration again swelling in her heart. Heather broke the spell when she pointed to the basement stairs.

"See that?" she asked.

"Stairs to the basement?" Bethany asked. "Sure."

"Not just that," Heather said. "You need to think back in time, right? To when this place first opened. It was different. I knew one of the assistant brewers. He worked here for a while. Downstairs, that was where the bottling line used to be. They packaged those big bottles back then; you know what I'm talking about?"

"The bomber bottles, yeah, twenty-two ouncers," Bethany said. "They're still around, just not so much anymore. Canning is easier, cheaper. One might argue that cans keep beer fresher, too."

"Well, whatever," Heather said, waving her hand at the unnecessary commentary. "So, now if you look at the back of the brewing tanks here—"

"The brewhouse," Bethany corrected.

"Ok, fine. The brewhouse. So, the back of that tank there, that's where they remove the grain."

Bethany looked, nodding. "Right, the mash tun. They need to remove the spent grain after the mash. Looks like they pull it out of the back port with this system. Probably with a big rake or something. That's a manual process. Lots of new systems these days have bottom ports and a mechanical arm inside the mash tun, which spins inside the vessel and pushes the spent grain into the open port."

"Okay, that's great," Heather said, a hint of irritation in her voice. "But check this out. There's a small lift back there, on the other side of that wall. They take the grain down the lift, through the basement, and back up another lift out onto the loading dock. Follow me, I'll show you outside."

They walked outdoors onto the wooden deck. Bethany took a sip of her beer, reveling in the flavor of the Pale Ale, its crispness mimicking the mountain air. She loved the generous dry hopping, an homage to this classic American interpretation of the style.

"Stop right here," Heather said, pointing to her right. "See this fence? Kind of protects the people sitting on the deck from having to look at the loading dock."

"Fair enough. I'd probably prefer not to look at a grain dumpster when drinking my beer. Ruins the ambience."

"But what is a fence on one side is a shroud on the other, wouldn't you say?"

Bethany frowned. "What do you mean?"

"My friend worked here, right?" Heather said. "I told you that. And this was shortly after the brewery opened. When the president was coming here for his summer vacations. He came to Jackson two years in a row, so keep that in mind."

Bethany took another swig of her beer, uncertain where Heather was taking this. She was not feeling patient now that the alcohol was seeping into her veins. She felt the familiar lift, the steady onrush of the high that added to the pleasure of drinking beer. Her career as a beer expert was not just about the hops. It was not only about the barley, yeast, water, or the beer making process. It was about the entire experience. And getting tipsy was the pinnacle of that journey.

"And in the year before that plane crash," Heather continued, "the president visited this brewery."

Bethany lowered her glass, swallowing. Her mind turned on that last statement, connecting it back to Heather's story in the brewpub. To the plane that crashed in the mountains.

"A man has to eat and drink," Bethany said. "Even the President of the United States. Did he have any of the beer? Did they get his endorsement?"

"That's the thing," Heather said. "He never made it inside."

"What do you mean?"

"I can't believe I'm remembering all this," Heather said. "So weird. So long ago. Haven't thought about it in forever." She paused to sip her beer, gathering her thoughts. "So, my friend, right? He was working in the basement that day. Doing a bottling run. Back then they used to ship their beer across the country, to Georgia and shit like that. Anyway, out of the blue these guys in suits are suddenly walking around the basement, checking stuff out, looking everywhere. Then they asked everyone's name. After that, they left."

"Secret Service," Bethany said.

"Right. We figured that out later. They were sweeping for the president's visit."

Bethany thought back to the basement stairs, trying to imagine the layout of the basement below the brewery. It would have been filled with equipment, bottles, and boxes. Probably a cold room. It was definitely a place the Secret Service would have searched.

"Now, understand, my friend didn't know anything," Heather continued. "About the president coming to the brewery, I mean. It was unannounced. And he's doing his job, right? Working the bottling line, monitoring the labeler and the capper. All the stupid shit he used to complain about. I remember he said the label glue would cause a terrible mess, a real pain in the ass."

"It sounds like they had a pretty advanced operation already," Bethany said. "A full bottling line for a new brewery is pretty unique, even now. Back then for a start up? Probably unheard of. Especially up here."

Heather shrugged. "I guess so. I don't know. I do know that bottling was always a problem and that my friend complained about it. And they'd fill the boxes with those—what did you call them—bomber bottles, and then stack them on wooden pallets, and pack them all up in stretch wrap. And then there was the clean-up."

"The nasty truth of production brewing," Bethany said. "The glory is in the final product. But the work leading up to that generally sucks." She took another long drink of her Pale Ale, appreciating in that moment all the hard work the brewers had devoted to this creation. As Bethany swallowed, feeling the beer slide down her throat, the prickly bite of carbonation still on her tongue, she wondered where Heather was taking this story. Bethany was down to her last sip and the beer list inside was inviting her back.

"It was during the clean-up that everything happened," Heather continued. "When everything made sense. It was after dark. My friend had been drinking during the bottling run, so he was pretty tipsy. And he was hauling garbage and whatnot up to the dumpster, behind that fence. Like I said, there's a lift back there from the basement to the loading dock.

"My friend comes up the lift. This is what he told me, right?" Heather's voice rose, nervousness and excitement climbing with her recollection. "He comes up the lift and it's dark and he's sort of drunk. And there's a ruckus going on, behind the fence from where he's standing. So, everything is happening right here, where we are. And he is on the other side of the fence and peeks over. What does he see? The president, standing right about here. Shaking hands, just a few feet away from my friend, all smiles and making new acquaintances and winning votes.

"Except my friend is really standing in the dark. At night—you can't see this now but at night—there really isn't much light over there. Maybe a bit, but it's mostly cast in shadow. And that's when everything got crazy. Nobody knows if this other guy came up from the basement somehow, or from behind the delivery truck, or was hiding in the dumpster, or was just shrouded in the shadows behind the fence, but all the sudden this dude is beside my friend yelling, 'death to the Nineteenth Amendment!' and apparently he had a weapon or something because a second later a Secret Service guy is over the fence, my friend is knocked unconscious, and this other guy is dead."

"Dead?"

"Yeah, like through the head. A single shot. They apparently had a sniper on that building over there." Heather pointed across the street, in the direction of the town ski hill.

Bethany finished her beer. "Holy shit," she said, swallowing hard. "And did that make the news? I don't remember reading about it."

"Funny how that was. Different times, right? No internet. Small mountain town. Yeah, it made some news. But not much. It was politically sensitive out this way, given the guy they took down."

"Yelling about the Nineteenth Amendment?" Bethany asked. "I don't get it."

"Ends up that he was affiliated with the Mormon Church," Heather said. "Well, a fringe group of the Church. Ultra-conservatives. Traditionalists who wanted to perpetuate and spread some of the most radical ideas of Mormonism."

Bethany straightened, alarmed. "Mormons? Wait, what?"

"Yeah. And yelling 'death to the Nineteenth Amendment' suggested he was protesting the president's speech the following day at Jackson Lake Lodge. You can probably read about that somewhere, I'm sure." Heather searched her phone quickly. "Yup, right here. August 26th. The president spoke at

Jackson Lake Lodge to commemorate the anniversary of the Nineteenth Amendment."

"But I don't get it," Bethany said. "This Mormon angle. Why would the president's speech matter?"

"I asked myself the same question," Heather said. "I didn't learn this shit in college and I was new to the area at the time. But I met some people who explained it, and then I was hooked. You probably heard of women's suffrage? The Nineteenth Amendment is really about the right for women to vote."

Bethany turned back toward the brewpub, taking a few steps. She needed another beer. Heather followed. At the door, Bethany paused.

"But why the hell would that matter? Of all the things? Women voting, it's totally normal in America. Completely accepted."

They walked inside and sat at the bar. Bethany tapped her glass, motioning to Mike for a refill. Heather, her beer still half-full, took a sip.

"Not for this fringe group," Heather said. "They wanted to turn back the clock. Do you remember the Waco siege in Texas? Cults and extremists have always been in the news. This event was just another version of that."

"But the Nineteenth Amendment?" Bethany asked, nodding to Mike as he served her Pale Ale. She was feeling good now, and would feel great after the next pint sank in.

"It wasn't just about the right to vote," Heather said. "It was about the old ways."

"The old ways?"

Heather took a long drink of her beer, staring Bethany in the eye. She swallowed, then cleared her throat. "Yeah, they wanted to bring polygamy back. End the stigma. Legalize it nationally. And suppress women again."

CHAPTER 3

TABLE MOUNTAIN

Bethany remained perfectly still. Her eyes were closed. She could feel the sunlight through a nearby window. A morning luster filled the room, beckoning her to wake. Nature did not care about her hangover.

She tapped the bed beside her. At least she was alone. Things had become a bit fuzzy as the previous evening had worn on. Nothing was impossible and Heather was a beautiful woman. Bethany sighed with a glimmer of personal satisfaction. She was glad she had not made a bad decision.

Her conversation with Heather flooded into her still-hazy mind. There was a lot to digest, a ton to think through. She stacked the mental inventory of information and clues into columns, a useful trick she had learned when still on the job as a Buffalo cop. It organized her thinking, made for easy retrieval of facts when she needed them, and helped connect all the dots as she worked an investigation.

Bethany reached the end of the list, taking a long moment to ponder Heather's big reveal. A few decades ago, the Secret Service had prevented an attack, perhaps an assassination attempt, on the President of the United States. The president had been shepherded away to safety. A Mormon protester was killed. And Heather's friend was taken into custody, eventually released once they determined he was in the wrong place at the wrong time. But, certainly lucky enough to have a story to tell. Bethany was surprised he had not sold it to one of the big news shows that had ruled the airwaves at the time.

"But here's the thing," Heather had said. "One year after all that went down at the brewery, that presidential cargo plane crashed on Mount Owen. And Jackson is a small town, right? So, you have to understand it isn't a surprise that a townie working the airport in the summer was also on the patio at the brewery when the whole thing with the president happened the year before, get it?"

Bethany had nodded, encouraging Heather to continue.

"Well, that townie said the Secret Service dude who jumped the fence—the agent that took down my friend and was there when the protester was shot—was the same guy, and the only Secret Service agent, that was on the flight when it crashed into Mount Owen."

That was a significant detail, but did it matter? Bethany did not believe in coincidences, instead believing connections to the truth lay hidden in the investigative minutiae. She breathed deeply, practicing relaxation, ignoring the stale beer on her breath, allowing her thoughts to drift through the information. Secret Service teams would be closely connected to the president. One year after the shooting it made sense not to involve a different agent with the president's second trip to Jackson Hole. And especially Jackson Hole after what had happened the first time around. That agent would have had a keen understanding of the environment, of the community, of the people. He would have researched the challenges and the risks. He might have even been a senior person on the team by then.

But why put him on the cargo plane out of Jackson? That made less sense. The news reports said the four-engine turbo-prop aircraft was carrying 35,000 pounds of jet fuel, presidential vehicles, and other equipment. It hit the mountain just below the summit around 10:45 pm, exploding into a fireball that could be seen throughout the valley. That intense fire only lasted a brief period and was mostly burnt out by the time rescuers reached the site at 4:30 a.m. There were no survivors.

The Air Force had blamed the crash on pilot error. A misreading of the radar. A failure to monitor the flight path relative to the surrounding, mountainous terrain. In total, eight crew members died. The Secret Service agent was the ninth fatality.

"And then, the weirdest thing of all," Heather had said, "was that it took almost twenty years to clean the whole thing up. I mean, I kind of get it. The crash happened at almost 11,000 feet. And except for the tail, the plane was pretty much obliterated. Big pieces were flown away—that was the easy part—but there were lots of small pieces and parts strewn across the mountainside. Hikers would kind of rummage through the area, you know? Pile things up. Maybe take a memento or two.

"But this is Jackson Hole. Everything is about the environment. Everything is about conservation. The crash happened in Grand Teton National Park. Someone should have been chomping at the bit to get that cleaned up—someone in the community, someone at the state level, just someone. But nothing. The crash site just remained. Almost like it was there for a reason."

Bethany rewound her thoughts to the previous night at the brewpub. She thought about the fence that hid the loading dock. She thought about the brewery basement and the lift that brought Heather's friend up to the area behind the fence, obscured from the president and his Secret Service entourage.

It seemed like a scene from a movie, a near-perfect approach for an assassination. Ok, sure, the Secret Service had searched the basement. But had they secured the staircase from the restaurant? Or the lift behind the brewhouse, the one that took the spent grain into the basement in the first place? Bethany imagined the Secret Service team walking the building, seeing the restaurant guests and the crowd at the bar, searching the kitchen and the restaurant coolers, the fermentation area and the glass-encased, refrigerated serving tank rooms.

But she guessed they never looked in the mash tun. Yeah, the assailant could have hidden himself in there once he realized the president was visiting, just waiting for his chance to pounce.

Bethany sat up, cringing at the pressure between her temples. She put her hands to her head. The last few beers might not have been the best idea—not at this altitude, anyway—but each one had tasted better than the last. By the end of the night, she had jumped to a delicious American IPA chock full of Simcoe and Columbus hops. Then over to a juicy, New England IPA. And then, finally, that Imperial New England IPA. Her nightcap for the evening. What had the bartender said? The alcohol content was something like 11 percent? She remembered the flavor of pineapple and blood orange. She could almost still taste it under the thick layer of morning sludge on her tongue. She vaguely recalled Heather saying something about being careful with a beer like that, about Bethany having a pint or two of water, about staying hydrated in the mountains. Bethany had shrugged off those suggestions. It was not her first time at the rodeo.

Was it possible that the Secret Service had missed the protester during their building sweep? Had he been inside the brewery the whole time, literally, waiting for the moment to slip out the back of the mash tun, down the lift, through the basement, and up to the loading dock? Did that even make sense? How would the protester have even known to expect the president?

Bethany fought against the fog in her head, resisting the urge to go back to sleep. Another hour or two of rest would help cut through her hangover and would probably put the conversation of the previous night into sharper focus. But Bethany felt the tug of urgency, that her minutes were too precious to lose.

The Mormon angle troubled her. Was it just a coincidence that it kept finding its way into the narrative? Bethany doubted it, again grimacing at the idea of coincidences. Patterns like this did not spring from nowhere—she had learned that on the job as a cop in Buffalo. She ran through the mental checklist. First there was Amanda Lang in Munich, then potential connections to Edward Roth's killer, and now this blast from the past back to a president with a penchant for visiting Jackson Hole. No, she decided, it could not be random.

Bethany swung her feet off the bed, resting them on the floor. She had to get moving before the day slipped away. She wiggled her toes, feeling the old, rough carpet tickle the soles of her feet. A shiver ran up Bethany's spine, then through her shoulders. She shuddered. Waking up was never easy, especially with a hangover.

She reached for her phone, pleased with herself that she had remembered to plug it in overnight. That was one of the pitfalls of loving beer—at least in the modern age. Too many damn things to remember. Plugging in your phone. Maybe even your laptop. Not losing your purse. Not misplacing your car keys. She was always grateful that she did not wear contact lenses, certain she would have slept with them in her eyes far too many times. Why couldn't a person just pass out and forget about it, like the good old days?

Bethany squinted, swiping the screen, suddenly anxious. Someone had texted overnight, probably this morning. Her heart rate quickened. A rush of heat flowed up her neck, adding to the discomfort behind her eyes.

"Let's meet in Wilson at the base of Teton Pass," Heather had written about one hour earlier. "There's a bar that you can't miss. I'll have my car. See you at nine."

Bethany groaned. Did they talk about getting together this morning? What was this even about? She read the clock in the top corner of her phone. Just a few minutes after eight. How far was it to Wilson? She checked her GPS. About fifteen minutes. She rubbed her cheeks. Thankfully she did not oversleep. A quick shower would have to do. And hopefully they had ridesharing in this town.

*

The driver eased his car off Highway 22, drifting into the parking lot of the only bar he knew that was at the base of Teton Pass. Bethany looked at the nondescript, red building. Its profile was low, its appearance suggesting the need for several thousand dollars of exterior upgrades. But could she doubt the formula for success? Her driver had spent the last fifteen minutes telling her about the place. Built back when Franklin Roosevelt was president. The subject of a documentary film. A place where cowboys, tree huggers, and movie stars all came together for drinks and dancing. It was a Jackson Hole icon.

Heather was standing in the parking lot beside her car, patiently waiting. A smile spread across her face as Bethany exited her rideshare. It was almost as if Heather was happy to be up so early after a night of drinking.

"Feeling a little rough today?" Heather asked.

Bethany pointed toward the front door. "If the bar were open," she said, "I'd suggest a little something to take off the edge."

Heather nodded, looking briefly at the building behind her. "I've spent lots of time in that place. In my younger days, anyway. Not so much anymore. The drive home is a killer. I used to live out here in Wilson, so that made it easy to party."

"Seems pretty lonely out this way," Bethany said. "I can only imagine what it was like ten or twenty years ago."

"Oh, it was really great," Heather said, the tone of pleasant reminiscences creeping into her voice. "Not so many distractions back then. Reading, hiking. Even writing kept us busy. Pretty healthy, actually. In a lot of ways, I really miss those times. They were quite simple."

Suddenly Heather stopped speaking, moving away from her car, an idea forming on her face. "Oh my God," she said, "I just remembered something. You and the whole beer expert thing! Wilson—this little town we are in right now. Here at the base of Teton Pass. Did you know it is the home of Wyoming's first modern microbrewery? It was founded here in the late 80's. I'm trying to imagine the bottle labels. I think it says 1988. We'll have to find one and check!"

"A microbrewery in *this* town?" Bethany asked. She knew the question was laced with doubt and hated herself for it. "Is there even enough population to keep a brewery operational and profitable?"

Heather laughed. "Well…," she started, drawing out that word to express there was more nuance to the story, "I don't think it qualified too much as a microbrewery. Not in the modern sense. It was pretty small. A little log cabin set up. They bottled and had some tap handles at the brewery. You could walk in and buy your drinking supplies for the weekend."

Bethany mused for a moment, trying to picture what Heather was describing. "Sounds a bit more like what they are calling a nano-brewery these days," she said.

"Ooh, and here's another thing," Heather said. "An interesting factoid for your beer knowledge. Do you have any idea who invented the modern glass growler?"

Bethany paused. Growlers were ubiquitous in America's craft beer world. A favorite and easy way to get fresh beer on draft from your local brewery. They were typically made of brown glass, were reusable and resealable, and held sixty-four ounces of your favorite beer. How many empty growlers did she have in her closet back home? Three? Maybe four already? Just the thought made her pine for being back in Buffalo. Maybe cruising down the highway for growler fills at one of the breweries in East Aurora. Then maybe a swing into Orchard Park before heading home. It was one of her favorite ways to spend a Saturday. Hell, since retiring and coming back from Munich, it was her favorite way to spend most any day.

"I give up," Bethany said. She was never one for trivia, even when the answer was obvious.

"The modern glass growler was first introduced by the Otto Brothers," Heather said. "That's Charlie and Ernie Otto, by the way, from right here in Wilson, Wyoming."

Bethany gave another look around with pessimism etched on her face. "Nothing personal, Heather, but I think I'll need to fact check that one."

Heather laughed. "You do that! I won't even do myself the indignity of proving it on my phone right now. You just look it up whenever you get the urge."

The urge was now, but not for a history lesson. All the talk about beer was making Bethany thirsty, never mind the dull ache that still sat behind her eyes. If there was one thing that she had learned along the way, sometimes the quickest way out of the haze was to cut right through it.

"Anyway," Heather said, "we have some driving to do. Hop in my car and let's hit the road!"

The climb up Teton Pass was surprisingly easy in Heather's dark blue Subaru Outback. The 2.5-liter, naturally aspirated, four-cylinder engine manhandled the steep, winding road as it powered around curves and charged toward the pinnacle of the pass at 8,341 feet above sea level.

"Maximum grade is ten percent on the pass road!" Heather yelled as she punched the gas coming out of a turn. "And you'll notice there are turnouts along the way. Places to park if you want to hike in the summer, or good for backcountry skiing and snowboarding in the winter."

Bethany looked out the passenger window, watching the pines flash past, her thoughts drifting back to skiing in Western New York. Those little resorts were mounds of dirt compared to the mountains in the Teton Range. Sure, Bethany loved her hometown ski hills, even if she visited them far too infrequently. They served as a quick getaway, a respite from life, an escape from the pressures of being a cop, a place to feel the wind rush against her face, a way to experience something other than the confines of her house, her former marriage, her police car, or her work desk during the depths of a Buffalo winter. But here in Wyoming, as the car kept climbing and the top of the pass never seemed to come, Bethany could hardly imagine the length of each ski run and the steepness of the terrain. She doubted her legs could ever handle it.

"Last time I was in the mountains," Bethany said, trying to find a comfortable topic, "I was south of Munich in a town called Garmisch. There's skiing there, too, as I understand it. Glacier skiing. *Zugspitze*, I think they called it."

"There are some glaciers in the Tetons," Heather shouted, her voice competing with the noise of the car's engine. "But mostly the snow melts off each summer, then comes in heavy during the winter. Check out the websites that show the seasonal snowfall totals for the resorts around here. We crush the competition."

Bethany listened but didn't entirely hear, her mind still back in Garmisch. *That was when they killed Louis*, she thought, remembering the gurgling sound of his last word through the thick wall, his throat likely slashed. And then the final gunshot.

After that, the Germans had driven Bethany into the mountains and dumped her on the side of the road. If she closed her eyes now, here in the Tetons, and imagined a hood over her head, the feeling in her body was eerily like that run-in with Nazi sympathizers. Sitting in a car, experiencing the sense of gaining elevation, the cooling and thinning of the air, the pressure changing in her ears. Even the engine noise was similar, although the whine of a Japanese engine hit different pitches than that of a high-performance German motor.

"You aren't so talkative this morning," Heather said, poking Bethany on the shoulder.

"Sorry," Bethany hurried. "Just lost in thought, that's all."

"Well, you can't have your eyes closed or be sleeping when you go over the top of the pass," Heather said. "Especially if it's your first time. In fact, you'll get a good view of the valley. Let me zip into the turnout for a second."

Heather jerked the wheel to the left, guiding her Subaru across the center line. The tires crunched across gravel and dirt, a light cloud of dust rising in the vehicle's wake. Moments later they came to a stop in front of a carved wooden sign that read: "Howdy Stranger Yonder is Jackson Hole" and beneath that, the subtitle, "The Last of the Old West."

"My friends and I have a long-standing debate," Heather said. "The figure on the sign that is pointing in the direction of Jackson Hole. Do you think that is a man or a woman?"

Bethany observed the sign for a few moments, picking out the details. "I'd say a female," she said. "Looks to me like she's wearing a dress."

"Or it's a male," Heather countered. "A cowboy wearing a hat, neckerchief, and chaps. That's my pick."

Bethany looked again, nodding her approval. "I could go with that, too," she said, but not caring either way.

"That's the view back to the valley," Heather said. "No big mountain peaks or anything. Just a nice look at some of the Jackson Hole community." She turned, pointing in the direction they were driving. "And that way takes us down to Victor, Idaho. You'll be in a new state in just a few minutes. Ever been to Idaho before?"

Bethany shook her head. She took a mental note that Idaho got the short end of the stick when it came to beautiful views. All she could see of that state so far was a bunch of pine trees. "Never really traveled too much as a kid," she said. "Moved quite a bit, but mostly in the Midwest. Ended up in Buffalo. Munich was pretty much my first trip abroad, outside of going there once with my parents when I was young. I'm pretty sure this is my first time west of the Mississippi."

"Consider yourself lucky, then," Heather said. "You've come to one of the most beautiful places on earth. Like I told you, I moved here from New Jersey and never looked back. It's expensive as shit to live out here, that's for sure, and I feel lucky that I got here more than twenty years ago and managed to afford a house when I did. I don't know how younger folks even stand a chance to get their foot in the door anymore. But I got situated and I'm firmly rooted in the community. There's really nothing that could convince me to leave." She shifted the car out of park. "Let's keep going."

The drive down to Victor took another fifteen minutes. They passed the "Welcome to Idaho" sign on the way down. Bethany took a deep breath at that moment, wondering if the air was any different in Idaho and if her body might react to the sudden crossing of state lines. To her disappointment, it was a complete non-event.

"When we crossed the border, the highway switched from Wyoming 22 to Idaho 33," Heather said. "I don't know who thinks of that shit, if it's just a pissing match between states or something, but it never made any sense to me."

Bethany blinked and they were already through Victor. She had expected more, like maybe some strip malls or chain stores or a wholesale superstore, but it turned out to be just a sleepy little town. "Any chance there's a good coffee shop around here?" she asked, the burden of the last night's drinking starting to weigh on her eyes.

Heather pointed her thumb over her shoulder. "You missed that chance back in Jackson. There's a place in the next town up, though, if you want to stop."

Bethany felt tempted to say yes. The quick rush of caffeine would pull her out of her drinking stupor, maybe put some pep in her step. But nothing pissed her off worse than a crappy cup of coffee. Was it too much to ask for some delicious, dark roasted java out here in the middle of nowhere? Something on the scale of French roast, characterized by an intense, almost smoky-sweet flavor? Something not too acidic, but with charred, roasted notes? Bethany appreciated the fact that lightly roasted coffees could give her a greater caffeine boost, and that most coffee experts claimed they were truer to the origin flavors of the coffee beans. Hell, as a beer judge she should prefer that nuance. But the higher acidity and an unsettling sweetness of many light roasts always made her stomach queasy. Couple that with the vagaries of a local coffee shop and the outcome might be disastrous, especially after an evening filled with too many beers.

"I'm not sure," Bethany said. "What little I just saw in Victor makes me worry about quality. Most restaurant coffees aren't to my taste."

"We'll pass by the place in a few minutes," Heather said. "In Driggs. That's the next town. 'Best Coffee West of the Tetons.' I think that's their slogan. It gets pretty good reviews."

Teton Pass. Best Coffee West of the Tetons. Bethany was starting to sense a pattern. Where the hell were these Tetons anyway? Everything, it seemed, had the word Teton in its name. She knew they had to be nearby. Maybe she should have made it a point to visit Grand Teton National Park before setting off on this goose chase. She vaguely recalled seeing the mountains from the plane, and after landing, but her mind had been elsewhere, focused on the investigation she was preparing to undertake. Were they somewhere distant, like a day's drive or something?

"What the hell," Bethany said, throwing caution to the wind. "I need a coffee. Support a local business, right? What's the worst that can happen?"

Driggs, Idaho was equally quiet. Just a bunch of generic business buildings lined the highway through town. Bethany sensed the expansiveness of the valley that housed this community and Victor, now miles behind them. It seemed to stretch forever to the north and was bounded by mountains to the east and to the west. Like Jackson, she thought, but quieter. She wondered why this little patch of America had seen much less growth and development than Jackson Hole. Notwithstanding Teton Pass, the towns weren't too far apart.

As if on cue, Heather spoke. "Shit, I'm really sorry but I just remembered that coffee place closed for good. I haven't been over here in a while. I totally spaced that."

"Probably for the better," Bethany said, secretly relieved. Glancing about the town, she wondered how the community could support most any business, let alone a coffee shop. Or, more importantly, a brewery.

Soon they turned right on East Little Avenue. "We'll be back in Wyoming in about ten minutes," Heather said. "We're about thirty-five minutes from the trailhead."

"The trailhead?" Bethany asked, a tinge of surprise in her voice.

"Um, yeah. Remember? We talked about this last night. We're heading to Teton Canyon Trailhead. We're hiking Table Mountain today!"

*

Bethany was poorly dressed for an active day outdoors. She wore a faded pair of denim jeans, a T-Shirt she must have purchased at the brewpub the night before, a light jacket, and running shoes that were breaking down from old age.

Bethany wondered how Heather had convinced her of this undertaking. The details were vague through the haze of several too many beers. She was open for a day of hiking but would have preferred a lot more preparation. Maybe Heather had described the beautiful meadows filled with fall flowers. Or perhaps intrigued her with the hope of glimpsing an elk, a mule deer, or even a black bear. But now, out on the trail, they climbed, climbed, and just kept on climbing. What started as a walk had become a serious effort. Bethany's legs burned with fatigue. Her lungs fought for oxygen.

"It's eleven miles round trip," Heather had said as they hit the trailhead. "We have to hustle. I know people that take twelve hours to do the whole thing, but we don't have that luxury. The days are shorter. The evening and nights are colder. We don't want to get stuck out here. Let's get going."

At least Heather had packed lightly. Thirty-two ounces of water each. Two energy bars per person. A quart-sized bag of trail mix. The limited extra weight was a blessing, but Bethany worried about the exertion and the eventual need for something decent to eat, though she found some solace in the carbohydrate reserves from the night before. Her mind felt dull, and her brain ached, but the beer kept feeding her body as they climbed 4,000 feet to their destination.

The weather was cool, and the air was crisp. The sky seemed to beckon them forward, an endless expanse without a cloud in sight, its pristine shade of blue the kind that Bethany doubted she could ever find in a box of crayons. Occasionally, between gasps of breath, she reminded herself to forget the agony in her calves, hamstrings, quadriceps, and glutes. Just find appreciation in the beauty that surrounded her. This landscape was the stuff of artistic majesty, a canvas of nature that filled every sense and overwhelmed the soul.

"Fucking shit," Bethany muttered. Above the tree line the wind hit a little harder, cutting through her thin jacket and cotton T-shirt. She could feel her skin prickling as sweat quickly evaporated. Heather was right. Get stuck out here and hypothermia would become a serious threat. Especially this late in the season when the warmth of summer had already graduated toward the earliest hints of another snow-filled winter.

"Not much longer now," Heather said, pointing. "We have a bit over one mile along this exposed ridge and then the final climb up the scree field to the peak. At the top we're at more than 11,000 feet above sea level."

Bethany trudged ahead, still wondering about the purpose of this hike. Heather must have had some compelling reasons, but they were lost memories after Bethany had found her drinking rhythm the night before and their conversation had faded to black. What was the benefit of hoofing it through woods and across treacherous rock fields, then up this final steep pitch? What did it have to do with the murder of Edward Roth?

"Oh my," Bethany said, surprising herself as the words slipped across her lips. She was on the summit of Table Mountain now, her legs quivering, her heart racing, her breath struggling to slow.

"And there you have it," Heather said, a triumphant note in her voice. "This is my favorite view of the Grand Teton. Standing here it almost feels like you're at the same elevation, staring right at it. Not an easy hike, but very manageable. It's even dog friendly, by the way."

"That's a bonus," Bethany said, indifference in her voice. She found the fact unimportant, though she knew plenty of dog lovers to whom such things would matter. She stared across the basin below her, marveling at the majestic mountain that loomed before her eyes. Here it was, the Grand Teton. The inspiration for the name of most everything in the area. Bethany could appreciate the reverence.

"How tall is the peak?" Bethany asked, pointing.

"Probably every local knows that answer," Heather said, laughing. "At least they would have a good guess. About 13,700 feet."

"Can you hike it like this?"

"Not exactly the same," Heather said. "You need far greater technical skills and equipment. And more time. I find this hike to be my preferred substitute. I've actually never summited the Grand and doubt I ever will. Made it up to the Saddle a couple times and camped, but that's been it."

A brisk gust of wind cut across the top of Table Mountain. Bethany's hair swirled and a wild strand stabbed her eye, breaking the pleasure of the moment. It was a reminder that Heather had come here for a reason, and that time was short. Bethany turned, noting the sun was beginning its descent toward the western horizon. The day was quickly coming to an end.

"I could admire the views for hours but let's cut to the chase," Bethany said. "I haven't asked. Kind of waiting on the big reveal. What's the reason for the hike?"

Heather raised her left index finger as if acknowledging that she had forgotten the larger purpose of their excursion. "Yes, of course," she said. "This wasn't a typical walk in the woods, was it? Do you remember last evening and the stuff we talked about? I mean, you were pretty reticent at first. But by the time you got to that glass of New England IPA, you had opened up quite a bit. Leaned in close, got your voice down to just a whisper. Told me about when you were in Munich and got caught up in this conspiracy. Nazi shit. A bunch of murders. Remember telling me all this?"

Bethany nodded, not remembering the conversation at all.

"And that the whole thing had something to do with the recent events in Berlin. But the kicker was the connection to some Mormon lady. A treasure of some kind. An underlying mystery to the whole experience that never sat quite right with you."

Bethany continued nodding, trying her best to remain composed. She had spilled her guts to Heather, sharing far more than she had ever intended. That was the problem with beer sometimes. Drops the inhibitions, makes for loose lips. She made a mental note to work on that aspect of her career as a beer expert.

"And then came the murder here in Jackson Hole. Well, technically over there," Heather said, pointing east across the mountain range. "News reports connected the shooter to Utah, possibly to the Mormons. And then the shit I told you about the president's visits. It all kind of clicked, you know?"

"What clicked?" Bethany asked.

"Here. The top of Table Mountain."

"Okay, and so we are back to the beautiful view?" Bethany asked. "Or what?"

"No, sorry," Heather said. "Remember the first town we drove through when we came down off the pass? Victor? We'll go back through there when we are done, by the way. Grab some beers at the brewery. You know that brewery I mentioned? The one in Wilson? They moved across the pass, built a bigger brewery, and then rebranded."

"Now we're talking!" Bethany exclaimed. "Though I'm surprised a brewery of any size can survive on this side of the mountains."

"Don't be," Heather said. "Victor was founded in 1889. It is a resilient little town."

"I'm sure that was pretty tough living back then," Bethany said.

"Rustic as hell, I'm sure." Heather said. "Nothing like we could tolerate today. But the founders of the town—and this is important—were the Cache Valley Mormons."

"What does that mean exactly? The Cache Valley Mormons."

"Don't quote me on this," Heather said, "but I've lived in Jackson long enough to have a decent idea of the story. By my understanding Cache Valley is a region down in Utah. It's about a ninety-minute drive north of Salt Lake City. So, a bit south and west of where the Idaho and Wyoming state lines connect."

Bethany tried to imagine a map of the United States, having little sense of the region's geography. She simply nodded again, urging Heather to continue.

"And the Mormon community has always been a significant portion of the region's population. Probably the majority now that I say it. Then think back to the late 1800's. America was nothing like it is today. No TV. No radio or telephone. Just endless land for those willing to explore it. And so, I'm guessing, somewhere along the line a group of Mormons from the Cache Valley area—maybe some families that were steeped in the tradition of polygamy, for all I know—decided they needed to expand their settlements. You know, for the good of the faith and all that."

"So, they settled Victor? And that second town we drove through, too?"

Heather pondered the question for a moment. "Driggs? It's possible, I wouldn't be surprised. It's named after Don Carlos Driggs. He founded the town in the early 1900's. I'm not so sure about his history, to be honest, but I'd guess he was part of the church since his son, Junius, eventually became president of one of the Mormon temples. In Arizona, I think. And you probably didn't notice this, but after Driggs we turned back east and drove through another tiny town, Alta, on our way to the trailhead. It was just after we passed back across the Wyoming state line. There's a tiny Mormon church tucked back in there. About eighty percent of Alta's population is still Mormon.

"Anyway, there's a question people ask in Jackson," Heather continued. "Maybe it's meant to be a joke. Why do so many Mormons live in Idaho?"

Bethany shook her head and shrugged her shoulders. She was certain this would be a knee-slapper.

"Because God can't see over the Tetons," Heather said. Then she paused, chuckling. "I always thought it was stupid. Kind of a mean joke. Now I wonder about that."

"Why is that?" Bethany asked.

Heather left the question unanswered, instead fishing in her pocket to pull out her cell phone. She tapped a code on the screen and moved closer to Bethany. "I took a screenshot this morning, so you'd be able to visualize it better."

Bethany scrutinized the screen, squinting to help against the sun's reflection. She lifted her hand, creating some shade, giving the image more clarity. It was a statue of sorts. A man standing on top of a ball. A simple horn or trumpet in hand, raised to his lips, as if preparing to blow a sound. And the entire statue was clad in gold.

"What is it?" Bethany asked, now confused.

"This is the standard Mormon statue, a big part of the art and architecture. You usually find it atop the Mormon temples. It's the Angel Moroni. Joseph Smith—that's the founder of Mormonism—stated that Moroni visited him on multiple occasions. Supposedly this angel was the guardian of the golden plates that eventually became the basis of the Book of Mormon."

"Golden plates?"

"Yeah, there's plenty to learn about that if you're ever interested. But that's not what matters for the purpose of this hike. Look."

Heather then raised her phone, pivoting her feet and swinging her arm so that the top of the phone appeared to rest on the peak of the Grand Teton. She tapped the screen again, the brightness rising, bringing back the image of Moroni.

"Some say the ball that Moroni stands upon is the top of the Grand Teton," she said. "And there were rumors in the valley that the attack on the president—and the plane crash the following year—were clear warnings from members of the Mormon faithful, from those that believe Moroni was more than just a prophet to Joseph Smith. They believe the angel is here today, preparing for the Second Coming."

CHAPTER 4

STRONG BEER

If this is what it felt like to be a jellyfish, Bethany hated it. The hike to Table Mountain had been tough. Trudging up through the changing altitude, each step had been worse than any stair machine she had ever used at the precinct gym. There would have been no way to get in shape for a climb in the Tetons without weeks, perhaps months, of acclimation in the mountains. And simple practice, practice, practice. Like shooting a gun.

But Bethany's walk down from the mountaintop had been more brutal than the climb up, with each step fighting against the relentless pull of gravity, using her quads and hamstrings, calves, and glutes to resist her body's full weight, all while keeping the pace at a brisk and steady walk. It was a race against nightfall and dropping temperatures, made more challenging by her crappy, unsupportive tennis shoes. Preventing a turned ankle on a rock or root was a constant worry.

Conditioning had never been Bethany's thing. Even as a cop she had struggled with the minimum fitness requirements to stay on the force. Her superiors and doctors always said the same things, doing their best to be supportive of healthy habits.

Lose a few pounds, Bethany. Focus on your heart health. Do some strength training. Your body will thank you.

Why start now?

They were back in Victor, standing inside the brewery's taproom. Bethany surveyed the taps and the beer selection. "I'll take the Imperial Stout," she said to the bartender, then looked at Heather. "Don't judge me. I need something to get my strength back. I can hardly feel my legs."

Heather laughed. "Yeah, that hike will take it out of you. I try to do it several times per season, and it kicks my ass every time."

"Stout for strength," Bethany said, enjoying the aroma of her Imperial Stout, then taking a long sip.

"Excuse me?"

"Oh, sorry. It's just an old marketing slogan I heard somewhere. Seems appropriate in this circumstance. Though, you know, some of the most famous Stouts are very light beers. Not the color or the taste, of course. Light in terms of alcohol, like 4.3 percent. This Imperial Stout is twice that. But the richness of dark grains, the focus on the malts. It does suggest more nutrients for the body."

Bethany glanced about, taking in the space. When they had pulled up to the brewery, the grain silo had been the only clue to the beers she was about to explore. Outside of that, the low-profile, tan building reminded her of a pole barn, not a brewery. *Certainly not a Munich brewery,* she thought, but then immediately reprimanded herself. It was not a fair comparison. Hell, the Munich brewery where the shit had hit the fan had been making beer since the 1300's. This brewery, founded in a small Wyoming town, was still just a baby. And, she dared not forget, the business had moved over Teton Pass to Idaho to be rebuilt from the ground up. Yes, it was unfair. The gritty unknowns of each American craft brewery were what made

Bethany's new career as a beer expert enjoyable and unpredictable.

"It will be dark before long," Heather said. "How about we finish up the day outside? I'll go find us a seat."

Bethany withheld a sigh. She was exhausted. And she liked feeling the vibe of the tap room. Sitting on the metal stools at the bar, just inches from the taps, was the experience she preferred. Looking at the colorful chalkboards, figuring out everything that was on tap. Smelling the lingering aromas of whatever batch they had brewed that day. Outside? Hell, she had spent more time in the great outdoors today than any day of her adult life.

"Sure," Bethany said, disbelieving her own response. "Let me just suck this down."

Pounding Imperial Stouts was not Bethany's thing but if they were going to sit outside, she wanted a beer more appropriate to the setting. "Go ahead and pour me a Brown Ale," Bethany said to the bartender. He pulled the tap handle and Bethany drained her glass, racing his pour.

"Take it easy on those," the bartender said. "The Imperial Stout is best enjoyed in moderation."

"Just one," Bethany said, holding up her index finger. "Pretty good beer, by the way. Thick. Picking up lots of caramel and roasted malts. Some hop spiciness. A hidden smokiness. I'd love to have some bottles of these in my cellar at home. Try one every year and compare my notes over time. I bet it would really mature and improve."

"Hey, Bethany," Heather called, standing by the door. "Come on out. I found us a spot. And some of my friends are here, too."

Bethany looked to Heather and then back to the bartender, smiling. He had given her a generous pour, right to the rim, with just a hint of foam. If she didn't know better, she might swear he was trying to get her drunk. Bethany's eyes met his and her hand curled around the cool glass, the Brown Ale inviting her to dive right in. *I'd go swimming with him*, she thought, surmising that there was a stream somewhere nearby where they could skinny dip together. *Probably another hike that would kick my ass. But it would be worth it to see what he's packing under those jeans.*

With the thought of water, she looked down at her beer, lifting the glass to her lips for the first sip. Of course, she hoped the creek water around here was not brown like her beverage. Was it even possible for anything outdoors to be nasty around here? Everything seemed so pristine and perfect. Brown water was the sort of thing she expected from the creeks that fed into Lake Erie and Lake Ontario back home near Buffalo, the ones that were known for monstrous steelhead trout, chinook salmon, and coho salmon. Some of her cop friends who gave a damn swore by those waters, claiming Buffalo was home to some of the best fishing in the world. A real hidden gem. But all Bethany could think about were the heavy toxins still buried under the water and silt of those creeks, a lingering gift from the old steel plants that had formed the backbone of Buffalo-Niagara's industry so many years ago. Now those poisons were a deadly part of the food chain, hidden in all the fish. It was nothing she wanted in her body. And if she was not going to eat the fish, then why bother catching them? No, it was easier to imagine Buffalo's creeks as murky and disgusting and leave it at that.

Bethany stepped outside. The sun was behind the western mountains. The evening air had turned decisively in the direction of freezing. She felt her face brace at the sudden biting at her cheeks. This would only add to the natural blush earned from both wind and sun during their long trek to and from Table Mountain.

"I was telling my friends about you," Heather said. "They are pretty intrigued by the story."

Bethany smiled, trying to keep her sense of apprehension at bay. About the last thing she needed was the story getting out—the reasons behind her visit, the history of what happened in Munich, her suspicions that Amanda Lang might be the mastermind behind the murder of Edward Roth. That was another oversight in her drinking binge the night before. If she had stayed sober, she would have considered the likelihood that Heather would spread the word. Small town gossip was probably rampant in mountain communities like this. But Bethany kept smiling, playing it cool. Maybe they would consider her half-crazy and get a good laugh at her expense.

Heather made quick introductions. "These are my good friends, Will and Genevieve. Will got to Jackson in the early summer about six weeks before I came to town. Been around ever since. Runs the Jackson Hole recycling plant."

"Reduce, reuse, recycle," Will said, flashing a peace sign.

"And his girlfriend, Genevieve. Or should I say fiancée now? You two have been together forever, it seems. I can't believe you aren't married yet."

"It's a spiritual marriage," Genevieve said. "We don't need a piece of paper or the state defining our commitment to each other."

"Hah, yeah, I get it," Heather said. "Genevieve is with one of the big conservation organizations in Jackson. They are all about protecting the wildlife and the habitat."

"It's been a challenge over the last twenty years, that's for sure," Genevieve said. "Trying to balance the demands of the wealthy with the needs of nature. People just want to build beautiful houses and make this their playground. And, of course, there's the tourism that drives the economy. We need it all to work together. We are always striving to find the perfect density of humans, both in the summer and winter months. It's a living lesson in ecological economics."

Bethany sipped her beer and smiled again. "Well, those are two words I've never heard used in a sentence together. Ecological economics?"

"Think of it as how human economies and natural ecosystems coexist," Genevieve said.

Bethany was confident she had never called anyone a tree hugger and decided now was not the time to start. These modern mountain communities, she was realizing, had been built on the backs of people who had experienced their childhoods in other parts of the country. But something had drawn them here and they had elected to call this place home. It suggested a special allure, an appeal that Bethany never felt in all the places she had ever lived—St. Louis, Memphis, Cincinnati, Cleveland, and, finally, Buffalo. She shivered. How was it that she was in this beautiful place, drinking an amazing Brown Ale, and she kept thinking about Buffalo? That damn city was like a pimple on her ass that would not go away.

"So, hey," Will said, moving past the awkward introductions. "I hear you're looking into that crash up on Mount Owen."

Acting surprised, Bethany waved her empty hand while sipping her beer. The Brown Ale was delicious, filled with robust malt sweetness and enticing hop flavor. There was little doubt they used Chinook hops in this one. And probably another hop varietal to aid the complexity. Maybe Centennial?

"Oh that," Bethany said after swallowing her drink. "I mean, I guess so. Heather just told me about it yesterday. Yeah, it's interesting. Kind of connects some dots for me, I suppose."

"Kind of?" Heather asked. "Unless you believe in coincidences!"

Bethany bristled, with even the mention of coincidences causing a visceral reaction.

"What I think Heather means," Genevieve said, "is that it seems the universe intended for us to meet." Her face lit into a broad smile across her wide, strangely attractive face. With Genevieve's brunette hair and thick eyebrows, Bethany's first impression of her had been unpleasant, almost laced with a tinge of repulsion. And Genevieve spoke with a monotone voice, as if her emotions had been sucked into the void of the ecological economics she called a career. But now her smile opened a new door into Genevieve's soul. Bethany felt drawn to her, waiting to hear Genevieve speak some more.

"That's awesome," Bethany said. She looked at Will. He was nodding in agreement.

"Like, Will and I have been up to that crash site over and over since it first happened. Kind of became our obsession, you know? Fits into both of our wheelhouses. Sort of the glue that made us a couple."

"Yeah, that's right," Will said. "You got the ultimate symbol of power—a presidential cargo jet—crashing into a mountain in the middle of the Teton Range. So, it was perfect for Vieve's area of expertise. Perfect for the stuff she does at work."

"And then all the debris that was left behind," Genevieve said.

"Lots of metal, of course," Will said. "But electronics, too. We packed a lot of it out to the recycling center. Did our part to help the ecosystem recover. Go up there now, and it's like you hardly would know the crash happened."

Will was built like a guy who could handle hauling metal fragments out from the wilderness. About six feet tall, his arms were as chiseled as his cheekbones. He wore shorts—something Bethany could scarcely believe with temperatures so chilly at night—that clearly articulated the strength in his quads. She was quickly becoming a secret admirer, and wondered how Genevieve, who must have struggled to stretch past five feet two inches in height, enjoyed her time beneath him, or on top.

Genevieve continued. "The thing is that every time we took that hike, every time we hauled stuff down off that mountain, we always had the same conversation that it just doesn't make sense. How in the hell did they crash into the side of the freaking mountain? Who does that? Passenger airlines fly in and out of Jackson all the time. Full sized jets, for crying out loud! If Jackson Hole has some treacherous terrain for flights, I'm sure as shit not gonna think the FAA or whatever it's called would allow for that airport to service the tourism industry."

"Yeah, we have little doubt about it," Will said. "Something had to occur that day that would have distracted the pilot. No experienced pilot—and especially not a military pilot—would fly their cargo plane into the side of a mountain."

Genevieve leaned in closer, taking a sip of her beer. From the color, Bethany guessed it was the year-round Golden Ale she had seen on the chalkboard inside. "After a while we started digging around. There were unsubstantiated reports of a small aircraft—possibly a helicopter—that came over the Tetons from the west, flying fast and low, into the airport's airspace. It's never been proven and remains only speculation. But if that helicopter did exist, it may have caused the pilot to change his flight path or take evasive action, which led to the crash."

"You're telling me a UFO buzzed the presidential cargo plane?" Bethany asked.

"In essence, yes. Nothing has ever been proven, like I said. Just some stories that were told around campfires over the years."

"We didn't have drones and shit like that back then," Will said. "And nobody ever claimed anything about a flock of birds blowing out an engine. When you're up on Mount Owen, you get a really good look at the valley. It's not densely populated, you know, and even less so back then. But there were still plenty of residents around to hear the unmistakable sound of a helicopter buzzing around. If that chopper was staged anywhere in the valley, we think somebody would have known. Someone would have come forward with a sighting or a hard claim. But nothing. Nothing at all."

"Which got us thinking." Genevieve said. "What's the best place to stay hidden from Jackson Hole?"

Heather nudged Bethany with her elbow, just hard enough for Bethany to spill a few drops of her beer. "That's kind of a trick question," Heather said. "You saw it today."

Bethany licked a couple drops of Brown Ale from her fingers, annoyed at Heather for the unnecessary poke. "I'm guessing the Tetons?"

"Behind the Tetons, that's right!" Genevieve exclaimed.

"We've hiked miles and miles of that terrain over the years," Will said. "We're convinced a talented helicopter pilot could find a place to land in Cascade Canyon. And then wait for the call."

"Up and over the mountains," Genevieve said. "They'd be on top of that cargo plane as it was making its climb. The pilot takes evasive action and wham!"

"Lights out," Bethany said.

"More like lights on," Genevieve said. "The fireball could be seen throughout the valley."

Bethany put her lips to her glass, starting with a sip before deciding to chug the last six ounces. She stifled a belch, relishing the buzz that was starting to set in.

"I'll grab you another," Heather said. "Same thing?"

"Thanks, actually I'll try one of those," Bethany said, pointing to Genevieve's glass. "The Golden Ale?"

"Thumbs up, yep. That's the one. It's one of my favorites."

Bethany watched Heather walk inside. Her mind was churning. If what Genevieve and Will were saying was true, then who wanted it to look like pilot error? There was no guarantee that the pilot would have taken evasive action that would result in a crash, so was there a backup plan? Shoot it down? Ram it? And why even bother with a cargo plane? What was onboard that aircraft? Or maybe the better question was, who was onboard that aircraft?

"We know it sounds crazy," Genevieve said. "We're not big fans of conspiracy theories and shit like that, but we've looked at it from every angle over the years. And then throw into the mix the protester getting killed at the brewery the year before. Plus, all the tensions about the anniversary of the Nineteenth Amendment."

"Ah, perfect timing," Heather said, arriving behind Bethany, a splendid glass of Golden Ale in her left hand. "I gave them the scoop on this twist to the story. Told them about our conversation yesterday."

Bethany accepted the beer with a tight smile, merely touching the glass to her lips. She had learned during her training to become a beer expert that it took three sips to overcome the previous beer's flavors on her palate. Take it slowly, let the taste buds adjust.

Will cleared his throat. "You can't separate the events. Everything occurred in a progression that culminated with the crash."

"And we would have declared the matter finished," Genevieve said. "You know, just amateur sleuthing to keep our minds active. Give us a reason for hikes or whatever. But then Heather tells us she'll be here and finds us outside. Gives us the two-minute update. We're like, blown away, you know? Now we're thinking the can of worms has been reopened. What happened back then wasn't the end after all."

Bethany tried to focus on her beer for a moment, taking the second sip, allowing the first hints of the new flavor to creep through to her taste buds. She was inclined to pound the damn thing, her throat had turned so dry, a typical reaction when her nerves kicked in. She had always carried bubble gum with her as a cop. That was the go-to solution when things were getting hairy and she could hardly manage a swallow. A little stick of something sugar-free usually did the trick. She preferred peppermint.

Bethany pulled out of her spiraling thoughts and looked at the three people she was with. She had known Heather for twenty-four hours. Perhaps even less. And Will and Genevieve for only a handful of minutes. And yet she had made the classic error of revealing too much to one person with a big mouth. Was it a subconscious desperation to find Amanda Lang? Was it her fear that something worse might be primed to occur, and she had to do something to prevent it? Bethany went for her third sip, finding instead a mouthful of beer sliding down her throat.

"Like it?" Genevieve asked.

"Mmmm," Bethany responded, raising her eyebrows in affirmation. The beer had a crisp body. Light malt sweetness. A delicate, floral hop aroma. And a reasonable amount of alcohol by volume. She could enjoy this Golden Ale all day. What wasn't to like?

"I need to be honest with the three of you," Bethany said, the courage from the alcohol lowering her inhibitions. "I wasn't looking to get anyone involved in this whole thing. I was doing some fact-finding, sure, and can't believe everything I've already learned. But I definitely wasn't looking for any sidekicks. What we're dealing with here, what I discovered in Munich, let's just say these people are ruthless."

"You think we don't know that?" Will asked. "All the evidence we've found? The story we have constructed?"

"Jackson Hole and over here in Teton Valley," Heather said. "These are quiet little places. Nothing happens. Hiking, fishing, camping, kayaking in the summer. Skiing in the winter. Drinking in the mud seasons. That's the normal pulse of things. Assassination attempts, crashing presidential cargo planes, and the murder of some famous economist just don't match the fabric of what we know."

"God can't see over the Tetons, remember that." Genevieve said. "Jackson is beautiful, sure. A great place for a vacation. The President of the United States. The Federal Reserve's annual meeting. On the surface, it makes sense that they visit here. But they keep coming back despite the trouble, as if inviting another incident. As if they want to poke the bear. Stir up a little shit and if they do, the world will hardly notice."

"God doesn't see past the Tetons," Bethany murmured.

"You know how, in the Cold War, they said the superpowers fought proxy wars?" Will asked. "The Soviet Union and America never went after each other directly—that was too dangerous with nukes and shit—so they fought conventional wars in places like Vietnam or Korea."

"That's what's happening here, we think," Genevieve said. "Little skirmishes. A fight between the big, bad U.S. of A and a small but mighty faction of separatists. Our government needs proof before they can go after their epicenter. They can't just swoop in and crush them, right? Not in a free country. So, they get as close as they can and keep rubbing noses in shit. Pissing people off. Making them react."

"Think about it," Will said. "If these separatists don't acknowledge the president as theirs. If they don't accept the Constitution, especially the Nineteenth Amendment. If they don't want to live under the economic decisions fostered by the gathering of the Federal Reserve. What is the final outcome? Everything is an affront to them."

Bethany again drank her beer, saying nothing, the story settling in. She had learned to accept that remarkable stories could be absolutely true. Working as a cop had taught her that. And not just here and there. No, she had experienced the painful depths of reality on a daily basis. Unbelievable murders. Child abuse. The list never ended. Television could never come close to the truth of things, no matter how crazy they tried to stretch their stories.

Finally, Bethany cleared her throat. She drifted her gaze across the faces of Heather, Genevieve, and Will. Her demeanor was somber. "So, it sounds to me like I'm not in the right place. Let's pretend I'm the government and I'm tired of fighting on the periphery. I want to go after the head of the snake. Where would that be?"

"Salt Lake City," they replied in unison.

CHAPTER 5

UTAH OKTOBERFEST

The air was different in Utah. Crisp and clean, without a hint of humidity, reminiscent of the high alpine air south of Munich. It was refreshing, though unsettling. Bethany Judge felt out of place in the Salt Lake valley, almost trapped. Mountains towered to the east. The Salt Lake stretched to the north. An empty expanse stretched to the south and west. She found herself longing for the confines and comforts of home, for the sweet, dank aroma that floated in from Lake Erie, blanketing Buffalo, and the surrounding towns. To Bethany, that smell was a mixture of dead fish and old pollution.

The Utah sky was perfectly blue, so pristine that Bethany was certain there had not been a cloud in days. This was the opposite of the cloud-filled skies that dominated Western New York from early fall until late May. She glanced up at the sun, squinting her eyes. Her skin felt crisp. Bethany made a mental note to add sunscreen to her morning routine.

Bethany dabbed a napkin to the corner of her mouth. She had been on a Mexican food kick since returning from Europe, burned out by the sausage and sauerkraut and bread and whatever else the Germans ate. *Good old Mexican food,*

Bethany thought. She hated to think how pathetic American cuisine would be if Germany had managed to win the Second World War.

"Thank God for other cultures," Bethany said to nobody, her mouth half-full of chicken, beans, and rice. Bethany had asked for a recommendation, something special, and the young lady at the hotel's front desk had not disappointed.

"Everyone loves the place near the airport," the receptionist had said, waving her hand dismissively. "I mean, I get it. It gets all the press. They have incredible mole and everything on the menu is delicious. There's even a second location, though I prefer the original. The lines can be long. Just wait until the snow flies. They have tall heaters lined up on the sidewalk to keep people warm. If you don't freeze to death, you can work up an appetite waiting outside for a table."

Bethany had grimaced at the thought. "Is there anything better in the area?"

"Oh, definitely," the front desk attendant had said, her eyes lighting with excitement. "Not too far from here, actually. About ten miles away. Best Mexican in town. I think they came from Texas, judging by the name. They have a cool old station wagon parked out front, covered with every sticker you could imagine. Takes up premium parking space, at that. That's the main downfall to the restaurant, to be honest. It can be tough to find parking. But it's worth it for the food."

Bethany brought herself back to the present, nodding her head with approval. She opened her phone and searched the restaurant, taking a few moments out of her day to award it a five-star rating. Little gems like this deserved some hype.

As did the young lady at the hotel. Bethany noodled on that for a second, wishing there was a way to rate individuals, not just businesses. She guessed it could be a million-dollar idea, but nothing that she could bring to fruition. There were more important things for her to do.

Bethany sat outside on the restaurant's small patio, enjoying the sun. The round table was far from new, its frosted glass and rusted metal attesting to many brutal winters and bright summers. She shifted in her chair. It had been cold at first against her backside but had warmed now with the day's rising heat. In front of her and above her, to the east, loomed the Wasatch Range. And somewhere back in that mass of mountains, Utah's version of the Oktoberfest was taking place today.

Bethany swiped her phone to open the screen but struggled to see. She lifted her sunglasses. It was hard to search for directions on her phone when looking through polarized lenses, but squinting against the mountain sun was equally difficult. Bethany held the phone closer to her face and searched the maps application.

"Up Little Cottonwood Canyon?" she asked herself. Her voice reflected a note of surprise. The map search said it was only thirteen minutes away. That was closer than she expected. She looked back up at the mountains. Everything seemed so massive here, so spread out. The mind could not take it all in, process the information, and estimate distances. But judging by the GPS, she would be safe to drive back to the hotel after a couple of Oktoberfest beers. She just had to limit her drinking.

Bethany turned her attention back to her food. She picked up a fresh tortilla chip and dug deeply into the massive side of guacamole. The bite went down with the satisfying smoothness of mashed avocado blending perfectly with the lime, garlic, jalapeno, and whatever else the talented chefs had secreted into their recipe.

"Jeeezus!" she exclaimed to herself, half aware that the word had slipped from her mouth. The food was not just good.

It was amazing. She remembered her cop friends talking about their favorite donuts being an *orgasm in your mouth*. Bethany smiled at the thought, then shook her head. They had never experienced a bite of Mexican food this good.

Slowly, Bethany's brain caught up with her now full stomach. As her hunger pangs subsided, her mind turned back to the drive down from Jackson Hole, and why she was here in the first place. She had rented a car and the trip had been uneventful, though memorable, the beautiful road winding through towns with unique names like Lava Hot Springs. A quick search in her phone had alerted Bethany to a brewery in Alpine, Wyoming, so she had made a pitstop to sample a flight of IPAs, then hit the road again. Once she had reached Interstate 15 it had been a straight shot to Salt Lake City, almost a snoozer. Six hours after leaving Jackson, she had arrived safely at her hotel in the city of Sandy, about fifteen miles south of Utah's capital. It had been Heather's recommendation.

"I stayed there with some friends during a ski trip," Heather had explained. "Needed to burn up some days on my ski pass. The hotel is close to both canyons, so perfect for getting up to the mountains."

That was when Heather had brightened. "Oh my God," she had said. "It's perfect timing. You have to visit the Utah Oktoberfest when you're down there. Probably nothing close to the real thing, but it gets voted as one of America's Top Ten Oktoberfest celebrations. It runs from mid-August through early, maybe mid-October. I think it's only open on the weekends, every Saturday and Sunday. Look it up on your phone! You have to check it out."

Bethany sidelined the memories of that conversation and brought her mind back to the mental notes she had made while sampling the IPAs during her stop in Alpine. Hands down, the one packed with fruity aromas and balanced with sublime bitterness had been her favorite. It had been hard for Bethany to settle for just one. But she knew it was never a smart idea to drink too many 7.5% ABV pints and then go driving down strange roads. Especially not in the middle of the Mountain West. No, not at all. Bethany had kept her enthusiasm in check. A flight. A beer. Another feather in her cap of beer knowledge. Another brewery checked off her list. But nothing that would impair her driving. For safe measure, however, she did get a six-pack of beer to go.

"Hangovers are half the fun," Bethany mumbled. That phrase was not part of the curriculum to become a beer expert, but she thought it should be. It was stupid, the sort of thing a cocksure teenager might say. Bethany was certain she had not coined the phrase. Most likely she had heard it somewhere along the way. Maybe from an old high school friend. Or the brother of a friend. Either way, it was one of those statements that was lodged in her mind, and it popped out of her mouth at the most appropriate moments.

Like now. Bethany was, she could admit, a little regretful. The six-pack she purchased had not lasted the night after she had checked into the hotel. It had whispered to her during the entire drive after leaving Alpine, a friendly seat-side passenger that kept reminding Bethany that she was not alone. And that her passenger was ready to party. She thought back to the artwork on the can. The hophead dude did seem like a guy out for a good time. Maybe it was his fault.

Bethany put her hands to her head. The fog from the six-pack sat heavy. She needed the Mexican food to kick in a little more. Take the edge off. Energy in her limbs would fill her mind with focus and help remind her that she came to Salt Lake City with a purpose. Somewhere nearby, perhaps within just minutes or miles, Amanda Lang might be at work, planning her next steps. Was it global domination they were after? Or some kind of cultish demand for religious and cultural freedom? Maybe something right in the heart of America? Any of it sounded plausible after listening to Heather, Genevieve, and Will. But at the same time, completely outlandish.

"Fuck it," Bethany said, standing. "It's Saturday. Let's see what this Oktoberfest thing is all about."

*

Bethany hit some unexpected traffic at the mouth of the canyon but within an hour she found herself at 7,760 feet above sea level, twenty-four miles from Salt Lake City and deep in the heart of the Wasatch National Forest. Mountains towered above both sides of the narrow canyon road and the unincorporated town that comprised the resort community. To Bethany, it almost felt as though she were enveloped by nature. Aside from the austere buildings with architectural stylings straight out of the 1970s, she could only see trees and rocks. And, at the highest peaks, hints of snow beckoned the coming start of ski season. Bethany shuddered. Winter would be here quite soon.

Suddenly, the sound of German polka music rose behind her, the beautiful tones of horns and accordions beginning their slow echo off the towering mountain walls that surrounded the ski area village. Bethany turned. The crowd was large and getting larger, streaming toward the event tent clearly labeled on the base area map. Bethany checked her watch. Exactly noon. She had a good six hours to see what all the fuss was about.

Bethany joined a line that snaked its way to a pop-up tent, where mugs were sold, and beer dispensed. That seemed an auspicious start. In less than ten minutes she was holding a half-liter glass filled with a Märzen-style lager, brewed by a Salt Lake City brewery.

"Don't just look at it," a voice said behind her. "That beer is made for drinking."

Bethany turned, half-smiling. The beer's deep copper color had caught her attention. Thinking back to her experience at Munich's Oktoberfest, she did not remember those Munich beers being nearly so dark. In fact, by her recollection they were nearly as yellow and fizzy as any standard American lager. Just with much more flavor, character, and kick.

"Point well taken," Bethany said. She took a deep drink, allowing the liquid to fill her mouth and coat her palate. Her eyes opened in surprise. Rich tones of malted barley, Munich malt and caramel malt popped to the front end of the beer. But the lightness caught her off-guard. It was thin, like no other Oktoberfest beer she had ever enjoyed.

Her new friend laughed and took a drink. "Judging by your reaction, I'm guessing it's your first time in Utah," he said after swallowing. "No, it's not the altitude that makes the beer like that."

"Like what?" Bethany asked. She thought the beer was delicious, but unique. Full-flavored but light and missing something that made it fall short of the Oktoberfest and Märzen beer style guidelines. But Bethany also knew she was not in Munich, and that American craft beers were morphing to the needs of their communities. As that happened, the style recommendations could always change.

"Alcohol content," he said. "What we're all here for, right?" He extended a hand. "My name's Ivan, by the way."

"Ivan," Bethany said, offering a brief wave instead of a handshake. She was not fond of swapping germs and could not know if he had washed his hands after his last bathroom break. "I was actually thinking that this is a very unique take on the Märzen," she parried. "For one, it is nothing like the beer I had at the actual Oktoberfest. You know, in Munich? And, because it seems to fall outside the style guidelines, whether you consider it a Festbier or a Märzen. It tastes delicious but, yeah, you're right. The lack of body and texture tells me they are way short on alcohol by volume."

"That's a Utah thing," Ivan said. "Our liquor laws have been fucked up here forever. Probably the most restrictive in the country. I sometimes wonder why breweries would even open in this state. But they did. And, hell, they've been successful. Look at you! We even draw out-of-state tourists to our Utah Oktoberfest!"

"Is it that obvious?" Bethany asked, unable to prevent a smile. She glanced down to look at her clothes, seeing nothing that set her apart from the crowd. "I'm here by chance." She eyed her glass, surprised it was already empty. Maybe that was at least one benefit of a lighter beer.

"I'm almost empty, too," Ivan said. "Quick, back in line while there's no wait. This is the best beer here, so stick with what you know!"

Ivan paid for both beers with his credit card. "Anyway, as I was saying," Ivan continued. "There have been some changes to the beer laws lately. I can't keep it straight. Hell, it hardly matters. It is what it is, right? I like coming up here for the annual festivities. It's really beautiful. Nice to take the tram up to the top of the mountain and hike around. You should check that out if you're interested. You might even mountain bike from the top back down to the village, just not after drinking! Bike down first, then top off the day with some brewskis. The only problem, of course, is the cost of these beers."

"They are pricey," Bethany said. "Thanks for paying, by the way. I'm happy to buy the next round. Or pay you for this one."

"No, that's not necessary," Ivan said. "It's my pleasure, really. It's just a running joke in the city, that's all. You save up all year for the Utah Oktoberfest and then spend all your money to barely catch a buzz. Get it? Expensive beer? Low alcohol content? It's a bad joke, I know. Something for the locals, I guess."

The first laces of alcohol reached into Bethany's mind, allowing comfort to drift over the conversation. She liked the idea of a challenge and was up for this one. "Well," she said, "how about we find out if we can catch a buzz?"

*

The event tent was packed with bodies, some lining up to order beers, others selecting food to eat. The festival band was on stage, playing its latest rendition of a polka song Bethany did not know. Husbands and wives, fathers and children, sweethearts of all ages filled the dance floor. Most of the men wore Lederhosen. The women dressed beautifully in ornate Dirndls. Bethany nodded in approval. Compared to Munich, the ladies were quite modest here. She had not yet noticed any breasts falling out of their tops.

Ivan pointed to a long table with two empty seats. "Let's grab those," he said.

Seated, Bethany took a deep breath, lightly gripping the handle on her glass stein. She thought back to the one-liter mugs at Munich's Oktoberfest. This one was half as big, nowhere close to what Germans considered regulation size. It did have a snazzy commemorative logo, so the mug had that going for it. The thought gave her pause. Beer glasses were not something she had much passion towards, but they did provide an avenue to relive the places she visited and the beers she drank. If she did not lose it or break it, Bethany figured she would have a nice memory every time she pulled the stein from her cabinet.

The music subsided and the band set down their instruments. The director announced into the microphone that they would take a short break. The dancers applauded the band's strong performance. The sound of voices rose in the room as conversations restarted. Bethany chuckled, quietly shaking her head. She always had bad luck with showing up just as bands left the stage. Coming all the way to Utah did nothing to break her lousy streak.

"So, what brings you to Utah and up to our awesome little festival?" Ivan asked. "Are you a beer person? One of those craft beer fans?"

"Something like that," Bethany said. She felt guarded and took note of the slight strain of an inexplicable tension toward Ivan. He had done nothing wrong, nothing she could put her finger on. But there was a lingering suspicion, a hair up on the back of her neck. Bethany could not ignore it. Trusting her gut in moments like this had made her a pretty good cop.

Ivan smiled. His teeth were white and straight. Almost fake looking. Bethany let her gaze hang on his face for a moment, long enough to gather an impression but not so long as to convey attraction. His eyes were swollen, thick on the upper eyelids and with bags underneath. He reminded Bethany of someone who had gone a round or two recently and was on the backside of healing his face. Maybe boxing or mixed martial arts. His slightly crooked nose confirmed he was not afraid to take some punches. Probably had paid to fix his mouth. But his physique told a different story. Thin arms. A protruding stomach. Maybe he was one of those *Fight Club* types, but not a serious athlete. Or maybe he got messed up in the wrong things sometimes.

Ivan reached over, grabbing Bethany's beer glass and breaking her thoughts. "Empty already? I'll grab you another one. Same thing, right? No reason to switch when we already have the best one!"

Bethany offered a thumbs up, saying nothing. She watched Ivan work his way through the thick crowd. He was clumsy in his movement, prone to bumping into people and not afraid to clear space with his body. A trained fighter, Bethany suspected, would glide through, using the narrowest of spaces between bodies to keep moving forward. Like a gust of wind. But Ivan was a wrecking ball. A bulldozer. A thug. Yeah, that was probably it, Bethany concluded. He was a street brawler, maybe a bouncer or a gang member, maybe the muscle for someone with a little bit of money. That was how he could afford the teeth.

She heard a voice beside her. Nasally, high-pitched, annoying. The kind that creeps into the ear like a bug. Once in, you can't get it out. No matter what other noises or sounds surround you, it is still the only thing you can hear. She turned her head in the direction of the voice. A thin, bespectacled man with combover black hair was seated beside her, facing partially away from Bethany. His left hand gripped a soda bottle. His right hand gesticulated wildly as he spoke to the person beside him, another man, equally gaunt and even more official in appearance.

"And this is what I need you to understand," the man beside her said. "We are a little more than a year out from the next election. You know as much as I do about what is going on in Washington. We have a president who is running roughshod all over this country. They may not have succeeded in removing him from office during his first term, but you can bet if he wins a second term they will be after him from the moment his victory is announced. And is that something we can afford? Imagine if they succeed! The alternative to that lunatic is only worse for us. We were worried sick during the first impeachment. What would happen if the vice president found himself in charge of the country? He is strongly Christian, and you know how that will turn out. All the Christian Conservatives will start spouting off again. Just like before. Remember that Southern Baptist pastor who supported the Texas Governor in his bid for the White House? Calling us a non-Christian cult? Saying that our beliefs disqualified Mormons for support from Christians?"

"Yes, yes," the other man said. "But that pastor was discredited at the time. His comments weren't well received."

The man beside Bethany scoffed. "Weren't well received? That's just putting veneer on the deeper truth. Institutional discrimination exists in all sorts of ways. Against people of color. Against people of different faiths. And while our church certainly is a child of the Christian tradition, there are many–a vast majority—who share that pastor's deep suspicion. He just had the courage to speak, to say it out loud. That we are a cult. That we brainwash. That our beliefs and traditions run counter to the prevailing winds that drive this country forward."

The other man spoke again, his voice resigned. "What can we do? Create a marketing campaign? Decry the abuse? I fear we would become laughingstocks, far worse off than we are even now. There are so many people who suffer, so many groups that are abused. We are just one of the multitudes. But we are kind and friendly people. And I pray that this—and our love as a community—will correct any misperceptions."

"I don't share your optimism, I'm sorry. We were persecuted from our first days. You know that history as much as me. We didn't keep slaves. We introduced plural marriage in the early history of the church. We had the potential as a group to wield political control. And so, our settlements were attacked by mobs. Crops burned to the ground. Homes destroyed. Families threatened. It is how we came to find Salt Lake as our home."

Ivan appeared in that moment behind Bethany, lowering a full stein over her left shoulder. Beer frothed to the top of the glass and over the edge, dripping down the side and onto Bethany's leg. She glanced back at Ivan, frowning. She appreciated his kindness and the free beer even more. But there was rarely an excuse for wasting a single drop.

"Feeling that buzz yet?" Ivan asked, grinning.

Bethany took a long drink. Surprisingly, she felt pretty tipsy. And a bit courageous. She was never the type to butt in on the conversations of other people, but the two men beside her had piqued her curiosity. They spoke like members of the Mormon community. She tapped the shoulder of the man beside her. "Excuse me," Bethany said, hearing in her own voice a hint of confrontation, "but I couldn't help but overhear some of your conversation. The things you were speaking about."

The man turned in his chair. Bethany was struck by his delicate, bird-like features. A narrow face with high cheekbones. A beak-like nose. Tiny eyes that darted back and forth as if searching for a worm. He leaned forward, looking at Bethany as if ready to peck out her eyes.

The other man did the opposite, leaning backwards, seemingly nervous. "Just a chat between old friends," he said, finishing his comment with a fake smile. Bethany wondered what he was worried about. Certainly not some lady striking up a conversation with them. Maybe they were offended by the beer in her hand, but she figured that was the point of the Utah Oktoberfest and unlikely the case. She did recall that the man beside her had been drinking a soda, and she found it curious that they would come here to celebrate if they weren't imbibing the traditional Oktoberfest beverage. There had to be a reason they would pick this location for their meeting.

Bethany took another drink, finding that action easier than wrestling with her thoughts. She realized, suddenly, that these beers weren't so weak after all, and were made more potent by those IPAs that she was still working off from the night before. She blamed her liver. It was still adjusting to the altitude and going a little slow up in the mountains. She remembered the warnings about getting more drunk at higher elevations just as she felt a wave of alcohol-induced euphoria sweep through her head.

The band returned and struck up a new tune. The tent erupted with noise. Undeterred, Bethany launched into a sudden interrogation, her tongue loose. "Old friends, huh? I had some friends in Munich. They are all dead, can you imagine that? And do you know what happened in Berlin? That disaster? So many lives lost? Do you think that was only about the professor? The German lady they talked about in the news? Doktor Herta Stocker? I was there. Can you believe that? Yeah, I was. You want to hear about my experiences with Mormons? Have you heard the name Amanda Lang? She's from Salt Lake City, too. Perhaps you've met?"

Bethany paused to take a long drink, allowing the malt-filled liquid to fill her mouth and rush down her throat. Her ire was up, she knew, and maybe it was the beer and the rising alcohol in her bloodstream that had tipped her scale off any professional balance. She felt a hand on her shoulder. Bethany turned to look and got a glimpse of Ivan, his lips moving but the words silent under the blare of trumpets and tubas. Then there was a solid thump against the side of her head, the sensation of cold glass on her temple, and the splashing of beer across her face and into her hair. After that, the world turned black.

CHAPTER 6

JUDGEMENT

"I think she's coming round."

Through her mental fog Bethany Judge recognized the male voice but could not quite place it. He sounded like an old high school friend, maybe a drinking buddy from back in the day. But that made no sense. She had fallen out of touch with everyone after graduation. She tried to tick through her mental inventory of Buffalo cops. People she had known on the force. Men with whom she had served, shoulder to shoulder. She felt a cool hand on her forehead, then a palm on her left cheek. The touch was light and tender. No cop she had known would treat her so kindly.

"You took a nasty hit," the voice said.

Bethany heard the word, but that also made no sense. A hit? She did not remember being in her police cruiser and had no recollection of an accident. A straw touched her mouth. Instinctively, Bethany wrapped her lips around it. She drew liquid onto her tongue. It was fresh, cool water. Very refreshing, but, for some reason, disappointing. She did not know why. It tasted good. The water relieved the dryness in her mouth, regenerating fresh saliva and making it comfortable to swallow. But the drink itself was very unsatisfying.

The thought slipped through her cloudy mind that water was a key ingredient in beer. Malt, hops, and yeast. And water. Maybe the most important ingredient, actually. Water made it possible to brew beer in the first place. Mix the crushed grain with the water. Turn it into a mash. Cook the grains at specific temperatures for the style of beer you are making. Rinse the grains with more water to extract the sugars from the mash. Take all that liquid—the wort—and boil it. Add hops. Boil some more. Chill rapidly. Add yeast. Ferment. And voila, beer!

Bethany opened her eyes.

"Got a beer?" she asked.

Her mind did not immediately recognize the face staring down at her. He looked familiar, like someone she had noticed once in a magazine advertisement. Or perhaps while checking out at the supermarket. He was not an old friend, and definitely not someone she trusted.

"A beer?" he said, and then he laughed. "I like your enthusiasm. You're determined to catch that buzz."

Bethany had heard that line somewhere before but struggled to place it. Something about catching a buzz. Something about never being able to. Something about weak beer that costs more money than it is worth. Her mind raced through muddy memories and suddenly Bethany recalled visions of mountains surrounding her. Then she remembered a beer tent filled with loud music. And two men speaking. She had eavesdropped. German music had started playing. Then, darkness.

She focused her eyes again on the man leaning over her. "Ivan?" she asked.

Ivan smiled. "Well, that's a start. You got bonked pretty hard on the side of your head. I'm glad you can remember my name."

Bethany lifted her hand, tentatively touching her temple. A small lump had formed. She winced instinctively. The pain was mild, but she knew it could be far worse.

"Who did this?" she asked.

Ivan pursed his lips. "Total accident. Do you remember that the band had just started playing again?"

Bethany struggled to replay the scenario in her mind. She could only recall brief snippets. The man beside her with the soda in his hand. He had been talking. A lot. And then she said some things. What had she said?

"I don't remember that exactly," said Bethany, half-grimacing. She again touched her fingers to her temple.

"I'm hardly surprised," Ivan said, leaning in close again to look at the lump. "You took a shot, that's for sure. The band had just finished their break, so the music started up. You were talking. Saying something to these two guys beside you."

Ivan stopped and pointed. Bethany followed his motion with her eyes. Two other men stood in the room. She had not noticed them until now and was not certain she had ever met them. Yet, both were familiar. One looked like a bird. The other appeared timid and afraid.

"Anyway, everyone got excited about the song," Ivan continued.

"It was the Chicken Dance," said the man with the bird-like face.

"The Chicken Dance, that's right," Ivan said, sighing. "It was probably the first time today that they played that stupid song. It's wildly popular, I'm sure you know. Really gets the crowd going. Flapping arms, wiggling hips. Starts slow and then speeds up, a little at a time, until it goes fast at the end. I'm sure you've danced to it somewhere along the line."

Bethany gave a mild shrug, not giving a damn about the Chicken Dance. She was getting worried about her current situation. Nothing good could come out of being in an unknown room with three strange men.

"Well, you would know it if you had," Ivan continued. "Da da da da da da dump, da da da da da da dump...." He paused, looking at Bethany expectantly. "Sound familiar?"

Bethany closed her eyes, annoyed. "Sure," she croaked. She had no idea where he was going with his explanation. A beer right about now, Bethany decided, sounded like a good idea.

"Yeah, see?" Ivan said, pleasure in his voice. "I just needed to jog your memory. Okay, so the music fires up, and everyone gets excited. People moving to the dance floor. Or just getting up to join in the fun. That's when the bad luck happens. Some kid who just turned twenty-one today. I found out he was celebrating his birthday with friends. He was already wasted by the time the Chicken Dance started. And who can get drunk on Utah beer, right? Hah! Anyway, he's got this full mug of beer and happens to be right behind you, swinging his arms and acting like an asshole. Then, wham! Smacks his beer stein right into the side of your head. You went down like a ton of bricks."

The memories swam back like beneath murky water, the events of the day finding some shape in her mind. The Mexican restaurant. The burrito that had left a hint of indigestion. The canyon drive. The Utah Oktoberfest. Meeting Ivan. The beers, weak but tasty. The men beside her, talking. The music. And then, darkness.

Bethany again touched her head. She probed the lump gently, testing the level of pain. She flinched out of reflex, but discovered the discomfort was more than manageable. In all her years as a cop, Bethany had never been shot or stabbed, or assaulted in any way. But she had suffered enough emotional wounds to know the depths of agony. This little knock on the head could never compete with any of that.

"Where am I?" she asked, turning her mind to the puzzle at hand. If this were a law enforcement situation, her first step would be to ascertain the setting and the personalities of the people involved.

The timid man stepped forward. His lips quivered as he spoke. "I had a room here at the lodge. We carried you up to the room."

"You look like you don't weigh very much but you're pretty solid," Ivan said, half-laughing. "Dense, I'd say. Lots of muscle. Must have been an athlete? You drink beer like a professional, that's for sure."

Bethany took a deep breath, hoping the influx of oxygen would clear her head. "Beer expert. I'm a certified beer expert. Beer is my thing."

The bird-like man stepped forward, affronted. "Let me say that while I respect your personal choices," he chirped, "such a profession would not be acceptable among our women."

The man's choice of words cut right through the remnant fog in Bethany's head. "Our women?" she asked, irritation coloring her voice.

"Mormon women," he clarified, "but truly all Mormon brothers and sisters. Are you familiar with the 'Word of Wisdom?' I'm sure that would be too much to ask, am I correct? Yes, I'm certain that's true. You see, the 'Word of Wisdom' is the common name of a section of the Doctrine and Covenants. Do you understand?"

Bethany closed her eyes, signaling she had no idea where this was going.

The bird-like man continued. "No? Then let me explain. You see, the text in the Doctrine and Covenants discourages us from drinking any alcoholic beverages, including beer. And hot drinks."

Bethany opened her eyes. "Hot drinks?" she asked, more surprised than interested by this last bit of detail.

"Generally interpreted to mean tea and coffee," he said.

"All the finer vices," Bethany said, dismissing the brief Mormon lesson with a shrug of her mind. She could not fathom a life without beer and coffee.

The timid man stepped forward, exuding a sudden air of authority. He took another moment to review something in his hand. Bethany was surprised to see it was her driver's license. "So now, Ms. Judge. I do understand that's your name, isn't it? A Ms. Bethany Judge? From Buffalo, New York, is that right? Visiting us in Utah. That's far from home. I should point out that we haven't formally met, of course. Our initial interaction was, sadly, cut short by your unfortunate accident. You were eavesdropping, do you recall? Listening to the conversation I was having with my friend here? You remember this, of course? In the beer tent?"

"Look, first off," Bethany said, weakly pointing a thumb towards Ivan, "his name I remember, but we only met outside in line for beers. And then we chatted a bit inside the beer tent. We barely exchanged pleasantries. I have a vague recollection of the two of you, that's it. Everything's fuzzy at best. Maybe it'll come back to me." She paused, using the moment to change her tone. She wanted to sound worried and confused. And vulnerable. "Could you at least tell me your names?" she asked. "And maybe what's going on?"

The timid man smiled in a way that reflected pity. He pulled his posture erect. His demeanor conveyed the need for no explanations. "Certainly. My name is Aaron Young. And my colleague here is Noah Gardner."

Bethany glanced at Noah. His name was perfect for a man who looked like a bird. He couldn't look like every animal on the Ark, she knew, but as for a feathered friend, he had nailed that one perfectly.

“As to what's going on,” Noah interjected, “that part hardly matters. We were at the Oktoberfest because it’s an important annual event for the community of Salt Lake. We always find it wise to be part of something bigger than ourselves.”

“That you sat beside us may have just been misfortune,” Aaron said, with the lilt of a question in his voice. “Your friend Ivan here said it was a random occurrence. The seats were vacant. He selected them out of convenience. A place to enjoy a beer and listen to music.”

“It’s a hazy memory at best,” Bethany said. “If that’s what he said, yeah.”

Ivan chimed in, sputtering his words. “Look, I’m telling you that’s exactly what happened. The tent was pretty full when we came in from outside. They were the first seats that I noticed.”

It occurred to Bethany that a strange dynamic was unfolding. When she first swam back to consciousness, Ivan was concerned for her well-being. Now he was nervous about these other two men. Maybe even scared shitless. Deference oozed out of his pores. To Bethany’s refined nose, the smell of fear had permeated the room.

Aaron touched his dimpled chin. His face was doughy, as if perhaps he broke a few Mormon rules now and then, maybe sneaking in the occasional beer at night behind closed doors. Or, more likely, when out with his non-Mormon friends. After a moment, he frowned and nodded. “Hmm, yes, of course. I can see how that would happen. I suppose that occurs all the time when strangers meet each other at events like this. People randomly elect to sit at open chairs beside people they don’t know. And soon they are listening to each other’s conversations, picking out the important parts and then interjecting at the most inopportune moments. Yes, I do suppose that happens all the time. Come to think of it, that happens to me most every day. Multiple times each day."

Noah picked up Aaron's sarcasm and chimed in. "Come to think of it, you're right. I stopped riding the city train because people were always doing that to me. And even when I am walking across Temple Square. When did people become so nosy and rude?"

"Now hold on, hold on," Ivan said. "We already went through this when she was still knocked out. I explained how I met her. Randomly, in line for beer outside the tent. We struck up a conversation—"

"My point exactly," Aaron said, interrupting.

"Oh, come on! That's how things go at events like this! You know that. You said it yourself! Be part of something bigger than you. I was there alone, and she looked like she might enjoy some company. I was trying to strike up a friendship, that's all."

Noah's eyes flicked in Ivan's direction. The way they moved, then focused, reminded Bethany of a documentary she had once seen about birds of prey. If her cop intuition had not been short-circuited by the knock on the head, she might have thought Noah was preparing for the kill.

"You weren't there, of course," Noah said, his words a peep. "No, conveniently not. Away from the table, gathering drinks for your new concubine. Perhaps to make the evening more enjoyable than the day? Or maybe a convenient ruse? Step away to ease the mood at the table. Especially for the two of us?"

Ivan glanced back and forth at the two men. Bethany could read the befuddlement on his face. Slowly, her mind was catching up to the trap that Aaron and Noah were setting. It was as if they were waiting to trip the spring when Ivan's neck was in the perfect spot. She looked toward Aaron, seeing now that he was blocking the door. Neither Ivan nor she would leave the room without a fight.

"What the fuck are you getting at?" Ivan snapped, his words a blend of anger, astonishment, and confusion.

"Or maybe you don't know anything about it," Noah continued, unperturbed. "If what you are saying is true, yes, perhaps that would be the case." He stopped and turned his head only slightly, returning his peripheral gaze to Bethany.

"She was, after all, so abrupt," he said. "Confrontational. Out of proportion for the environment and the event. A complete and obviously inebriated stranger suddenly haranguing two leading members of the Mormon Church. So, perhaps it is time you both tell us why Ms. Judge thought it prudent to ask us about Amanda Lang?"

CHAPTER 7

A LITTLE BIRDIE

He was a quick one. That was a strange thought to be having, Bethany knew, but it was a fact. The one that looked like a bird had the speed of a hawk. When he attacked, it was quick and decisive. Next thing she knew, Noah had yanked her up and pushed her face into the wall. The pain already in her head amplified. She tasted the sweetness of blood in her mouth. The sound of Ivan yelling filled her ears.

"Hey, what the fuck!" Ivan shouted. "Take it easy! What the hell are you doing?"

Bethany heard the unmistakable sound of a fist connecting with Ivan's soft, unsuspecting stomach. A *wumpf* of air rushed out of Ivan's mouth as the hard-moving punch landed below his solar plexus. Ivan's voice silenced immediately.

"Please be quiet," Bethany heard Aaron say. He clearly relished the power he had over Ivan, now sounding more sinister than timid.

Noah's hand pressed firmly against the back of Bethany's head, keeping her face planted into the wall. She could taste dried paint and blood on her tongue and thought for a moment that a beer would solve that problem. "Guys, guys," she said, bubbles of blood rising between her lips, then popping. "There's gotta be some mistake here."

Noah spoke in her ear, his breath minty fresh. "No mistake. Of the four of us, only two were totally sober. My friend Aaron. And me. The two of you? Maybe you say you had only tried a sample or two. Maybe had one beer. But maybe your perspective is skewed by Satan. Maybe you count three as one. Or maybe you just lose count. Maybe you were here the day before. Perhaps you have been drinking for days in a row. Whichever the case, Aaron and I know our minds are clear. We don't suffer the effects of alcohol. But we do know that we were having a private conversation and that you were listening. And this caused an inexplicable eruption from you. Why in the world would you mention Amanda Lang?"

Bethany felt memories of the day flood in. Her brain gained a spark of clarity. "Aaron," she said, her voice gently pleading. "Please don't hit Ivan again. He really doesn't know what's going on. Truly. He's just an innocent bystander, a guy I met in line at the beer tent."

Noah spoke quickly. "We're giving the orders here. You're in no position to make demands. Or even requests. Do you understand that?"

Bethany nodded. She felt her face trace a streak of blood up and down the wall.

"And there are no accidental meetings, no innocent bystanders," Noah said. "Do you accept that? Some people may choose to believe in coincidences, but really these are examples of divine orchestration. The Hand of God in our lives. Perhaps your friend Ivan, here, was just another man you met today. But that meeting led to the next step—you walked into the beer tent. And then your new friend selected the seats beside us. Was that just by chance? Just a coincidence? I think neither when it provided the opportunity for you to overhear our conversation.

God, you see, wanted us to meet. He ordained it with the dawning of this day and all the days past. The trajectory of us meeting today has always been part of God's creation."

"And violence?" Bethany asked between gritted teeth. "Force? Is that in God's plan? Wouldn't He promote something more kind than this?"

Aaron snickered behind her, then did something that caused Ivan to yelp in pain. Noah pushed Bethany's head a bit harder into the wall. "You know nothing about God. You know even less about the Latter-Day Saints. Our founder, Joseph Smith, believed in capital punishment. 'Blood for blood according to the law of Heaven.' Let the blood of our enemies spill on the ground and have the smoke of it rise up to God. That is our righteous belief. Like Joseph Smith, I promise you that we will wring a thief's neck. Understand and believe that. So, tell me, why were you stealing the words of our conversation? Why did you ask about Amanda Lang?"

Bethany remembered now. She had let her tongue slip. Despite their low alcohol, the beers had snuck up on her and, with it, her professionalism had waned. She had been less of an ex-cop and more of an amateur sleuth, coming straight out and asking what they knew about Amanda. She ran some potential excuses through her mind but concluded there was no way to backpedal from the mess she had created. Taking a big breath, Bethany started speaking.

"I met Amanda in Munich. That's in Germany in case you didn't know. Long story, but I was over there for a vacation of sorts. Recently divorced. Just finished up my certification as a beer expert. I'm sure that doesn't appeal to you so much, given your convictions, but there is an overwhelmingly large community of people in this country that supports what we call the craft beer movement. And I discovered I have an extraordinary palate, so I received training and gained this certification.

"But that was what took me to Munich. I wanted to explore the specific beers of the region and, more importantly, visit Oktoberfest. Create a catalog, so to speak, of Bavarian beer styles in my palate's memory. Except the trip took quite a different spin. I found myself caught up in some things. A murder, actually. I was an innocent bystander. Kind of like Ivan, here. Just in the wrong place at the wrong time. And next thing you know, I'm drawn into a far larger, far more dangerous situation. That's when I met Amanda Lang."

At the mention of Amanda's name, Noah increased the pressure on the back of Bethany's head. She grimaced against the pain as her cheek bone pressed into the unyielding wall. A tear trickled from the corner of her eye, down to her nostril, tickling and itching before it dripped to the floor.

"Nobody just meets Amanda Lang," Noah said in a low growl.

"I found that out myself," Bethany said. "She tricked a lot of people for a long time. And then she killed them. People she must have considered to be friends somewhere along the way. They all seemed close. She was so good at it. The lying, I mean. I trusted her. I never expected she could do the things that she did. And then, what she supposedly stole. Or took. I don't know how to look at it. But it must have been worth millions. I'm telling you that I never knew anything about her until it was too late."

"And yet," Noah said, "here you are today. In Salt Lake City. At the Utah Oktoberfest. And out of the blue you interrupt our conversation with a mention of her name?"

Exasperated, Bethany heard desperation rise in her voice. "I'm looking for her, okay? She sent me a postcard. To my home in Buffalo. I got it shortly after returning from Munich.

Kind of a taunt, I think. *Come find me.* That sort of thing. Or maybe more of a *fuck you.* Either way, it doesn't matter. It finally ate me up enough to come out this way. Try out some Utah beers and look for Amanda Lang. Sounded like a nice distraction to me."

From behind them, she heard Aaron snort. "Probably the only person in the world who ever traveled to Utah for the beer," he said. Bethany could hear the sarcasm in his voice but could not tell if he was doubting her story or was trying to lighten the mood.

She guessed the latter. With a mild shrug, Bethany lowered her tone and tried a version of what Ivan had said earlier. "I saved all year and barely caught a buzz. The beer tasted good, but yeah, I get your point."

Almost imperceptibly, the pressure against the back of her head eased. Noah leaned in close, as if deciding his next move, his breath hot and loud in her ear. Bethany's mind floated back to her cop friends in Buffalo. Some of them had liked to hunt for wild turkey, and they had told stories of the adrenaline-pumping excitement of being pinned against a tree, unable to move but close enough to the birds to hear them inhale and exhale. She had wondered sometimes what would compel a person to sit motionless in the forest for hours, all in the hope of shooting a turkey and hanging the tail feathers on the wall. *Perhaps if the final moments of the hunt were like this that thrill could be addicting,* she thought, and then brought her mind back to the present. The sound and tempo of Noah's breath was coming down, a bit of relaxation creeping into his demeanor.

"You're better off not looking," Noah said. "You won't like what you'll find."

Aaron piped in again. "But don't you think that would help us?"

Bethany felt Noah turn. The motion was slight, probably just his head, as if he were throwing a nasty glance in Aaron's direction. The pressure on the back of Bethany's head increased again. Apparently, Aaron's choice of words had irked his partner.

"I'm not so sure about that," Noah said. "*Loose lips sink ships*, as the old saying goes. Even up here in the mountains, not to mention down in Salt Lake City. And our friend here has quite the mouth, doesn't she?"

"But she wouldn't know, would she?" Aaron asked. "How could she? She's not from around here."

"There's truth to that, yes," Noah said, contemplatively. He turned back to Bethany, speaking just above a whisper into her ear. "I don't want you to think I'm exaggerating with my next words, okay? Hear me clearly. There was a good chance that saying Amanda Lang's name would get you killed today. Probably the only reason you are still alive is because of where you said it. Or what happened to you just as you said it. If any of her people were at the Oktoberfest, they weren't supposed to be. Not unless she sent them to spy on the event, to watch for things of her choosing. But if you had said her name down in Salt Lake City? That would have been a different story."

"Killed you on the spot," Aaron said. "They're ruthless."

"And her people can be anywhere, watching and enforcing that we bend to her will," Noah said. "We're all beholden to her commands, however they arise." He relaxed again, this time taking the pressure entirely off Bethany. He grabbed her shoulders and eased her around until she was facing him. Bethany looked at Ivan, their eyes locking. He knelt on the floor at Aaron's feet, looking disheveled, confused, and very scared. She tried to convey confidence and calm, doubting her success. Bethany guessed that she looked like crap, but she was seldom self-conscious of her appearance. This was not the time to start.

Ivan's eyes flicked to the door and then back to Bethany, pleading. Bethany blinked her eyes slowly, signaling it was a bad idea. There was no use making a break for it. Between the lump on her head, her sore face, and the toxic edge of a hangover, Bethany knew she would not last one second in a fight.

"Which was the reason we were here," Noah continued. "To be honest, the Oktoberfest is about the only place we think we could meet these days. I don't even trust my own home. Or my car. Just too many ears out there."

Aaron helped Ivan to his feet. "Here you go, my friend," Aaron said. "I'm sorry for everything. I take no pleasure in hurting others, please believe me. Can I get you a glass of water?"

Ivan nodded, his tongue involuntarily wetting his lips. "What the fuck is going on?" he asked, the words quavering as they passed across what sounded like gravel in his throat.

Noah smiled, releasing a small laugh. "It seems we are friends after all," he said. "At least I hope our judgement is correct on that account. Please, I beg of you both, don't prove us wrong."

"Hold on," Bethany said, trying to make sense of the sudden flip-flop. "One second you're pushing my face through the wall and now this?"

"There's no easy way to tell it," Noah said. He stopped, as if realizing something. He glanced about the room, his eyes darting to the ceiling and to the corners. "Aaron, would you turn on the television, please? Give it some volume, too."

Aaron obliged, and after a few long moments Noah continued.

"To be honest, I don't know if the television will help us now or not. But that's what happens in the passion of the moment, right? Get a little sloppy. Like you did in the beer tent, mentioning her in the first place? Oh well, it seems you didn't know, and we can't change things now, can we? Just hope for the best and keep moving forward."

Noah cleared his throat and continued. "If it isn't obvious already, yes, we're both Mormons. And make no mistake about the fact that we cherish our beliefs and our religion. We don't sway like so many others do. We weren't at the Oktoberfest to bend the rules a bit, sample some beers, get a little jovial, and then return home to our families to pretend like nothing happened. No, what I said before was true. We needed a safe place to speak. And so, we chose a place among the broken."

"We prayed they would not be here," Aaron said. "Her followers, I mean. But, then again, we could never be certain of that." He disappeared into the bathroom, turned on a water spigot, and returned moments later with a paper cup filled nearly to the brim. Aaron handed it to Ivan.

"You keep saying *they*," Ivan said, his voice croaking this time. He held up a finger to signal a brief pause, took a deep drink of water, and then cleared his throat. "Who are you talking about?"

Noah nodded deeply. Excitement was now etched into his body language. "Precisely the point," he said. "We don't exactly know that. There's a war happening now. Prophets and leaders fighting for control. They build alliances and betray each other. Mormonism tends to be seen by most Americans, I'd venture to say the entire world, as one belief system. Give it a name and move on. Mormons! You can read about Joseph Smith and Brigham Young, visit Temple Square like any tourist, and you know most everything you need to know about Mormons. But that is far from the truth! Ridiculously far! It's like saying all Christians have the same beliefs. Perhaps they have the same underlying beliefs, conceptually, but the driving forces of Catholicism are different from those of non-denominational

Christianity, for example. The Pope, I dare say, doesn't preach the Prosperity Doctrine like so many Protestant Christians espouse, am I right? Think of it like that. Or something like it because that's what we have within the Mormon community."

"Splinter groups?" Bethany hazarded.

Noah contemplated the question for a moment, frowning. Finally, he appeared to accept her assessment. "I suppose that's a good description," he said. "Except there's a problem. This in-fighting could set the Mormon people back decades, tarnish our reputation, make us laughingstocks. Most of us are moderates, but that is no longer an option to these splinter groups, as you called them. They are the fundamentalists, you understand. The hard-core believers, and those that want a society led by an iron fist. Traditionalists. Adhering to the letter of the law."

"They have managed all of this under a cloak of secrecy," Aaron said. "Nobody is talking about it. You won't find stories on television or the internet or in a newspaper. Yet the battles are happening. We know they are, because we have seen firsthand what happens to the moderate thinkers like us. Those who did not know better at first not to speak their minds. And those who later were unafraid to do so. They have all been silenced."

"Silenced?" Ivan asked.

"For the most part, permanently," Noah said. "The Great Salt Lake Desert, the Sevier Desert, or somewhere up in the mountains. There's plenty of places in Utah for a person never to be found again. But others, for whatever reason, were spared. Maybe they were more pliable. Perhaps they were the ones that could convince their little flocks to join the larger cause. We don't know exactly."

"Hitler convinced a nation," Aaron said. "Remember that."

At the mention of Adolf Hitler, Bethany's mind rushed back to Munich. Amanda Lang had not only stolen riches, but perhaps also the doctrines and teachings of the Nazi party. Or, better said, the tricks the Nazis had used to win the support of the German people. That was one hell of a set of souvenirs for Amanda to have brought back home.

Bethany shook her head, bringing herself back to the conversation. "Listen," she said, "I get it. At least I think I do. But what's it all about? What are they after? Unifying the Church? Becoming a Mormon version of those mega-churches all around the country? Or maybe another version of the Catholic Church?"

Noah touched the side of his nose, then pointed at Bethany, acknowledging her last question. "Another version of the Catholic Church?" Bethany asked again.

"As best as we can figure, yes," Noah said. "But with that, you have to look beyond what might be in your mind right now. This isn't just about 17,000 Catholic churches in America. Or the 1.2 billion Roman Catholics around the world. It's bigger than that. These Mormons want to establish their own country. They want to be like Vatican City. Only far larger."

CHAPTER 8

ROCK SPRINGS

Amanda Lang despised Rock Springs. She hated being relegated to the southwest corner of Wyoming. She longed to be home, in the Salt Lake valley, in the place that Brigham Young had discovered nearly two centuries past. He had been leading his people away from persecution, away from those in the fledgling United States who did not believe his vision and did not understand his writings. The non-believers had only seen a threat, and the Mormon community had suffered under the yoke of their oppression.

She abhorred them for it, all those people then and all the non-believers today. She detested many things, she realized at that moment. The spirit of divine retribution burned deeply in her stomach. She stopped writing and looked above her desk, setting her pen beside her notebook. On the wall hung a portrait of the Angel Moroni, trumpet in hand and raised to his mouth. She understood the symbolism. The Angel was preaching the Gospel of Jesus Christ to the world. And calling people to repentance.

Amanda looked down at her notebook. The ink words she had just written were still moist, yet she did not remember writing them, nor having the thoughts that produced them.

"Every man and woman who turns to God in genuine repentance and faith will be saved."

"By this ye may know if a man repententh of his sins," she whispered, "behold, he will confess them and forsake them." She smiled. Quoting from Doctrines and Covenants had never been her strength, but she had improved since returning from Munich. Devoted study. Prayer. Her understanding of Joseph Smith's revelations was rising each moment of every day.

A soft tap on the door broke Amanda from her thoughts. "Yes," she said, a slight tone of irritation in her voice. "Come in."

The door opened slowly. It creaked gently on dry hinges, reminding Amanda of where they lived and of what they were suffering through. It was for a much greater good. Thanks to her success in Munich, they had all the money they could have ever imagined. She could fix the hinge in a moment with the snap of her fingers and a sharp command. But she refused to spend a penny on lubricating oil. Or other luxuries. She would bring repentance to the world. With the horn blow of the Angel Moroni, she would bring people to their knees.

A man stepped into the room. His face looked young, but graying temples and thin crow's feet beside both eyes betrayed the first stages of advancing age. At six feet, three inches, he was taller than the average Mormon man. His crisp, white shirt hid a strong, athletic body. His face was clean-shaven, and his white teeth flashed as he spoke.

"Something concerning has happened," he said.

"Is that so?" said Amanda Lang. She cringed with a sudden touch of anxiety, immediately wanting one of the beers she had enjoyed during her Munich stay. Yes, she had broken so many rules during that mission. Yes, she had repented after every drop of alcohol had passed over her lips. But her sins had been for the greater good. It had led to success and put them where the movement was today. The time was getting nearer, she could feel it. Swallowing hard, repenting once again for the urge to drink, she sat up straight in her chair and spoke.

"These aren't the times for cryptic, half messages, Malachi. Speak what you know. And always be prompt about it. Time is becoming of the essence."

Malachi Bradshaw took a deep breath, pausing. Amanda held her gaze upon his face, her own features fixed with stolidity. Her mind, however, churned opposite. Malachi was supposed to be a rising star. A future leader of their faith. He had been hand-chosen, one of dozens of orphaned children the church had discovered in the city of Barlad, Romania. Members of the church had traveled to that godforsaken country—appropriately known for stories of its blood-sucking vampires—and discovered tens of thousands of abandoned children, a remnant of the social policies under the communist leader Nicolae Ceausescu. They had saved those that they could through adoption, bringing them to America under the umbrella of the Mormon faith. Malachi had been given the name of the Old Testament prophet because it meant *messenger*. Yes, Malachi was meant to deliver great news to their people, and that news was coming soon. Had the elders made the wrong choice?

"Accounts from the Oktoberfest indicate someone was making inquiries about you," Malachi said. "A woman. A non-believer."

"A non-believer at the Oktoberfest," Amanda said, musing. She looked at the small calendar on her desk, pondering the time of year. The height of the summer had passed, and ski season was still a couple of months away. "That's hardly a surprise.

You are talking about our Utah Oktoberfest celebration, I presume?"

"That's correct. She was heard saying your name, perhaps nearly shouting it to the two men who may have strayed, the men we had sent our people to observe. It happened quite suddenly, I'm told, and then she was knocked unconscious."

Amanda blinked, holding back any appearance of shock or surprise. "Unconscious?" she asked.

"Misfortune, it seems," Malachi said. "Someone struck her inadvertently with a beer mug."

Amanda nodded, her mind drifting back to Munich, to the real Oktoberfest. She knew how the beer could grab hold of you, loosening the soul, opening the body to careless movements. She imagined some inexperienced Utahn, perhaps even a Mormon hoping to slip under the watchful radar of her growing power, drinking for the first time, tipping back a mug, then two or three, and becoming oblivious to the world around them. And then cracking this poor woman upside the head. But she wondered why this woman had mentioned her name. She most certainly could not be some random stranger, a person from the streets.

"These accounts that you speak of," Amanda said. "Did they provide a description of her? Any kind of details?"

"I asked that also but there's very little, I'm afraid. It all happened quite fast and then she was down on the floor. Lots of concerned people surrounding her, yelling for doctors and the like. You can imagine the scene."

"Oh, yes," Amanda said. "I most certainly can." Images flashed in her mind again from the Munich Oktoberfest, this time of people passed out all around the Theresienwiese, the festival grounds where the annual event was held. No physicians in Germany worried about those drunks, of course. Not unless they were not waking up. Germans tolerated and even celebrated public inebriation, especially during Oktoberfest.

"The only thing they mentioned was her accent," Malachi noted suddenly, bringing his right hand to his chin, trying to remember. "Yes, something about that."

"Accent? Was it German?" Amanda asked, concern rising in her voice. The riches she had stolen from the Munich brewery could never be considered safe; she knew that. But after the events in Berlin, with the death of Herta Stocker and so much damage done to that movement, Amanda had hoped the threat was greatly diminished.

"No, no," Malachi said. "Nothing even close to German. We were fortunate, in fact. One of our people recognized the woman's accent. He had recently visited Hill Cumorah. She spoke like people from that area."

Amanda's eyes widened. Hill Cumorah was for Mormonism the equivalent of the Holy Land for Christianity. Like Moses with the Ten Commandments at Mount Sinai, Joseph Smith—the founder of the Mormon religion—was believed to have climbed Hill Cumorah in 1827 to receive the golden plates from the Angel Moroni. Later, Smith translated those plates into the Book of Mormon.

"Hill Cumorah is in Manchester," Amanda said, her voice turning to steel. She visualized a map, seeing the tiny village nestled just off the New York State Thruway, almost halfway between Lake Ontario and Canandaigua Lake.

"Yes, of course," Malachi said. "Manchester, New York. The woman had an accent from the region, I'm told. Quite distinguishable."

"And Manchester is about one hundred miles from Buffalo," Amanda said, a mixture of acknowledgement and relief rushing over her like a wave. She leaned forward across her desk, looking blankly into the wall. “It appears Bethany Judge is finally here.”

“Bethany Judge?”

Amanda sat back in her chair, trying to put on an air of calmness. “An old friend. An acquaintance, really. We had the opportunity to meet in the past.”

“On your mission trip, perhaps? Did you have any luck bringing her to the true understanding of the Restored Gospel?”

Amanda said nothing, shaking her head instead. She was not inclined to offer details to Malachi. He did not understand many things about the movement, about what she had done and what was to come. She knew it was unreasonable to expect anything more from him. He was still too ungroomed, more muscles than brains. Malachi might not understand Amanda’s mission trip or know that one in four Mormon missionaries were women. Or perhaps he had a subconscious bias that blocked his awareness of that fact. Amanda had been special as a child. Extra special, in many ways, and she guessed that Malachi had seen plenty of women at the Missionary Training Center suffering through the same sixteen-hour days, learning the six basic lesson plans designed to take the potential convert through to the final step of baptism. Like him, those women had every aspect of their behavior scrutinized, from how they spoke, to how they smiled, to how they behaved and appeared. The training taught them facial expressions, listening skills, and how to create common ground with a stranger. But he had probably forgotten about how powerful the women could be.

Amanda felt the hint of a smile tug at the corner of her mouth, recalling the day she had first met Bethany Judge. Creating common ground. That had been the tool that had started it all. And led to her success. Malachi was still green enough to have a hard time believing it, but women were good at the missionary schtick.

"A non-believer, then," Malachi said, his tone shifting to displeasure. He left the rest of his opinion of this new stranger, Bethany Judge, unsaid, his words shifting instead to caution and protection. "Is she a threat to you? To us?"

"When you no longer fear the darkness, then that is the moment to fear the most," Amanda said.

Malachi bowed his head in silent reverence at the quote, whispering a prayer in remembrance of its author, Patrick James Armstrong. The Mormon scholar, educator, and religious leader had died well before Malachi's time, but the man had been a preeminent leader of the church, serving as a member of the Quorum of the Twelve Apostles of The Church of Jesus Christ of Latter-Day Saints from 1981 until his death in 2004. The man was Malachi's hero, his inspiration. A man among men, blessed by God in all ways imaginable. Thanks to prayer and the power of the Heavenly Father, Patrick Armstrong had survived World War Two as an infantryman. He had returned from war only to enlist in service for the Church as a missionary overseas. He later earned a master's degree in political science and then worked for four years in Washington D.C., first for the federal government, and later for several Utah senators.

One of those senators, Malachi knew, formed the foundation of his beliefs today. The senator had written a book, *To Be a Mormon,* and it lay on Malachi's bedside table, a long-ago gift from Amanda Lang. It was dog-eared, the result of her nightly readings and constant study, and now his. The senator had been an apologist in many ways, but no matter, because every movement of true power begins with an able foundation. He had been exactly that for Amanda Lang. Now, the senator's knowledge was passing to Malachi and to all who followed Amanda Lang's leadership.

"So, are we there?" he asked. "Is the voice of this non-believer coming from the pitch black?"

Amanda raised her eyes, shaking her head. "No," she said. "It isn't that. Just my hubris, that's all. I poked the bear, as the old saying goes. Kind of taunted her with a postcard after I returned from Munich. I invited her to visit if I'm being honest. I was curious to see if she'd come."

"If she isn't welcome, we'll ship her away," Malachi said. "Or neutralize the threat. We don't need her announcing your name in public, making a spectacle! Subterfuge is the strongest weapon in our arsenal."

"It is, yes," Amanda said, thoughtful. "Our puppets have done so much for us, though, haven't they? We have made endless advances, yet we receive no credit."

"*You* receive no credit," Malachi said, correcting her.

Amanda nearly blanched, realizing her own error. It was so easy to retreat into the confines of the church's fundamentalist teachings, believing in the patriarchal perspectives assigned to women's roles. Yes, she was exploiting those beliefs, but to her advantage. The church's Kingdom on Earth awaited her forthcoming success.

"I'll remind you of the words of C.S. Lewis," Amanda said, "'Pride gets no pleasure out of having something, only out of having more of it than the next man. It is the comparison that makes you proud: the pleasure of being above the rest. Once the element of competition has gone, pride has gone.'"

"Yes, of course," Malachi said. "It's just…"

"There is no *just*, Malachi," Amanda said. "Refer to your teachings, to your notes and to our conversations. My rewards shall come. I don't need words from you, or titles from anyone."

"I'm sorry," Malachi said, the aggressive tone in his voice shifting back to humility. Amanda liked that about him. He had an ability to master his emotions, a willingness to be malleable, an openness to her coaching. Not everyone was like that. Certainly not most men within their movement. And even less so when the leadership was coming from a woman. Yes, that was a shortcoming of the society her people had built, but it was not insurmountable. Even Joseph Smith's wife had served as scribe during the translation of the Book of Mormon. And she was also the subject of one of the church's early revelations, including how to compile the church's first hymnal. And she had formed the Relief Society as a self-governing women's organization within the church, now one of the oldest and largest women's organizations in the world.

Yes, if Emma Smith could have played all those roles, then Amanda knew she could also. And even more. But for now, she had to keep pulling on the puppet strings.

"There's no time for sorry," she said to Malachi. "Errors or misjudgments—we learn from them quickly and then move them to the past. *Charity never faileth*, but we succeed by decisive action, lest the actions of others crush us first. And, for that matter, we have spent far too long mired in the information you have shared with me. We can speculate about Bethany Judge, talk about her all we want, but that gets us nowhere closer to my goals. The time for action is now. Call Senator Young."

CHAPTER 9

SENATOR YOUNG

Soft mountain light filtered through the window, into the room that Senator Orin Young called his office. This was his escape, the place away from home where he could calm his mind, collect his thoughts, and soothe his body. On mornings like this, when the room's darkness slowly rose through shades of grey and eventually into the brilliant sunshine that averaged 222 days per year in Salt Lake City, he considered himself the luckiest man alive. Only God could have ordained for him to call such a beautiful place home. Only his Creator could have provided the wisdom and wits to rise through the ranks of the Church. And only his Savior would have placed him at the precipice of winning the Republican Party's nomination for the president of the United States.

"Thank you," Senator Young said, looking up at the woman standing in front of him. She was beautiful, with long brown hair that dripped funnels of curls off both shoulders. Her equally brown eyes held his gaze for a long moment, faking a smile. Her lips were slightly open, showing the bottom half of her recently whitened, top teeth. He wondered if she was going to say something back to him, like *you're welcome*, perhaps. Or maybe ask for some money. She had never done that in the past, not even once in their two dozen overnight meetings in this little sanctuary. She just came when he bid her presence. Then they spent the night tangled together, forgetting their beliefs, and ignoring the fact that they were a short walk from Temple Square, these fleeting moments about the animals inside them both. Mostly him, if he were being honest with himself. There were some urges he just could not escape. But she always came willingly. And spontaneously through his mastery of her flesh. Yes, she certainly enjoyed it as much as he did.

"Things will be getting busy very soon," Senator Young continued, lowering his eyes to the papers on his desk. "Lots of distractions to deal with." He grabbed the thin stack and quickly lifted it, tapping it on his desk to square up the documents. He liked a neat office, liked keeping his things in order, and liked knowing where everything was at a moment's notice. Important files, pens, staples, paper clips, his office phone. But if that was the case, he wondered why he had pushed her onto the desk in the throes of passion, brushing everything onto the floor when she had wrapped her legs around him. Now he had created a mess that he needed to clean up.

Her voice was low, sweet, and sultry. "I'll keep you relaxed," she said. "Do you want to relax now?"

He looked up and saw she was smiling. Really smiling. The creases around her eyes, the slight wrinkles in her forehead, the way her lips quivered up at the corners—those clues displayed the pleasure she felt in moments like this. Teasing him with the things she said. The naughty suggestions. The offers that were impossible to refuse.

Senator Young leaned back in his executive chair. The spring tension held firm, holding him ergonomically poised at the perfect height above his office floor. He cherished this chair. It wasn't some sort of *Made in China* crap that might last a year or two, not at all. His supporters had discovered someone special to custom build this perfect piece of office equipment. An Amish convert to the Mormon faith. A person who had been raised in the art and craft of creating fine furniture. This chair from America's heartland—from the beautiful state of Ohio—reminded him each day of the power and grace of God's word. If the Amish could see the clarity of the Restored Gospel, anyone could.

"Don't I look relaxed?" Senator Young asked. The question slid off his tongue with mocking jest. He kept his eyes fixed to hers. Sitting naked in his office felt unnatural, perverted, but at the same time empowering. He was hiding nothing from her. Age had softened his chest and wrapped an extra ten inches around his waist. The skin on his arms had started to soften and sag. The bags under his eyes looked unnaturally dark, as if he had forgotten to wash away mascara from the day before. But what did she see? Certainly not the flaccid, diminutive penis of an aging, poorly endowed man. Just the erect tower of a virile leader. A real man, always ready. There was no relaxation when it came to these pleasures in life.

"Mmmm," she purred, cocking her head to the side. "I see your assistant is ready for work."

Senator Young swelled with pride. Every time they played this game, a fleeting thought passed through his mind. *No fucking blue pills needed.* This was all him, and his assistant was the spelunker that explored every cave and crevasse and orifice it could find. Hers just happened to be some of the best in his sixty-two years of exploration.

"Take a closer look," Senator Young said. "Ask him yourself."

She stepped around the curved edges of his desk, her hip brushing against the dark-stained wood. He heard the brief swoosh of her pencil skirt, the hushed sound raising excitement in his chest. She stopped in front of him, lowering her hands to her hips, then down her thighs. She gently pinched the skirt, pulling it up, exposing her knees. "But they are already so red and tender," she said, playfully. "It will hurt to kneel and look *really* close."

Senator Young followed her gaze toward her knees, stopping briefly to admire the shape of her breasts beneath her tightly fitted blouse. They had been so firm in his hands. Her nipples had been like hard candies in his mouth. Involuntarily, he licked his lips. She stepped closer, lifting her left knee to his face.

"See?" she whispered.

"Aww, baby, I'm so sorry you're hurt," he said. "I promise to get a new carpet soon."

"You've been saying that forever!"

"Budgets are tight," he said. "You know that. If it was just so simple—"

She interrupted him, her voice now high-pitched and squeaky. "Kiss it. Make your little girl feel better."

An excited knot formed in Senator Young's throat. He loved it when she spoke like a prepubescent teen, perhaps even younger than that. And she played the part well, sometimes even dressing for the occasion, usually coming to visit with all her body hair shaved clean. He had friends who hated this kind of stuff, but not him. It felt natural. A part of his Mormon heritage. A reminder that his long-dead grandfather had married two teenage girls when he was well into his sixties. As a child, Senator Young had loved that man with all his heart and had spent a lifetime modeling himself after the stories of greatness he had heard about his grandfather over the years.

"Anything for my little girl," he said, leaning forward with his lips puckered.

He saw the flash of movement coming from his left, knowing at that moment he should have prepared for this. He was so powerful and so revered, but he was such a willing victim, never really taking the steps to protect himself until it was too late. Her palm connected with the side of his face, coming in high and a little bit back, cupping his ear. The impact of flesh on flesh filled the room with a hollow smack. Just as quickly the sound diminished, swallowed by the books that lined the shelves and the draperies that framed the windows.

"Jesus!" he exclaimed. "Fuck!" The words spilled out, but he was not entirely sure he had said them, not being able to hear himself through the piercing hum that filled the space between his ears. She grabbed his chin and turned it upwards, glaring at his face.

"You're such a bad boy, aren't you?" she cooed, punctuating the question by pressing her knee into his lips and nose. "Aren't you now? Such a bad, bad boy?" He closed his eyes, enjoying the sensation of her weight against him, smelling the blood on her knee. Something about the musty scent of coagulation urged a primal response, a desire to ravage her further, to punish her and to love her all the same. He touched his tongue to the scab, reveling in the salty sweetness that teased his palate. It was like the ultimate dessert, the senator thought, a sample of flavor from inside her body, far more of a delicacy than the tastes from just kissing and sucking and licking her skin.

He heard a soft noise, no louder than a whisper, and felt her knee slide further across his right cheek until it touched his ear. She drew closer, bringing now her other leg beside him. His nose touched her waist just below the belly button. He closed his eyes and took in the aroma. Yes, she was excited. Not angry with him. This was the way she liked to play. His mind drifted to the memories from the evening before, between her legs, her thighs smooth and lotion-soft, her hips writhing against the gentle caresses of his tongue and the warmth of his breath. The senator wondered if she was remembering that now, inviting him back for an encore performance. He turned his eyes up, the look questioning.

"Now, dear Senator Young, do you think you have earned that?" she asked. "You do know the rules, don't you?"

He let his hands settle onto the roundness of her backside. Firm, powerful, perfectly shaped. That was the feature he had first noticed on her, an ass to beat all asses. He had known from the first moment that he needed to make it his, to touch and to fondle in the execution of his sworn duties for the State of Utah. Senator Young believed it to be right and just. The Utah way. The Mormon way. His wife might care, but she would eventually understand. As would his children and, certainly, his constituents.

Senator Young's cell phone rang. "Duty calls!" she said, pushing away and restoring an air of professionalism. She flattened the front of her pencil skirt, the remnant warmth of the senator's breath enough to ease the creases. "You should probably answer that."

Senator Young frowned. Everyone knew there were only certain times during the day when he accepted calls on his personal phone. This was not one of those moments. Perhaps this was another one of her games, a way to take him from aroused to frustrated and to build up some kinky tension. Or maybe this was another one of those pervasive robo-calls. Despite all his power, even though he had co-authored a bill to stop spam callers, he was not immune to their ceaseless assaults on personal privacy.

She reached for the phone, mimicking the ringtone that emanated from the tiny speaker. "Dah dah dah, doo doo doo," she sang, placing it into his hand. He smiled at the effort. She suffered from some degree of tone-deafness, and he loved her even more for it. God, he knew, made everyone according to His plan.

He creased his eyes, pondering the number on the lighted screen. The area code showed 801. The Salt Lake region. He hesitated. More than likely the number was a computer-generated ruse from some obscure corner of the world, intended to trick him into answering the call. The senator knew that it only took one time answering one of those fake calls to open Pandora's Box. After that, it was hell to close.

But something felt different today. Like it was worth the risk. Or a necessary risk. Yes, that was it. Necessary. Repentance for all the things he had done with her last night. A call to action on this new day. Like his son's favorite character in the Avengers movies, Spiderman. *With great power comes great responsibility*. And, right now, his Spidey-Sense was tingling. The hair went up on his arms. A shiver ran down the back of his neck. He swiped the screen and put the phone to his ear.

"Hello, you've reached Senator Young," he said, carefully reciting the simple and friendly phrase his political consultants had crafted. Always act forthcoming, available, and confident. Sage advice, and it had cost him hundreds of thousands of dollars to get it. He sucked in a deep breath, repeating in his mind that last word. *Confident*. "I'm very pleased you called me today. How may I be of assistance?"

A pregnant silence followed his question. Senator Young glanced over, his eyes raking the belly of the woman he had ravished so many times. He wanted to make a child with her, knowing it would be the most beautiful creature on the planet. She was certainly fertile, he knew that for sure, because her period was always a point of contention. She hated having sex during her time of the month. He didn't mind, rather enjoyed it if he were being honest with himself. There was something dirty and savage about it. But when it came to making babies, that was a two-person process. At sixty-two years old, he doubted his sperm count was up to the task.

"Senator Young," a voice said through the phone, barely audible. It was a man, not remarkably forthright with his diction, the words as much of a statement as they were a question.

The senator perked up. He was honestly surprised to have a live person on the phone. "Yes, of course," he said. "How may I be of service?"

He heard an audible sigh, so loud as if it were in the room with him. He moved the phone in front of his face, staring quizzically at the screen, confused. The sigh came again. The senator looked up.

She was across from him, seated in his favorite plush chair. It had been a gift, something he had treasured at the time because it was upholstered with fabric that matched the navy blue of the Utah state flag. And, because it was the first gift he had received as senator. But mostly because of what his wife had done to him on that chair the night he had put it in his office.

But now *she* was in the chair, her pencil skirt lifted over her hips, her panties pulled to the side, her fingers massaging that spot she enjoyed the most. "Service this," she mouthed, then leaned her head back in silent ecstasy.

"Senator Young?" he heard again, this time clearly through the cell phone, this time obviously a question, and this time with greater urgency. The senator put the phone back to his ear, regaining focus.

"Yes, yes, I'm sorry," he said. "We must have had a bad connection for a moment."

"Zion is in peril," the voice said.

Senator Young snapped to attention. Was it time again? So soon? “I understand,” he said. “What do you need from me?”

“Everything,” the voice said. “First thing tomorrow morning. Now listen very carefully.”

CHAPTER 10

FLOWERS AND PLANTS

Bethany was not a big fan of nature walks. Today was no different. Her head still felt tender and her face ached, but at least the remnant weight of a hangover had stopped pressing on her mind and body. Ivan did not seem to be enjoying himself either, huffing down the trail as if he had never exercised in his life. All the warnings about altitude rang through her mind. Bethany wondered if that was part of their misery. Without being able to look at her phone, it was impossible to know how far Salt Lake City was above sea level. Knowing her audience, she figured it was not a good time to ask the question. Maybe someday she would have a chance to find it out for herself.

Whatever was happening, this was possibly the oddest turn of events that Bethany could have imagined. The situation with Noah and Aaron had started bad. Really bad. And then, for reasons she still could not fathom, everything changed. And then changed again. First there had been distrust and violence. Then they had been building trust. Perhaps a friendship. And then Noah's phone had buzzed. He had made that curious face, like when a bird cocks its head to search for a worm. And after he had answered, he just listened. He never said a word, but his demeanor changed. Officious. Detached. As if he had received an order.

And then the conversation had just stopped. Any air of kindness and understanding had vaporized. Noah and Aaron had transformed back to the gut-punching, face-smashing thugs they had been when Bethany first swam back to consciousness. All business. Neither thoughts, opinions, nor questions were allowed. They never gave a reason; just told Ivan and Bethany they would spend the rest of the evening in the hotel room. The discussion was done.

"Tomorrow morning we'll go to our car and take a ride," Noah had said.

Bethany trusted her gut. It had served her well as a Buffalo cop. Today, she was confident its powers were still purring like a fine-tuned engine. She just had to pay attention to it. Sometimes that was the hardest part. Shutting out all the noise. Collapsing all the emotions. If she could stay level-headed, her brain could process the information that was being chucked its way.

When they had gotten in the car that morning, it had helped to keep her eyes closed. She had focused on her breathing, but her mind still had wandered back to when she was a cop, back to the years when nothing good had ever happened in Buffalo. The economy had always sucked. Taxes were too high. Crime was on the rise. And the Bills could never win a Super Bowl. Her mood had brightened at that last thought. Maybe this was the year when that finally would happen. It was the one glimmer of annual hope for a city lost to hopelessness, and she shared with other Buffalo residents the blood-borne enthusiasm for a professional football outcome over which she had no control.

When Bethany's eyes had drifted open again in the car, she had felt swallowed by a sense of foreboding, perhaps because she had been crammed with Noah into the back seat of the small sedan, perhaps because the phone call had put a pause on Noah's willingness to talk. She had wanted to ask a question about where they were going or what was happening but suspected he would just give her a sideways glance, as if some mystery remained unsolved in his mind. Sometimes it was better to just stay quiet and let things unfold, especially after taking a knock on her head.

Up front, Ivan had sat in the passenger seat and stared out the window. She had thought back to randomly meeting him outside the beer tent, remembering it fully now, and marveled at his abrupt change. He had been so garrulous and gregarious. Now he was silent and brooding. Throughout her law enforcement career, Bethany had seen plenty of people shift personalities like that, but usually they were being hauled away in the back of a cop car. Then the perpetrator became the victim, acting like the plug had been pulled, the fun was over, and they were facing an as-of-yet undetermined time of extremely limited freedom. Or even worse. She had stared hard at Ivan for long parts of the car ride, drilling her eyes through the back of his head. He was definitely in that space, acting like an animal on its way to being euthanized.

Aaron had been the driver and Bethany had sat to his right, behind the passenger seat. He had offered her nothing except hands placed perfectly at ten and two, eyes fixed on the road, and a mindful driving style that never breached the speed limit. They had descended the canyon, that was for sure, but there had been little she could discern by way of landmarks. More trees. More towering mountains. Lots of rocks and the occasional trace of remnant snow high up on the peaks. Everything had looked the same. She saw the occasional turnout with parked vehicles. For the briefest moment, her mind had imagined people out there climbing the sheer rock faces that lined the road. Then she had toyed with the thought that she might enjoy rock climbing, but quickly brushed it away. The fear of falling was far too deep of a phobia for Bethany. She figured there were lots of reasons for that fear, but most would remain unknown unless she cozied up to a therapist and succumbed to dozens of sessions of self-discovery. In the end, though, Bethany knew the *why*. Her fear of falling was a simple fact. There was no reason to doubt it. No reason to test it.

Bethany had been six years old when the spine curdling terror had first found her, high in a barn's haymow with her friend, where they had found a nest of kittens hidden inside the maze of hay bales. They had played with them until the fall sun had dipped below the trees, and shadows inside the barn had widened and darkened. "Let's go," her friend had said with perky enthusiasm, standing to brush the hay from her clothes and hurry to the ladder. To Bethany's memory, that was when the barn had swallowed her friend. She had simply disappeared from sight. Not a sound, not a scream, not a thud. Bethany's heart had skipped a beat, the moments lengthening and driving dread into her chest.

"Come on, Bethany!" her friend had suddenly yelled. Impatience had rattled in her voice. Bethany had tried to stand but had felt no strength in her legs. She had crawled over to the square opening in the floor, feeling the stiff hay poke at her hands and knees. Tears had streamed down her face when she had reached the hole and the top of the ladder. Looking down to where her friend had stood with her hands on her hips and head cocked to the left, had felt to Bethany as if she was staring into the recesses of the earth.

"I can't," Bethany had said, sobbing.

"Can't what?" her friend had asked, realization dawning. "Climb down? You're afraid? A scaredy pants?"

Bethany had felt the warmth of urine creep into her jeans and heard the laughter of her friend as she ran off to find

Bethany's dad. When he finally came, her father had chuckled as he climbed the ladder, a forlorn smile on his face as he had lifted Bethany into his arms and eased his way back down to the barn's concrete floor.

"Not so bad, right honey?" he had asked as they walked together, side-by-side, out of the barn. She had not answered. The shame had burned too deep, lingering even to this day.

Inside the car, coasting down the canyon and through the seemingly endless number of twists and turns, Bethany had nearly laughed out loud at the useless memory. There was little value musing about the long-distant past and the humiliations she had suffered. There was no reason to contemplate new hobbies or pretend to still be a cop. Her goal was to travel and explore the world of beer, simple as that. It was time to get her life back on track.

"We're here," Aaron had said, breaking the silence that he had held the entire drive. Bethany had noticed that Aaron spoke in an ominous baritone and wondered why that had not struck her before. Perhaps he had said too little up until now to make the impression, or maybe the knock on her skull had confused her senses. This time, though, it had been noticeable, like the moment of truth had arrived. As Aaron had swung the car into a parking space, Bethany had leaned forward to look out the front windshield, seeing a brown, stone building that fitted neatly into the surrounding terrain. Several other cars had also dotted the parking lot. The letters on the front of the building had told her exactly where *here* was:

"Utah Botanical Garden," Bethany had whispered beneath her breath.

They had walked into the building, but only for a quick pass-through. Noah had pulled a card from his wallet, flashed it to the person standing vigil at the entrance, and they were waved up the stairs.

Now they were on this fucking nature walk.

Bethany found no more pleasure hiking today than she had climbing Table Mountain with Heather. She could admit that Utah Botanical Garden was beautiful, but it was too late into the fall season to enjoy the flowers and plants. The summer months were the time to visit, she thought, wondering if she would ever have the chance to return to test her theory.

Adding to Bethany's indifference about the hike was the simple reality that Noah and Aaron's agenda was not about admiring the various plant species. They kept walking, trudging along the dirt paths that wound further and further away from the parking lot and the building and any sense of civilization. Before long, they were beyond the various exhibits and well-groomed gardens, simply wandering trails amidst the natural plants that flourished at the base of a butte that towered above them to the northeast. She found herself looking up toward its summit, wondering how difficult that hike would be. It did not look terribly high, but the trail appeared to get rather steep in certain places. Worst of all, the walk to the top appeared to consist of lots of loose stones and complete exposure to the sun. She grimaced at the thought of making the climb. She was not in the mood for any of this. Even still, she took a deep breath and pressed on, the gravel crunching beneath the soft soles of her shoes.

Bethany noticed that her mental clock had stopped ticking. Maybe it was the surprisingly warm temperatures, the dearth of beer, the knock on the head, or the rhythmic cadence of their footsteps overlaid with the heavy breathing from continuous walking. In some ways, it felt like they had been on their feet for hours, perhaps hiked for miles, but she knew it was far less than that. The sun had just barely made its way above the Wasatch Mountains and a morning chill still hung in the air. Despite the exertion, a shiver ran down Bethany's spine.

Suddenly they reached a fence, suggesting they had come to the end of their little jaunt. Noah and Aaron stepped aside and spoke to each other in low tones, glancing about at their surroundings as if to get their bearings.

"Are we lost?" Bethany asked, her voice tinged with aggravation. She was in no hurry to get to wherever they were going, but she certainly had no desire to keep traipsing around the Utah wilderness. Whatever was happening, the least her kidnappers could offer was to know what they were doing.

"Not lost," Noah said, surprising Bethany with a response. "We weren't paying attention to the signs."

"Kind of lost in thought," Aaron said.

Bethany exchanged a glance with Ivan, a kind of *what the fuck* expression on both of their faces. They had departed the hotel room up in the mountains that morning and driven to the Utah Botanical Garden without a word being spoken, and now this? It was beginning to feel to Bethany like the height of incompetence, reminiscent of how the Buffalo Common Council had screwed up every aspect of managing that city. Over the lifespan of her career as a cop, she had come to disdain the city's leaders for nearly every decision they made or failed to make. That same situation seemed to be happening here.

"What are we looking for?" Bethany asked, pointing at the fence. "Seems to me we hit the end of the road. Unless you plan on going over it."

Noah looked at the fence, as if imagining himself perched on the top bar. Bethany guessed it was about fifteen feet tall. This was not an obstacle they could easily hop over. Even when she could meet the physical fitness standards to become and remain a Buffalo police officer, she hated scaling fences. *Fucking haymow*, she heard herself thinking. Even a fence half this height would challenge her deepest fears. Bethany felt a nervous thickening of her throat. She swallowed hard.

"It's back that way," Aaron said, pointing for them to retreat down the path. He squeezed past Bethany and Ivan, being careful not to tumble into the bushes. "Excuse me," he said.

Bethany and Ivan let their eyes meet again, their faces full of questions. *Excuse me? What kind of situation was this? A kidnapping?* More like a *kind*-napping. Bethany's thoughts lurched back to Munich, to those moments when she had been locked away in the darkness of a room, listening to the muffled sounds of an interrogation, and then to the screaming and the gurgling and then the gunshot. Her friend, Louis, had been the unlucky one. But she had been spared a similar fate, set free near Garmisch in the mountains of southern Germany. Bethany broke her gaze with Ivan, looking now at the Utah mountains that surrounded her, somewhat sad that they could not match up to the majesty of the Alps and Germany's famous *Zugspitze*. Travel, she realized, did have its benefits. The ability to compare the mountain ranges of Utah and Germany would have never happened if she had stayed in Buffalo.

They continued walking until Aaron stopped and pointed at a sign that read *Rock Pile Road*. "Here we are," he said. "We walked right by it, sorry about that. We're going this way. It's not too far now."

Aaron let Ivan past, then stepped in behind him. Bethany followed, with Noah taking up the rear. "It's not far now," she heard Noah say, repeating Aaron's words more as a comment to himself than to anyone in the makeshift troupe. And he was right. Boredom and exhaustion made every minute stretch into eternity, but within moments they reached another dead end. Another section of fence closed off the route up to the top of the butte. To their right, a modest, dilapidated, and abandoned building crumbled in the sun. Bethany guessed right away that the structure had meant something once, but time and weather had been its enemies. The stone-covered exterior had peeled away in places. Large chunks of brown, tan, and red rock littered the ground. The roof and windows were missing. Bethany thought back to the run-down parts of Buffalo, knowing the Queen City had fallen to shit over a short period of time. Some of its most famous buildings were now tenements. Many of its most glorious neighborhoods were now slums. Age was brutal to everything unless lavished with love and attention. That was true in Western New York, the Western United States, and the whole world over.

This structure seemed rather far from the parking lot, Bethany realized, to have played much of a role for this botanical garden. She supposed it was possible that visitors once had parked higher on this hillside, descending to the garden rather than starting with an uphill hike. She turned in a circle, shielding her eyes from the sun, but saw nothing to support her suspicions.

A movement inside the decrepit building caught her attention. Something or someone had been obscured among the low shadows, staying clear of the morning sun. It was now moving into the open. She heard Aaron mumble something that was unintelligible to her, but loud enough to catch Noah's attention. "Ah, you are here," Noah said, his voice simultaneously cheerful and fawning. "We apologize for our tardiness. We took our guests on an inadvertent trail hike."

The figure emerged in the crumbling doorway. Sunlight now poured through the open roof, creating a massive backlit shadow void of distinctive features. If it were a man, a woman, or something entirely different, Bethany could not discern. She squinted, then raised her hand again to shield her eyes. It was only when the shadow finally spoke that Bethany realized she had been holding her breath.

"Welcome to Rock Pile House," the friendly male voice said.

CHAPTER 11

RELAXATION ROOM

He hated this type of thing. Normally, lacing up his hiking boots did little more than create a feeling of foreboding, a dreading of the ceaseless marching, the *one foot after the other* drudgery that so many people in the Mountain West found somehow exciting and—dare he imagine it—exhilarating. But he did love her, and that was the reason he did this cheerfully, with an abundant heart. At least for today.

He was traveling light and did not have the benefit of darkness to conceal his movement. He had made the two phone calls and then she had given him orders. "Get your rest," she had said. "You'll need to leave very early. And take the rifle." She had not even pointed down the hallway to indicate where it was. He was aware of its location. He had used it several times before. He was becoming good at this part of his job.

And, admittedly, he loved his compact sniper rifle. Whoever had engineered the weapon deserved a gold medal for ingenuity. The damn thing came with a hefty price tag, but it was a dream to work with. It broke down easily to be carried in the pack he strapped to his back, each part being no more than eighteen inches in length. Altogether, the unit weighed a mere ten pounds. When he was in position, it would require less than one minute to reassemble. At that point, it was ready to fire. And he was confident after many times practicing that the rifle's modular system would ensure that the barrel realigned with the receiver exactly the correct way. The combination of locking lugs, alignment pin, and barrel nut were an engineering marvel. There was absolutely no risk that the rifle would be off zero. Accuracy was guaranteed.

He had to hurry. It was impossible to guess the timing of how everything would play out, and whether her expectations would meet reality. There were so many moving parts, so many unknowns, but still he believed in her vision. He had driven through the pitch black, then the rising light of dawn, and finally with the first hints of early morning sun at his back, barely feeling any sign of relief when he pulled into the parking lot and saw the sign for the Utah Botanical Garden. Instead, anxiety rose in his chest and up into his head, filling his mind with a thickness that made it difficult to keep his thoughts organized. He glanced around the parking lot, wondering if any of the cars belonged to them. The effort was futile, of course. There was no way to know what they were driving. He was haunted only by the dreaded sense that the whole thing could be over before he could get to the Relaxation Room and then into position.

But there was no reason to ponder what he could not control. He inhaled deeply, trying to calm his nerves, quickly reversing the vehicle. Another car honked, startling him. He raised his right hand apologetically. That would have been his fault. He hadn't even looked for other traffic in the parking lot, his mind was racing too fast. Talk about messing things up. A car accident would have done a good job of that.

He gave the accelerator a light push and the car eased forward. He turned a few hundred feet later, soon easing the car off the pavement and pushing the gear shift into park. This was where the real work began.

Across the road to his east was the Relaxation Room Trailhead. He had heard about it, but never actually done this hike. Not like he had ever *wanted* to do the hike. That was almost laughable. He would rather have his nails ripped out than do this voluntarily. But it was a popular trail for Salt Lake locals. A relatively easy, 1.25-mile hike to the top of the butte. The starting elevation was at 5,000 feet and the net elevation gain was 980 feet at the top. A jaunt like that would not be too bad if he had the luxury of taking his time, but he was going to be practically running the trail, and with a ten-pound backpack adding weight to the effort.

Oddly, his vehicle was the only car parked at the trailhead. He knew that was bound to change, and likely quite soon. This trail pulled in the locals and was known for being crowded, for the most part with hikers. Bikers liked some of the other nearby trails, and he would cross those paths along the way. Yes, there would be other people out there. At least eventually. He was going to have to be as smart as he was good.

He moved swiftly from the car and started east, crossing the road before entering the woods. About one hundred yards ahead, he tested the waterproofness of his boots as he splashed through a small stream, one that he imagined would have been an important source of water for the people that first settled the area. Shortly after that he broke into the open, stopping briefly to catch his bearings. To his right, a large office building stood vigil over the confluence of the Relaxation Room Trail and one of the popular biking trails. He mused for a moment whether a guard might be standing atop the building, and if someone might call out to demand the reason for his trespassing. He shook his head at his momentary indulgence and quickly moved on, knowing the glass-wrapped building did nothing more than reflect the brilliant Utah sunshine, throwing a bit of extra warmth into the start of his climb. He looked up toward the ridge he was about to ascend, exertion and excitement pounding his heart. There was no time for hating the thought of the climb to come, only for action. He got his legs moving and powered onward.

He passed a trail sign that offered options to consider instead of his objective. He avoided any temptation to contemplate an alternative plan, feeling his pace quicken instead, adrenaline now overriding any sense of physical and mental exhaustion. Each step came easier now, and the fast walk turned to a slow lope, then to a consistent jog. He never considered himself a runner and least of all a trail runner, but his efforts in the gym were paying off now. High intensity interval training, especially when done with an altitude training mask, had prepared him for the unexpected. The social media advertisement for the training mask had promised to make his respiratory system stronger, with unmatched stamina, endurance, and recovery. He would have to remember to go back and post a five-star review for the product, he thought, if his physical performance continued as well as it had started.

He separated his mind from the growing effort by thinking back to how this whole adventure started. She was wily and demanding but, in the end, she had needed little to turn her burning expectation into a loving request. Just a quick change of tone in the way she said the words. And, with it, a slight smile that turned up the right corner of her mouth, met with a softening of the skin around her eyes. All those things had melted his heart, weakened his knees, and made it easy to simply say yes. He had been moving constantly ever since.

And little more than fifteen minutes after leaving his car, after all the twists and turns of the exposed trail, he made the last ascent and came to what the trail maps said was the Relaxation Room.

It was tempting to stop. All around him, sandstone slabs were carefully constructed to form armchairs, sofas, and ottomans. It was a beautiful spot to enjoy the panoramic view of Salt Lake Valley and the Oquirrh Mountains, maybe sip on some water and just watch the sun continue to rise. He could stay here and relax for a while, maybe even until sunset.

He shook his head, breaking from the brief reverie. He wondered how people fell in love with hiking, thinking that maybe all the advertisements he had seen rang true to some people. There was glory in the sweat, and even he felt an inkling of pride that he was strong enough to have done the climb so well. Young people would probably want an award or something. At the least a selfie to commemorate the moment. Anything to celebrate a job well done, even if that had been done rather poorly. As for himself, in the end, he really did not care for accolades. Those were for the weak, for the people without purpose, for those that filled their leisure time with meaningless activities. His work would determine the future of the movement, the future of their people. The only thing that mattered now was the task he had been given.

The Relaxation Room had been an easy landmark to find. There was no patting himself on the back for that minor success. From here, the going got tricky. He pulled a compass from the backpack and determined his bearings, then started down the ridge, heading back in the direction of the Utah Botanical Garden. He was after more elevation and a good vantage point. From where he was now, there were no real choices.

The question at this point was speed versus stealth. The slow way would put him high upon the ridge. He could slip into some brush, blending into cover to limit the risk that, somehow, he might be seen from below. The faster route meant moving along the east side of the ridge, below the brush. He could travel quickly across the scree field, but that exposed him to anyone that might be looking up in his direction. There was always the possibility of a witness taking random photos or videos. He cursed the advent of cell phones, allowing himself a silent moment to question God's wisdom.

But this was not the time for contemplation, and certainly not a moment for sacrilege. The answer was obvious. Time was of the essence. The fastest way was his only choice. He had known that from the moment he turned the key in the ignition and raced away from Rock Springs.

His hiking boots made easy work of the loose rock and uneven terrain. He hugged as tightly as possible to the edge created by the vegetation, hoping this would break up his silhouette to anyone that looked in his direction. So far, he saw nobody on the trail. He whispered under his breath a quiet thanks that, perhaps, the Angel Moroni was blessing his work.

Sweat beaded on his forehead, a result of his exertion and the rising morning temperature. He wiped it away with his forearm, wondering about the changing of the season. He sensed he should be more worried about a sudden snowstorm, not this Indian summer weather. But fall was always unpredictable in the Salt Lake valley and today was no different. Tomorrow might bring a complete change. Rain, or maybe plummeting temperatures and a good dose of the white stuff. Something told him the ski weather forecasters were scouring the computer models for signs of the first significant snowfall. Hope sprang eternal for Utah sportspeople and every season had its enthusiasts.

Following the shape of the terrain, he suddenly crossed the ridgetop. Instead of looking down to where he had started his gaze fell squarely on an immaculate stone building that seemed to blend into the natural surroundings, and its parking lot dotted with cars. Now he had a clear view of the Utah Botanical Garden. He was getting close.

He squatted, aware that if he were not cautious, he might be seen from below. His rational mind told him that was overkill, that there was no reason for anyone to suspect the job he had been sent here to do. Perhaps, in fact, his attempts at being clandestine could draw more attention to his movement. But sneaking around was part of the excitement, and he had to admit to that. It was like having a role in a movie. There was something exhilarating about playing the part. Today, he was an assassin. A reincarnation of Orville Lagrange.

As he scurried through the low brush and rocks, careful to stay in a low crouch, Orville's name kept drifting through his mind. He wondered how it would feel to live like Orville, to possess thirteen wives and have God bless him with dozens of children. He pondered how it must have felt for Orville to rise to lead a polygamous fundamentalist Mormon group, and all the glory that came with his ascension.

Orville was another one of his heroes and mentors. He had lived his life like Caleb, who told the doubting Israelites that they would conquer and take possession of the land. That was how Orville had operated, simply taking what was his and killing those that opposed him.

He stopped, pushing away his thoughts of Orville Lagrange, and shielded his eyes. The sun's glare yielded to the width of his hand. There it was. The Rock Pile House.

In his mind, the clock started ticking. He needed to have the sniper rifle assembled and ready in less than one minute. He started, relying on hours of countless practice. The rhythm of his routine was simple. It was built upon the names of people Orville Lagrange had killed: James Lagrange. Robert Tuft. Noelle Martini. Dan Robert Best. Albert B. Chesterfield. Mike Chernosky. Susan Chernosky. Billy Phillipi. Mark Chernosky.

The last piece fell into place. He was ready.

The tripod rested on a large stone. He checked the rifle's foundation once, then twice, confirming there would be no unexpected movement when the time came to squeeze the trigger. He sprawled flat into a prone position, moving a few rocks that happened to dig into his hip points. He wished at that moment for a thick blanket or a mat to lie upon, just something to make things a little more comfortable. He might be stuck here for a while.

He let the rifle slip into his shoulder pocket, that fleshy, muscled area that would absorb any recoil when the bullet was fired. He brought his breath under control, exhaling slowly out of his nose, and let his right eye settle in behind the scope. The picture he saw swam for a moment as he swung the barrel in the direction of the Rock Pile House, searching for a line of fire.

Blood Atonement. That had been Orville Lagrange's legacy of revenge. The LDS Church may have denied the doctrine since 1889. Early church leaders may have called it a *fiction.* And later leaders might have called it a *theoretical principle.* But Orville knew that early Mormon leaders—including Brigham Young—had promoted the Doctrine of Blood Atonement during the Mormon Reformation.

He smiled. The scope caught a brief reflection of his teeth, but he did not pause to take notice. His thoughts were elsewhere, reveling in the glory of the moments to come. Once he squeezed the trigger, he would forever etch his name into the history of Blood Atonement. Malachi Bradshaw. The Enforcer. And Amanda Lang's greatest defender. For that, especially, his rewards would be great.

CHAPTER 12

WATERMELON

Bethany Judge had big dreams. Not in the sense that she had high aspirations. She had never been that type of person. Even as a cop, she had satisfied herself with a mediocre career, one that had been more like the steady hum of an electric wire rather than the rising trajectory of a rocket ship. She had preferred it that way, finding some degree of comfort knowing the relative predictability of each workday—if the job of a police officer could ever be predictable. Throughout her career she had done her best to stay out of any workplace politics and had kept her head down enough to never be considered for a leadership role. Career advancement had been a non-starter, as far as she had been concerned. Thank God that was all behind her.

Because now there was this whole beer expert thing. Bethany R. Judge. *Beer Judge*. Bethany smiled inwardly every time she thought of that nickname, of how Frau Doktor Herta Stocker had just made it up on the spot when they first met in Munich. That little play on her name. So creative. Herta had summarized in two quick words Bethany's biggest aspiration of her life. To drink and understand beers of all styles, from all around the world. Traveling and exploring, visiting breweries and meeting brewers, attending beer festivals and becoming famous in the process. Hell, maybe even write a book or two, like Herta had suggested. And stay in Munich for a while to be with her. Too bad Herta was dead.

The shit had hit the fan in Munich. And Berlin. Even now, back in the States. Bethany knew some of the truth of what had happened overseas and suspected much of what was happening now. She felt an odd compulsion to do something about it but, when she let her mind relax and just listened, Bethany could still hear the steady sound of complacency. Her lack of desire and commitment. Comfort in the status quo. Fear of success.

Yet here she was, a Level Four beer expert. It was one of the most prestigious titles on earth. Less than two dozen people had completed the program, and she counted among the ranks. When she remembered that, her heart swelled with pride. It had not been easy to complete the four levels, with each progressively more difficult than the last. But she had done it at record speed. First, she had knocked out the Level One exam. Nothing to it. She had learned how to think and talk about beer, about how to serve beer, and things that put beer quality at risk. That exam had been like snapping her fingers.

Then she had crushed Level Two. She was in good company once that was done. About 4,000 others could claim the well-rounded knowledge of beer styles and service that came with the certification, including an understanding of beer styles and flaws according to taste and smell.

Level Three was intimidating but Bethany took it down like a good Pilsner. Quick and easy. Introduced for people who wanted to take their beer knowledge up another notch, Level Three usually took several years of practice and tasting. But Bethany had needed just months to prepare for the multiple written, oral, and tasting components of the day-long exam. Everything had clicked into place.

She had moved straight to Level Four after that. The coveted designation as a professional beer expert. Every aspect of beer knowledge was challenged in that curriculum, from the technical to the aesthetic. The success rate was next to zero. Everyone had warned her it was a grueling and heartbreaking journey. Be happy with Level Three and just move on.

But Bethany R. Judge had found her calling. The reason she had been put on Earth. Nothing had stopped her from her destiny.

However, afterwards and ever since, when she looked at herself in the mirror, she was haunted with the question as to whether there much of a difference between "Buffalo cop" Bethany Judge and "beer expert" Bethany Judge. The simple and honest answer was...no.

And at night, deep in sleep, her mind making sense of the tragedies that had shaped her life and of the horrible things she had witnessed as a cop, dreams churned through Bethany's brain, a rich tapestry of images that built upon themselves night after night in ways Bethany never understood.

Which made the floating watermelon very strange. It just hovered there above the ground, about six feet, roughly the average height of a man, and kept talking at her. The thing had eyes and a moving mouth. Bethany squinted, trying to make sense of what she was seeing. A bright light shone behind it, making the watermelon look like some type of solar eclipse. It was saying so many things that Bethany found herself enthralled by the words.

Like many dreams, this one just seemed to go on and on. Endless. Bethany tried to wrench her mind free, taking control of the dream by charting a different course. Sometimes that worked. This time, it didn't.

She felt surrounded by people. Not a big crowd. Just a handful. More likely, only a few. Yes, a small contingent stood on her periphery and, if she looked, she might be able to see their faces. But that did not matter. Even without faces, she *knew* who they were. That was the thing about dreams. God was not in the details.

The watermelon had a lot to say. It even had a name. If Bethany guessed, it was the most important watermelon in the history of watermelons. It spoke with a clear, crisp cadence that made Bethany listen closely, but in the recesses of her mind she was curious that her dream had conjured up the watermelon's pleasant speaking voice. An ugly Buffalonian accent would have made more sense. That was how Bethany spoke, with a nasally tone and a peculiar emphasis on hard "a" sounds. She still said stupid words, like *youse*. It was the reason people sometimes gave her confused glances, almost as if they pitied her upbringing.

There was a sudden glint behind the watermelon, a reflection of sorts that caught Bethany's attention. It was there, then it was gone. And then it was back again. Was someone in her dream sending a signal? Was it some sort of morse code? That was when the watermelon popped. Exploded, really. The juice and rind and seeds burst across Bethany's face, covering her chest and arms. And what was left of the watermelon fell to the ground in a heap.

Except that was not what happened. And none of it was a dream.

*

"*Welcome* to the Rock Pile House," the tall, backlit figure said again, this time putting special emphasis on the first word. Noah and Aaron took that as some kind of signal. They crossed their hands at their waists, closed their eyes, and bowed their heads.

"My name is Senator Young," the man now said. "Senator Orin Young." He turned his head slowly, leveling his gaze at Bethany and Ivan. "You've not heard of me? That's a shame, I suppose. It suggests you aren't engaged in the politics of this nation. Are you not concerned with the struggles of our country?"

"I'm very aware of who you are, Senator Young," Ivan said, now also bowing his head. "I'm sorry. The sun is behind you. And everything that is happening. This is all so strange."

"Yes, I suppose that might be the case," Senator Young said. "This is all rather sudden, isn't it?"

"And our apologies for her ignorance," Aaron said, speaking on Bethany's behalf. "She's from Buffalo."

Senator Young tipped his head to the side and took a step closer. "Wyoming?"

"New York," Aaron said, in a tone that suggested everyone from the western United States would ask the same question.

"Ah, New York," the Senator said. "I suppose that might provide some excuse for her. If nothing else, my esteemed colleagues from her lovely state have tended to overshadow my efforts. Though I am often in the news, of course. Is she not aware of my aspirations for higher office?"

"I don't believe so," Aaron said. "She seems not to know very much."

"That is the trouble with our democracy, isn't it?" Senator Young said. "And a microcosm of what I intend to fix." The senator stepped forward again, now gesticulating slightly with his hands. "You see, I lead a people that, rather unfortunately, have been forced into silence and submission for decades now. We feigned ignorance to lower our profile as a community, to blend in, to reduce persecution. And, in the process, we lost our compass. We lost the passion that led us to this beautiful valley. Our Promised Land."

Senator Young turned slightly, admiring the view that stretched out before him. Now there were buildings and highways as far as the eye could see. And even planes lifting off from Salt Lake City International Airport. But his gaze seemed to see something different, as if flowing across eternity. "I sometimes think back to how it must have been," he said. "To the beginning, yes, but mostly to that moment when Brigham Young first laid eyes upon the land that was meant for us. We see things so differently now, don't we? Our world is fast. Transient, in a sense. Zip zip, we buzz around in cars, going here and there at speeds our forefathers could not have comprehended. And without the slightest effort on our parts, outside of the effort needed to fill up on gasoline, I suppose. What toil and trouble that is! Hah!

"No, our tribe moved at the speed the Lord intended when they arrived here. They absorbed everything they were given and then possessed the beauty and bounty of this land. Why? Because they had the time to process the moments. All of them. Yes, not just any single moment, like we live today. They were on foot. Or in wagons. Perhaps riding horses. Imagine that! Up there, behind us, to the East, first resting their eyes on this majestic blessing. Do you think they imagined they had stumbled upon Eden? I certainly do."

Senator Young laughed quietly. Speaking again, his voice was quieter and less excited. "See, I let my thoughts get the best of me. I am passionate about these things, admittedly. It is woven into the fabric of who I am. I represent my people in Washington, and I can't separate this love and commitment from the duties I am sworn to uphold. No, they are truly one and the same to me. And, sadly, the rest of our country is blind to it. This new lady friend here proved that today.

"Not that I blame her. Buffalo, New York? I've never heard anyone speak highly of that city. In fact, always the opposite. Is it just a victim of the times? Did enough people like her stop caring and the city followed suit? You do know that cities—like all of society—are a living organism, right? They must be tended to, no different than our bodies. If we fill ourselves with poison, like tobacco, caffeine, alcohol, or drugs, our physical beings will collapse upon themselves. We erode from within and without. Eventually we perish. A city like Buffalo is the same. Yes, now that I say this, I do see a vision. A future great speech. Even dying bodies can be healed. Miracles have been witnessed, haven't they? Christ raised Lazarus, did he not? We have many cities in this country that can be just like Lazarus."

The senator paused only briefly, collecting himself. "This happens, my moments of clarity. They are blessings. When I am consumed by the spirit. My colleagues in Washington like to say I have brainstorming sessions. Or diarrhea of the mouth. I know that's the modern parlance attributed to moments of spiritual passion. It is as if an entire nation—supposedly founded under God—has forgotten the Gifts of the Spirit. And we are all different, you know? I mean, there are only so many Gifts available, right? Isaiah enumerated seven gifts of the Holy Spirit. Have any of you determined yours? Wisdom, understanding, counsel, fortitude, knowledge, piety, and fear of the Lord? No? Perhaps you should spend some time in study and self-reflection. You may find clarity understanding the gifts assigned to you.

"Though if you were Mormon, I'd remind you of something different. Of our seventh Article of Faith. 'We believe in the gift of tongues, prophecy, revelation, visions, healing, interpretation of tongues, and so forth.' Women can receive these gifts, by the way. We offer equal opportunity in that fashion, hah! And all it takes is some serious effort on the part of the recipient. Some diligent seeking and righteous living. That's not too much to ask, is it? For a gift from our Lord? I think not. Sometimes I think that God is speaking through me in moments like this when words simply pour forth like a waterfall. Perhaps this is what is meant by interpreting tongues, don't you think? Divine inspiration is like the ether. I hear it, though it is silent. What emerges are the words spoken through me.

"But I'm surprised, to be honest," Senator Young continued. "Buffalo, New York? I imagine the city was in some ways blessed. You know that Joseph Smith lived nearby, don't you? Yes, he was born in Vermont but moved his family to western New York by 1817. A similar gift, you see, because it was there that he received two visions! You know where he saw the most important vision? Where he found the golden plates? The ones he interpreted into the Book of Mormon? Why, that was just down the highway from Buffalo these days. What do they call it up there? The New York State Thruway! Another toll road in that poorly managed state. An endless tax to feed the ceaseless needs of New York City."

Senator Young took a breath to collect himself. "Manchester, New York. That's where it happened. That's where you find Cumorah. It's easier to call it Mormon Hill, I suppose, but I hate the fact that our lazy society demeans it with such disregard. Would they call the Rock of Calvary 'Jesus Rock' or something that debased its importance? I think not!

"Ah, see, now I ramble," he said. "Diligent seeking! I can't always hear and breathe from the ether, can I? We still live on earth. Oh, how to keep the channel open to the spiritual world! My search for that answer will never end. And, for that matter, I will never stop my quest to improve the lives of our people. Mormons first! Others may quake at that proclamation, but it isn't meant in anger, nor is it meant as a threat. Simply a horn blast, like that from Angel Moroni. A call to the world to come to us. We are congregating and the entire planet is welcome in our embrace.

"We can't do this with the fools steering the ship. You know that, right? Of course, you do. You're from Buffalo! A city of the blind leading the blind. How can those leaders ignore the plight of its body? I find it unfathomable! I am not one for endless debate and lack of action. No, I take steps for meaningful change. When the Lord speaks to my heart, I do not hesitate. That is how I will lead our country when I'm elected. Decisive leadership.

"And leaders take action. I am not afraid to make difficult decisions. When Amanda Lang calls, I know it comes from God because she has diligently sought her spiritual gifts. She has worked hard. She lives righteously for the good of our cause. I have not questioned what she asks of me, and so I am here, fulfilling her request, even if it pains my pride to yield to the whims of a woman. No matter! The Mormon body is one flesh, and where one succeeds, we all succeed.

"And we did. I stopped their endless, crazy talk about the economy, but the entire Mormon community was beside me in that victory. My people see that and know that. They are rallying behind me. Meeting after meeting, and those so-called economic experts get their faces on business television and their quotes in the paper. What do we get? Ridicule! Oh, yes, nobody wants us to matter. What are we? A joke? No, we are eternity!

"That's where he is now. Do you think he met God? Based on his last name, I thought he might have been Jewish. Edward Roth. What a stupid person. Everyone thought he was smart. His education and degrees said he was intelligent, but he wasn't clever enough to consider me, was he? Did he think God would let man tinker forever with the gods they were putting before Him? Money and the economy and interest rates? What a disgrace! We should be working for the Kingdom of G—"

CHAPTER 13

PARK CITY

Bethany knew a rifle report when she heard it. Maybe it was her years of training as a cop and all the time spent at gun ranges. Or maybe she could credit her dad for taking her deer hunting in Pennsylvania. In western New York they could only use shotguns during deer season, but they allowed real guns down in the Keystone State, and the first time she heard the resounding *crack* of her dad's hunting rifle it had been seared into her memory forever. Now, she heard a similar sound bouncing off the surrounding landscape, the vastness of Utah swallowing it for eternity.

What made less sense was the blood and brains that sprayed her face and the gaping exit wound that appeared suddenly in the head of Senator Orin Young. He had talked incessantly, confusing Bethany's perception and making her imagine strange things, as if in a dream. Then this happened. Bethany's mind spun like a roulette wheel, finally landing on the question as to whether *God* was the last word Senator Young had tried, but failed, to speak. She found irony in that thought but doubted the senator would have appreciated her musings.

A body slammed into her, knocking Bethany off balance. She heard Aaron's voice yelling, a cacophony of noise amidst the swirling chaos of Senator Young's collapsing body, and the sensation of being dragged to cover behind the decrepit walls of the Rock Pile House.

Suddenly, Ivan's eyes were staring into hers. "Are you okay?" he asked. "Are you shot?" His right hand came up to her face and Bethany felt a slick, warm sensation as he wiped blood away from her eyes. He moved quickly down to her body, patting her shirt for any indication of a bullet wound.

"I'm fine," Bethany said. She pressed her back against the wall behind her. Without a weapon to protect themselves, she felt more annoyed than scared. She had a conceal and carry permit but had stopped packing a firearm the day she had retired from the police force. A weapon had seemed unnecessary in her new career. And rather stupid, if she were honest with herself, given all the beer she planned to drink. Somewhere up in heaven, Bethany was willing to bet some dead cops were having a good laugh at her expense right about now.

"What the fuck is going on?" she asked.

"Don't know," Ivan said. He pointed with his thumb to some distant point hidden behind the wall that protected them. "Somebody took a shot from back there. A hunter? Maybe just an accident?"

Bethany looked over to the lifeless body of Senator Orin Young. A dark red puddle of blood stained the tan, almost colorless stone upon which he had crumbled. Before long, she knew, sun and rain would bleach away that blood forever. Nature's harshness would never allow that blemish to remain.

"Not a chance," Bethany said. "Whoever took that shot, it was intentional."

"A sniper?"

Bethany nodded, thinking. The Rock Pile House backed up to the butte. She had noticed it when Senator Young had been pontificating but had not paid close attention. Was the top of the butte closer than she remembered? She scooted on her backside down the wall and peeked around the corner.

"Careful!" Ivan said.

"The shooter was up there," Bethany said, trying to estimate the distance. "That's a long shot. They knew what they were doing."

She took another moment to scan the hillside below the summit, knowing every extra second with her head exposed put her at risk for a well-aimed bullet. There was a chance that more than one person was involved in this, but she saw no indication of anyone advancing on their position. After another few moments she turned back and rested against the wall.

It dawned on her that she was alone with Ivan. That was a surprising turn of events. Her gaze floated across the surrounding sagebrush, looking for signs of Aaron and Noah. She was confident there had only been one gunshot, but perhaps she had failed to hear subsequent rifle reports in the confusion that erupted after Senator Young's head popped open in front of her. There was a chance either or both were also dead. Bethany felt a moment of comfort at that thought, but quickly chastised herself. She had never been a big fan of people dying, even when they appeared to deserve it.

Suddenly, a cell phone rang. The sound came from her left, muffled and too distant to get an exact bearing on the sound. She looked over to the body of Senator Young as the phone rang a second time, listening intently. There was a chance it was his phone and that the open terrain was confusing her senses. The ringing paused briefly and then continued. No, it was not the senator's phone. The noise was coming from her left, somewhere among the sagebrush. In that same instant she heard

Noah's voice. He spoke a single word, both questioning and urgent, like a hatchling waiting to be fed.

"Hello?"

Bethany listened, only hearing wind, the rustling of leaves, the creaking of branches, and the sound of Ivan breathing beside her. His breaths were shallow and fast. She worried he might hyperventilate but pushed her concern aside. There were bigger issues to deal with now. After what seemed like an eternity, she heard Noah speak again.

"I understand," he said.

Noah popped up, showing no reluctance to expose his entire body to the unknown shooter. He crouched forward slightly, as if ready to pounce at any moment. His eyes appeared to look in every direction and his head darted back and forth, perhaps searching for prey. Bethany was struck with the memory of a velociraptor from one of those sci-fi movies she used to watch when she could not sleep. She fought to recall the movie's title, knowing it was an easy trivia question, but vacated the effort when a sudden gust of wind billowed Noah's sweat-stained shirt. He reached the back of his hand to his forehead to wipe perspiration from his pale face.

"Aaron!" he barked. "We're in the clear. Get out here, come on! They gave me the call. We have some cleaning up to do, we need to hurry!"

Aaron stood slowly, uncertain about following Noah's orders. "What are you talking about?" he asked. "Who called?"

"He did." Noah said, leaving any elaboration unsaid. "Now, come on. Anyone could hike out this way. We don't want to explain what happened here, do we? Or have to eliminate someone who stumbles upon us? Outside of the simple reality that he's dead, the senator is too recognizable, even in this condition. We need to deal with this fast."

"Deal with it?" Aaron asked. "What the fuck, Noah? We have no tools to bury him! What are we supposed to do?"

Noah surveyed the area, thinking through their options. After a moment, he pointed to the fence that somehow shaped the perimeter of the Utah Botanical Garden. "There," he said. "We need to get him behind the fence. That should keep people from finding the body. And then we'll bury him under a pile of rocks. Make it harder for animals to get to him, give the body time to decompose." He pointed to Ivan and Bethany. "You are part of this, too, so let's go. Grab an arm or a leg. And once we're done, we need to get to Park City. Amanda wants a meeting."

*

The work was tough and disgusting, but Bethany's mind had been focused on Noah's last statement. *Amanda wants a meeting.* She pondered the possibility that the trail to the top of Table Mountain, and now to the ruins of the Rock Pile House, may have finally led back to the woman she had met in Munich. As Bethany had placed the final stone that covered Senator Young's face, she knew in her heart that he had deserved a better death and funeral. But then she thought back to Munich and to the murder of her friend, Louis, remembering the moment when she had heard through the concrete wall the last sounds of life leaving his body. She tried to imagine the final thoughts of Louis's dying mind, guessing they had been a combination of fear and confusion. Maybe eventually relief. Whatever the answer, she guessed the senator had not experienced something similar. Death had come too quickly for him to have given it much thought.

Nobody said a word after they left the Rock Pile House, trudged back to the car, and started the drive to meet with

Amanda Lang. Bethany was not too surprised by that, figuring that each of them was experiencing some degree of post traumatic shock. A high caliber rifle round blowing open a man's head tended to have that effect. Bethany stared blankly out the car's window, trying her best to stop the images of Senator Young's last moments from playing over and over in her mind. After a while, she just quit. She had learned a trick or two as a cop about how to shut out bad memories, but this was all too fresh. She needed a little more time to pass. And a different environment, somewhere to decompress. Bethany took some comfort knowing that she was not alone in her suffering, guessing the others were brooding over what they had just experienced at the Utah Botanical Garden. And, for that matter, what was next to come.

They stopped at a small gas station in what felt to Bethany like a less desirable part of Salt Lake City. She hated being in a strange town and not knowing exactly where she was, but this felt like the type of place where random shootings might occur. Bethany craned her neck to see if the clerk inside was protected by plenty of bulletproof glass. She afforded herself a small chuckle, betting Senator Young would have appreciated her gallows humor.

"You need to get cleaned up," Noah said to Bethany. "We all do, really. But you took a lot of blood spray when he got shot. I'll get the key for the outside bathroom."

The bathroom mirror told Bethany more of the story. The dirt and dust from hauling rocks and covering the body had turned the red blood into some shade of brown. From afar, she guessed it looked like a regretful patch of freckles, passable enough to not catch anyone's attention. But beneath the stark white light inside the gas station restroom, there was no mistaking it for what it was. Lots of blood. And probably some brains and bone and hair. At that moment, she wondered about

Senator Young's blood type, then felt a pang of concern. She likely had taken some spray into her eyes. Maybe even her mouth. She frowned. Rule number one as a cop was expecting the perpetrator to have some type of blood-borne pathogen. HIV. Hepatitis. Even if the person wore a clean-pressed suit. Sometimes especially so. You always took the necessary precautions.

"There's no going back on this one," Bethany said, looking in the mirror. "It is what it is at this point."

She got the sink water as warm as she could, and still not nearly hot enough for the job. Bethany pushed the soap pump several times until a nice puddle formed in her hand, then grimaced. The bathroom soap was the creamy blue kind, replete with a cheap gas station scent. She hated perfumes. They gave her headaches and confused her olfactory system, making it difficult to taste beer. Scent-free shampoos and soaps, those were the friends of a beer expert. But this time there were no options. She slapped her palms together, rubbed vigorously, and applied the soap to her face.

"Ah, a new woman!" Noah said after Bethany emerged thirty minutes later. "To be honest, I was starting to get worried. If there had been a window in there, I might have thought you had escaped! But I see you were taking your time getting back to some semblance of normal. That's good, that's good. Wash away your sins and all that kind of stuff. Well, anyway, it gave Aaron some time to get some fresh clothes for you down the street. They should fit just fine, maybe a bit baggy. Go back in and change. After that, we should all take a turn, shouldn't we? We want to look presentable."

Sixty minutes later they arrived in the heart of Park City, Utah. The streets were quiet. Bethany was surprised, feeling like she had a sense of the town's reputation, and that what she knew demanded a far different scene. Lots of hustle and bustle. People hitting the restaurants and bars or popping from one art gallery to the next. Perhaps things would be different during the heart of ski season. As if reading her thoughts, Noah cleared his throat.

"Here are some worthless factoids for you," he said. "You saw the training area when we exited the highway? That's a remnant from when Salt Lake hosted the 2002 Winter Olympics. The region was big for skiing before then, but certainly has grown since. If I'm not mistaken, the largest North American ski resort is here in Park City. But who knows, right? So many mountains continue to expand, it's almost a tragedy. Oh, I suppose I should ask. You are a skier, right?"

"Not really," Bethany mumbled. "A bit as a kid in western New York. Some as an adult. Smaller resorts, nothing like this. There was a free tow rope and a small hill in East Aurora. My parents would take me there sometimes."

"Hmm, yes," Noah mused. "Keeping children busy and happy is always the challenge, isn't it? Well, the skiing would be far different here, I'm sure you can imagine."

Noah continued. "This is historic Main Street, though far different than what we might have experienced one hundred years ago or more. Today, it's just a shopper's paradise, don't you think? Look at all the galleries and stores, restaurants, and other attractions. You could get lost here for hours wandering about. There's really no need to vacation in Park City to ski, if buying things or exploring food is your pleasure. And, for that matter, artisan drinks. Ah, here we are!"

Bethany glanced first to her left, noting only a parking garage. A moment later they passed under what appeared to be a chair lift. She imagined it ran nonstop during the winter, hauling skiers and snowboarders from their vehicles up to some drop-off point on the mountain. Today, however, it sat idle.

Noah pulled into an open parking space on the side of the road. "She's in there," he said, pointing to his right. "Let's not keep her waiting any longer."

Bethany leaned forward in her car seat to look at the building, her mood lifting at the sight of the large window facade and, behind it, the copper tanks of a craft distillery. Had they asked, she would have suggested they hold this meeting at a brewery instead. Under the circumstances, though, she was not going to look a gift horse in the mouth.

Inside, the restaurant was open and airy, and bled straight into a beautiful bar at the front end of the building. Bethany felt transported back in time, to an era her mind associated with western movies and television shows she had watched as a child. The wooden walls, floors, and ceilings created an Old West atmosphere. Only a handful of small windows allowed light to creep into the room. Eight large opaque ceiling fixtures cast a soft glow. Bethany paused to take note of the chandeliers. They were round, creating a pleasant visual offset to the squareness of the room. Circular artwork also decorated the walls, and the square dining tables could be opened into round tops. Inwardly, Bethany smiled. She appreciated the genius of the interior decorator that had designed the space. It was the sort of skill Bethany could appreciate because she possessed none of that talent herself.

Bethany brought her thoughts back to the matter at hand. They were here for more serious business than her ruminations about craft distillery aesthetics, and the events at the Utah Botanical Garden just hours earlier underscored the point. With that thought, an image of Senator Young flashed into Bethany's mind. Anxiety and panic raced through her limbs, nearly causing her legs to buckle. Bethany fought for composure, conjuring the coping skills that she had learned as a cop. They had made life tolerable back then, helping her recover from the daily horrors of murder, child abuse, suicide, or car accidents. She hoped they would do the same now.

In that instant, she noticed a woman standing behind one of the tables, then saw her wave them over. Bethany's eyes widened with the realization it was Amanda Lang, fitter than ever, wearing a blue and white athletic dress that complimented her tanned skin, her hair now chestnut brown and shoulder length. Bethany remembered none of these visuals from their time together in Munich.

It hardly mattered now.

CHAPTER 14

FRENEMIES

"Fancy meeting you here," Amanda said, a glint of ill-timed humor in her eyes. "I sometimes thought we would never meet again. To be honest, I wondered if you had made it home from Europe in the first place. Lots of people died over there, right? For all I knew, you were one of them. And when I looked you up to send you that postcard, I found out you aren't the only Bethany Judge on the planet. There's actually a professor out there that shares your name! Isn't that a lovely coincidence? You and the whole fiasco with Professor Stocker in Munich. And then it turns out you have a namesake Professor Bethany Judge here in the United States!"

"I don't believe in coincidences," Bethany said dryly.

Amanda waved her hand dismissively and took a seat. "Don't be so serious. Look, honestly, I thought you might have pursued Herta to the ends of the earth, especially if you had realized what was going on. Did you ever figure it all out?"

Bethany nodded. "It took a moment. Actually, after the long walk in the English Garden with her. You told me to take her there, and nobody showed up as planned."

Amanda laughed. "It was a gamble on my part. Too bad what had to happen to the boys. I don't take pleasure in things like that. I hope you believe me. But they were part of the collateral damage, right? They had their mission. I had mine. They thought they were smart. I was smarter. It doesn't pay to underestimate me. Anyway, I thought you'd have a hard time giving up whatever connected you to the professor. Was it love? Lust? Or just some kind of stupid infatuation? I guess it doesn't really matter. I just worried that you might have been in Berlin when everything happened. What a disaster, right? Herta was an example of a person that couldn't handle power. She thought she could, but she was wrong. Perhaps we are the only two people who really know that truth about her. But that's all in the past. We move on and live in the present. For today. As for me, I'm happy that you are alive. That's all. I'm not certain that I am happy to see you, however. Yes, that I can say."

"You did invite me," Bethany said.

"Hah, yes! I suppose that is true. I'm a sucker for postcards, like back in the days before cell phones and all this social media crap. There's something to be said about a random photo of someplace showing up in your mailbox."

"With a nice little message," Bethany finished.

"Well, of course! What else are postcards for? I suppose nostalgia or curiosity or maybe even kindness got the best of me, though, didn't it? I know all too well your love of beer. I dare say that we Utahns are holding our own in that category."

"So, you bring me to a distillery?" Bethany asked.

"Not optimal, I agree, but we have a broader audience, don't we?" Amanda turned her attention to Noah and Aaron for a moment, offering a limp-wristed salute. "Thank you for your service today."

Both men nodded, saying nothing. Amanda motioned for all four of them to take a seat at the table, then looked quizzically at Ivan.

"And this other gentleman is?" she asked.

"His name is Ivan," Bethany said, her voice cold. Whatever she had stumbled into, Ivan did not need to be involved. Her mind raced for a way to extricate him from this meeting. She needed to think of something fast. If not, Bethany worried Ivan would become another one of Amanda's casualties.

"Welcome, Ivan," Amanda said, pointing to a chair. Her eyes encouraged him to sit.

"Thank you," Ivan said, acting on Amanda's silent command.

"You know that, as a rule, Mormons don't drink," Amanda said. "Bethany, you will remember we chatted about this back in Munich. I'm not going to belabor my thoughts on that Mormon belief. Hell, I'll admit to everyone here and to God that I drank enough beer to fill an oil tanker during my mission in Germany. But it served a purpose, and my success is all the justification I need to have strayed from our teachings."

Amanda paused, surveying her audience. "And so, we are here in this distillery with my good friend Bethany Judge. Did you know she is a certified beer expert? What a comical aspiration, but we all long to be recognized for our talents, don't we? What's a wine expert again?"

"Sommelier," Bethany responded.

"Ah, yes," Amanda said. "Is that French? The word sounds so refined, and you do pronounce it tolerably well. Even with your Buffalo accent. A bit on the nasally side, I would say, but French has never been my strength. Understandably so, I'm sure you can guess. Historically the Germans and the French didn't get along so well. And you remember the whole story about my parents, about how—"

"Was any of that true?" Bethany asked, interrupting.

"About the murder of my parents?' Amanda asked. "Most certainly. Look, if you don't believe me, I'm sure we can find old news stories about it. Maybe there is something on the internet, I don't know. But I assure you there would be something in the Mormon archives. Old newspaper microfiche, at the very least. I just don't know, exactly, because I never bothered to look. I refused to torture myself by reliving that pain. What was done was done. I plotted my course. I planned my vengeance. I kept moving forward, not looking back."

A server approached the table, saying nothing. He looked at Amanda for direction.

"Yes, of course, I am so sorry," Amanda said. "Please, bring the order that I requested." She looked around the table, her face a radiant smile. "I planned ahead before you arrived. You brought an extra friend but that isn't a problem. I'm sure you are all parched and in need of refreshment. Hard work deserves its reward!"

The server hurried toward the bar and returned moments later, placing tasting sheets on the table that described some of the distilled spirits produced on-site and the ones they would sample today. Bethany tuned out the world for several minutes, pushing away thoughts of Senator Young's gruesome death as she soaked in the information on the sheet. She imagined each sip and the kaleidoscope of flavors that would cascade across her palate. Her mouth filled with saliva, a Pavlovian response to the forthcoming experience. Bethany sighed appreciatively when the waiter delivered their flights.

"And bring her a beer as well," Amanda said. "The Pilsner that is brewed in Salt Lake. German style. She'll like that one."

The server departed again. Without touching any of the small glasses in front of them, the rest of the table joined Bethany in reading the descriptions of the distilled spirits that now awaited their judgement. Bethany's heart gushed with excitement. As with any tasting, it helped to get an expert's perspective and then use that knowledge to build her own. According to the tasting sheet, one of their bourbons would convey sensory notes of vanilla, candy corn, cornbread biscuit and caramel apple. It sounded absolutely tantalizing.

"Ah, here it is," Amanda said, breaking Bethany's focus. She watched the server place a beer bottle and glass on the table. "I'm sorry it isn't on draft, but we are in a distillery. What else should we expect? They need to serve their own wares, right? And, besides, look at the bottle! A true European half liter! Isn't that wonderful? I thought you would appreciate that little touch, and the fact it is brewed in the Pilsner style, as well."

"Thank you," Bethany said, rubbing her hands together. She appreciated Amanda's kind gestures and was touched that the difference between bottle and draft would even cross Amanda's mind. Bethany wrapped her hand around the bottle and lifted it to inspect the label, the cold from the glass a striking contrast to her warm palm. Bottled beer did not bother Bethany. In many ways she felt it was a great avenue to understand the nuances of a brewery. Bottles were like tiny capsules that revealed the capabilities of the brewer, the recipes, and the attention to detail during production and packaging. Unless the bottles were past their freshness date. When that happened, it threw everything down the shithole.

Amanda nodded, as if acknowledging all the thoughts that had passed through Bethany's mind. "We must keep our beer expert happy, mustn't we?" she said. "I've thought about that a lot. Do you remember how we first came to meet in Munich? I had wondered how I might break the ice and earn your trust, but your love of beer made everything so easy. So natural. You and I just kind of flowed into each other, didn't we?"

Bethany sipped the rye whiskey sample. Her mind played with the words used to describe the drink. Cinnamon. Nutmeg. Clove. And the stated goal to create the spiciest rye whiskey in the world. She suddenly coughed, her face reddening. The booze had a kick, and Bethany now understood why the inventors had been clever enough to register a trademark with an exclamation point after its name. Bethany fought to catch her breath and regain her composure.

"We aren't really here to reminisce about Munich," Bethany finally managed. "Or are we?"

Amanda gave her a pitiful smile. "That's funny," she said. "Get caught up in life's memories and I lose track of the business at hand. No, you are correct. Munich is in the past. Well, I suppose not entirely, right? Professor Stocker's handiwork is still playing itself out. It chills me to think of what might happen to our water. Aren't you worried? What do you think it was? There's speculation everywhere, from an old Nazi weapon to some type of new technology. But I'm sure you know all about that."

Bethany thought about other things she knew, like the execution of Senator Young that day and his unceremonious burial plot beneath the rocks. She killed the memory at that moment, resolving that it was also in the past, no different than Munich, and that her path forward began here. She laughed, a sense of emotional freedom washing over her, and shifted in her seat like a giddy teenager. The first effects of alcohol were creeping into her brain. She still had the glass of rye in her hand and punctuated the laugh by tipping the rest of the drink into her mouth. She swallowed, this time neither choking nor bothering to relish the flavors.

"I worry about water because it is ninety-five percent of beer's content," Bethany said after swallowing. "The main ingredient. If we don't solve the water problems that arose in

Berlin, what will happen to our beer? Nobody seems to think about this in America. Why should they? Everyone is crazy about hops these days. The flavor of hops. The aroma of hops. Blah, blah, blah. I get sick of hearing it and I'm a beer expert, but sometimes I can't hear another word about hops knowing that we can lose every beer on the planet if we don't focus on the thing that matters the most. Saving the water. No water, no beer. So, yes, I am very concerned."

Amanda shrugged, lazily glancing at her whiskey tastings that still sat untouched. "We're Mormons around here," she said. "At least most of us in Utah are. We care less for the—what did Nietzsche call it? The *fair brunette*? Yes, that's it. A lovely turn of phrase, even if Nietzsche's true aim with those words was to eviscerate what he saw as the collapse of the German spirit. The love affair to which young German scholars succumbed, ceding their spirituality and the instinct of self-preservation to the siren song of beer. *Where would one not find the gentle degeneration which beer produces in the spirit*? That is Nietzsche's question, not mine. Even so, I know the allure. In Germany, I needed to act as a German, not as a Mormon, and so I drank my beer. More of it than I wish to admit. And did it help me succeed at my work? Yes, I would argue it did. But would I pledge loyalty to the beverage until death? No, I would not. Nietzsche was correct to criticize the false logic of those who proclaim allegiance to beer ahead of the loftiness of spiritual goals."

Bethany lifted the other rye sample, took a cursory sniff, and tossed the tasting in her mouth. She swallowed fast, grimacing slightly as a shiver ran across her shoulders. She smacked the glass back on the table with more force than she intended but was glad it added emphasis to her next words.

“You should know by now that I don’t understand the first thing you are talking about,” Bethany said. “I’m from Buffalo. I was a cop.”

Amanda cocked her head to the side. “Are those reasons or excuses? You see, this is precisely the point in many ways. We allow life’s temptations to subvert our thinking, to set us upon the wrong path. Nietzsche was not a Mormon and for that I could never consider him a great thinker. But he saw in the temptations of his time the gutting of the German spirit. Is that any different than what is happening now, in our country? Aren’t the internet and other unseen forces morphing our behavior? Beer dulls the mind to this, you know. And now we are awash with beer *and* poisoned water. We are doubly damned.”

“Germany’s beer culture is connected to a historical distrust of the water supply,” Bethany said, this time taking the smoked whiskey tasting glass into her hand. “You know that, right?”

Amanda waved away Bethany’s words, smiling slightly as Bethany polished off her next sample. “Of course, I’m aware of that,” she said. “If they didn’t boil the water, people died. A pretty common problem a couple centuries ago. And perhaps our problem once again. Did you know that German brewers recently warned against fracking? You know, as a method to extract oil or gas? They claimed it would endanger the water supply and put the country’s beer industry at risk. They asked the same question before this whole Berlin explosion fiasco: how can you make world-class beer with subpar water?”

Bethany tossed her fourth sample into her mouth and immediately swallowed, forgetting to examine the drink for the tasting notes she had anticipated when it was first served. She pushed aside the empty whiskey glasses and expertly poured the Pilsner into the glass. A thick head of white foam formed atop the golden liquid as small bubbles raced to the surface. Bethany held the glass up to the light, observing the color and the carbonation, then wafted it beneath her nose. She inhaled deeply, pulling the aroma to the depths of her nasal cavity.

"It takes a few sips to cleanse the palate," she said in a reflective tone, placing the glass to her lips. She took a long sip. "Especially going from whiskey to beer. It will be hard to know how good this beer is, at least right now. A pleasant and appropriate bitterness comes right through. Yes, it does. And that's true to style. But, honestly, I'm not sure it matters, Amanda. I'm confused. Why are we even here, having this conversation? It doesn't make any sense."

"It does, dammit!" Amanda said sharply, slamming her palm on the table. Two of her whiskey tastings toppled over, spilling their contents. Amanda set the glasses upright and used her napkin to sop up the mess. She glanced from face to face at everyone at the table, words perched on her lips, as if cautious as to what she would next say.

"I'm sorry," she continued, her tone hard and unapologetic. She turned her eyes back at Bethany. "I forgot the rest of you were here. Noah. Aaron. Perhaps you can take our other guest for a stroll down Main Street. Bethany and I need some time to ourselves."

Noah flew from his seat and sank his claws into the shoulders of both Aaron and Ivan. "Let's go," he said. "Be quick about it."

They moved in graceful unison and were soon out of sight. Moments later, they passed the front window outside, walking in the direction of what Bethany remembered was Main Street. To any other observer, they were a group of friends out for a drink and a stroll. Perhaps even a purchase or two. Bethany knew differently. Despite the warmth she felt across her limbs, she worried about Ivan and could not help but wonder what would become of her unfortunate new friend.

CHAPTER 15

KEEP SWEET

"You think I'm a liar?"

Bethany brought herself back to the moment. She blinked her eyes and took a long swig of Pilsner. This time, the malt pushed into her palate, guided by the balanced hop bitterness. The next sip, she guessed, would supplant any remnants of the whiskey that had coated her tongue. She noticed the remaining full whiskey tastings. Perhaps Ivan and the others were too unnerved to test the samples, or perhaps they did not suit their tastes, nor their cultural norms. Whatever the case, Bethany felt remorse at their missed opportunities. Though more whiskey was not likely for her today, none of the tastes deserved an unceremonious dump down the sink.

"A liar?" Bethany asked, unable to strip the sarcasm from her tone. "What from our experiences together in Munich would lead me to that conclusion?"

"The part that mattered the most," Amanda said. "About my family. Everything else was a stretch of the truth. Ok, a significant stretch of the truth. But the part about my family, about what brought me to Germany, about what they did to my parents—all of that was true."

"And that should overshadow everything else? The deception? The murders?"

"Yes, my dear friend, it should." Amanda said. "In Munich you told me that you knew so little. A child of Buffalo, New York. You even said it again today. Ignorant of the world, or perhaps indifferent. But now here you are, in the world. Isn't that true? Such a far cry from the senselessness of being a police officer, now you find yourself touching the pulse of what really makes the world tick. The dirty reality of things. Imagine if Herta hadn't failed. Where would the world be now? Everything hinged on a moment of misfortune and now the fork in the road brings us here."

"But what is here?" Bethany asked. "A part of the world bound by rules I don't really care about, and certainly don't understand. I'll remind you—my focus is on beer. I'm a certified expert, for fuck's sake! I'll drink whiskey, but I don't understand it. Same with wine. But beer? That's my everything. Preferably fresh from the tap, but this bottle did just fine, thank you."

Amanda cleared her throat. "There you go again. So afraid, aren't you? Open your eyes to this, Bethany! The entire Salt Lake valley, do you know how it came to be settled? Do you understand the torture that my people endured to find this home? I can see from your eyes that you don't, and more so that you don't care."

"I strive to keep it simple," Bethany said, holding up her beer glass. "I care about the stories that brought me this."

Shaking her head, Amanda frowned. "We're a shit show, you know. Not you and me, sorry, I don't mean it that way. I'm talking about the Mormons. We strive for this ideal on Earth—we call it Zion—where mankind works and shares with the goal of a common good. It is inspired by heaven and yet we are persecuted, seen as some derivative of socialism or communism, driven from our homes, arrested, and even murdered. That is *our* history! Here on this continent. How can that even be possible? Aren't we supposed to provide for freedom of religion in this country?"

Amanda touched the remaining whiskey tastings in front of her, as though contemplating a sip. After a long minute she pushed the drinks away and looked up at Bethany. "But it hardly matters, right? Because the ideal is never achievable. We are broken creatures, awaiting redemption through our Savior. My entire life I have been told to '*keep sweet*' and put my doubts and questions *'on the shelf'* rather than challenge the status quo. But is that really possible with all that has happened in our Mormon society? One corrupt leader made way for another, who opened the door for the horrendous actions of the next. Can our fundamentalist believers ever truly believe again, Bethany? Can I ever believe again?"

Bethany finished her beer and waved to the waiter for a refill. "I'd be lying if I said I understood a single word of any of that," she said.

"The stupid cop from Buffalo," Amanda said. "Yes, you play that part extremely well. I'm sure you heard the stories about the Fundamentalist Church of Jesus Christ of Latter-Day Saints. Somewhere in that beer-soaked mind, the story is there to be remembered. Do polygamist marriages ring a bell?"

Bethany shrugged her shoulders, remembering vaguely that Heather had mentioned the subject, and shook her head.

"Come on!" Amanda exclaimed. "One of our church leaders had nearly sixty children. And then one of his boys turned out to be a real bad apple once he was all grown up. Ended up being charged with arranging marriages between adults and underage children, then for incest and sexual misconduct with a minor! You're a cop! How can you not know this?"

Bethany tried to smile. “Utah isn’t Buffalo,” she said. “Why would I ever start to care about what happened out here?”

“Good question, my beer drinking friend,” Amanda said. “Except don’t talk about it in the past tense. It is happening today.”

Bethany grinned, enjoying a recollection. “Remember how Herta called me—”

“Stay focused, Bethany,” Amada urged. “You’re getting closer to the truth you seek.” Amanda placed both of her hands on the table and leaned forward, her eyes digging into Bethany’s. “Do you truly know so little?”

Bethany shook her head again, confirming Amanda’s question. “Maybe because of the heavy metal in Lake Erie. I swam there as a kid. And it was probably in my drinking water.”

“Oh, for crying out loud!” Amanda said, leaning back. She stared hard at Bethany, finally sighing and drooping her head. “I would have thought that Munich opened your eyes. Maybe it helped you remember things you learned in your life but never thought were important. Maybe it made you curious. Isn’t that what brought you out here? Curiosity?”

The waiter finally returned with Bethany’s beer. “Go ahead and bring another,” Bethany said, pausing her conversation with Amanda to fill her glass. She took a moment to watch the foam rise to the rim, threatening to break over the edge. As if by magic, though, it stopped its ascent at the last possible moment and slowly began settling back into the golden liquid. Bethany smiled, knowing a perfect beer pour was a hard-won talent. She celebrated with a thorough gulp that drained away half of the seventeen ounces she had just poured.

“Yes,” Bethany said after she swallowed, using her fingertips to wipe away the foam at the corners of her mouth. “I blame curiosity. I was a cop, still am in so many ways. Edward Roth’s murder in Jackson Hole caught my eye. I looked on a map and realized it wasn't far from Salt Lake City. I thought of your postcard and decided to pay a visit."

Amanda nodded her head thoughtfully. "I truly wondered about that decision. The postcard, I mean. And I probably still do. Why introduce the unknown into your life, right? Not as though we have the situation at hand. No, not at all. And then all the sudden you are here." Amanda paused, tapping her index finger on the table, deciding her next words. "I wasn't surprised. Like a moth to a flame."

Bethany squinted, briefly sensing something hidden in those statements. "Moths are stupid," she said. "Like me. Kind of like when you said some things that made absolutely no sense, almost as if you were speaking your own language. Was it a code of sorts?"

"A code?" Amanda asked. "I'm sorry. I was frustrated. Rambling. What was it?"

Bethany paused again as the waiter placed her third half-liter on the table. She nodded a thank you, drank the second half of her most recent beer, and poured a fresh glass, again admiring her skill. "I don't recall exactly. You mentioned something about being sweet."

"Keep sweet," Amanda said in a hushed whisper. "Yes, the calling card of our fundamentalists. The words serve many purposes, but mostly for control. To keep the doubters silent. To maintain the power of the abusers. Young girls are told to '*keep sweet*' to remind them of their submissive role, mostly in marriage. In the end, it is a simple directive for how people should conduct themselves, even in situations they find horrible."

Amanda leaned in closer. "And that bleeds right into the other control phrase. *'Put it on the shelf.'* Have you heard of that one? No? I would have guessed people said it outside of the

FLDS. Maybe just not in Buffalo. Is that city a black hole of American culture or something?"

"Don't shit on Buffalo, okay?" Bethany said. "It's a dump, but it's still my home."

"No offense, no offense," Amanda said, a smile creasing her lips. "I'm just giving you a hard time. The boys in Munich had lots of laughs about Buffalo."

Bethany took another long drink, studying the beer as she swallowed, feeling the crisp carbonation on her palate and the slight sting of bubbles in her throat. She knew Amanda was testing her, but why? Was there any value to connecting the past to the present? What did Munich have to do with Utah? With Edward Roth?

"Put it on the shelf?" Bethany asked.

"Yes, of course." Amanda said. "Look at me losing my train of thought. You'd think I was the one doing the drinking! *'Put it on the shelf'* is another control phrase. A way to stop the questioning of someone who senses they are being controlled. Why these rules? Why these restrictions? Why, why, why? And to each of those questions, the answer is to *'put it on the shelf.'* The answer will come. God will answer when he is ready, but now is not the time to be asking."

"Seems there's lots of control going on out here," Bethany mused.

Amanda merely smiled. "Buffalo, you know, is rather central to the Mormon story. Maybe not the city itself, but not too far east. Have you heard of Hill Cumorah?"

Bethany raised her eyebrows and pursed her lips, refusing to acknowledge the memory of Senator Young mentioning Hill Cumorah before he was shot. She took a deep drink and shook her head. "Sorry," she said. "I got nothing."

Amanda sighed. “Ah, well. A blank slate then. We’ll leave it at that. Perhaps it isn’t the worst thing, is it? So many things are happening, so many wheels are in motion.”

“Amanda, please,” Bethany said, her voice pleading. “I’m trying to understand. Trying to connect the dots. You’re not giving me much to work with.”

“Of course, yes, I apologize. There are so many things to share. It is difficult to know where to start.”

“You said some letters.” Bethany paused, trying to recall Amanda’s words. The rising influence of alcohol in her bloodstream was disrupting her memory. “F-something.”

“Hah, that’s hilarious!” Amanda exclaimed. “I’ve never heard it said like that before. Almost like you’re trying to soften your profanity. F-that! F-something!” Amanda stopped, chuckling as she composed herself. “But all joking aside, it is FLDS. That’s short for the Fundamentalist Church of Jesus Christ of Latter-Day Saints. You want a dictionary definition? It’s one of the largest fundamentalist denominations and one of the largest organizations in the country with members that practice polygamy.”

“Polygamy again? You mentioned that a minute ago.”

“Marriages with multiple wives.” Amanda said. “There’s no easier way to describe it. And hence the reason to *keep sweet* and *put it on the shelf*. The men—especially the husbands—don’t need their multiple wives and children asking questions about this arrangement, do they? I mean, it’s a sweet deal for the guys. The FLDS holds that plural marriage is essential to salvation. At least three women for every husband, that’s the magic number. But why stop there? Especially for the leaders of the FLDS church. They are called prophets. One of our most famous prophets had at least fifteen spouses. And the one who followed him? Guess how many widows he left behind. No idea? Most estimates say at least seventy-five.”

"Seventy-five wives?" Bethany asked. The thought made her thirsty, but this time only for the briefest of sips. She imagined the size of the house, or the number of houses needed to pull those relationships together. And then, what about children? "I suppose there were also kids in the mix?"

"Maybe sixty-five," Amanda said. "Possibly more or less. And then one of his sons had something like forty wives. But some reports say there were far more, in the seventies. It is impossible to know, I suppose. And who knows how many more children were produced from those relationships. Shocking, right? But a nice arrangement for the men! The husband gets to pick who he lays with each night. They are the leaders, the priesthood. No wonder they want no questions. No wonder the women are told to '*keep sweet.*'"

"But," Amanda continued, "they failed so miserably. Government and the law caught up to them. One of those prophets is in jail for his foul actions. He should be equally punished for his terrible teachings, but I suppose that hardly matters. He will most likely die in prison as it is."

"I can't help but want to chuckle," Bethany said. "You make fun of Buffalo, give me a hard time because I'm from there. And yet all these insane things are happening here in Utah. Shouldn't you point the finger at yourselves?"

"And now you land upon the truth," Amanda said.

"The truth?"

"Precisely that. Pointing the finger back at ourselves. Looking in the mirror. Do I like what I see? Absolutely not. You think that the death of our past prophets changed things? Is jailing one of them going to stop the fundamentalist movement? Hardly! He has preached from his prison cell, passed messages to his followers. And his people? They doubt the claims and the charges against him. To them, it is all fabricated! They think it is just another example of when the government raided Short

Creek in 1953. Tearing the FLDS families apart again, that's what they say, and the first way for the government to achieve that is to cut off the head of the organization. So, the true believers? They have gone into hiding, further underground, blending into society. And now that they are there, they are building a political consensus by exploiting the center."

"And why would they bother with that? With compromise?" Bethany asked. "If they stray from their core beliefs, what does that accomplish?"

Amanda touched her nose, then pointed her index finger at Bethany. "Precisely," she said.

"I'm not following you."

"Look, Mormons don't get persecuted just because they're Mormons," Amanda said, then paused, thinking. "Okay, maybe sometimes. People are people, right? Protestants and Catholics don't get along sometimes. That type of thing. It has gone on for centuries. People always find reasons to dislike each other because of different belief systems. But when it comes to hating Mormons, look no further than our belief in Zion. The concept of an ideal community. Most Americans worship a different god."

Bethany pondered Amanda's choice of words, spinning the beer glass on its base. "We're a Christian nation for the most part. What God do you mean?"

Amanda smiled. "A god with a small g," she said. "Capitalism. Simple as that. Claim a communist plot or a socialist agenda and the capitalist stalwarts flash their claws. Anything that suggests the rights of the group supplant the rights of the individual. But Mormons see it differently. The road to Zion begins with working together to the best of one's own ability, to affect the greater good of the whole community."

"It doesn't sound like such a terrible idea," Bethany said. "Teamwork yields the best results. *Two minds are better than one*, as the old saying goes."

"Maybe, but the ideal of Zion can't exist side-by-side with capitalism. It simply can't. Capitalism is for the individual. Zion is for the community. That's why Mormons chose to congregate large groups in certain areas. It started mostly in the Midwest. Illinois. Missouri. Safety in numbers, but what then? Exploit the democratic system. Vote each other into positions of power. Become the community leaders by free and fair elections. It was easy because they dominated the local population."

"Sounds diabolical," Bethany said.

"It depends on your perspective," Amanda responded, shrugging. "It's the way the system was built. Mormons gamed it."

Amanda paused suddenly, sighing. Bethany noticed a sadness creep into Amanda's face, followed by a deflated slump of the shoulders.

"Didn't work out so well," Amanda said. "Initially, I mean. Ignore where we are sitting now for a minute. Imagine, if you can, the mid-1800's. Back east, as I mentioned, the non-Mormons didn't take too kindly to the changes in political leadership. And they weren't too fond of who was in charge and what it meant for their individual wealth and property. So, they did what was common back in those days. They persecuted, murdered, and ran the Mormons out of town."

"I'm sorry it happened," Bethany said. "But those were different times."

"I appreciate your sympathy, but was it really so different? Have people changed at all, or have they been forced into a box that controls their fear and hate?"

"I've seen my share of man's inhumanity," Bethany said. "You don't have to try hard to find it."

"You can find it right here," Amanda said. "Joseph Smith founded Mormonism. He was killed in Carthage, Illinois, along with his brother, Hyrum. There was a threat of violence against their people in Nauvoo, Illinois, so the Smith's called out the militia. And then they got arrested. Persecute the Mormons in Nauvoo! Persecute Joseph and Hyrum Smith! Anyway, a mob broke into the jail where the brothers were being held. That was the end for them."

"When did this happen?" Bethany asked. "We learn nothing about this in school."

"1844. A long time ago, but still only yesterday," Amanda said, her voice melancholy. "Yes, history is the story of the victors. Seldom do they share what happens to the downtrodden. Perhaps there is rising sympathy for the losing stories in modern society, but human nature doesn't change. To the victor go the spoils, and that includes what is taught and learned. What happens to people like the Mormons will forever be a sidebar or, worse, a footnote. Unless, that is, we become the victors."

Bethany sat up straight, realization dawning. She leaned forward in rapt attention. "Is that why?" she asked.

Amanda produced a sad smile. "Why what, Bethany?"

"Why you did all those things in Munich," Bethany said, and then lowered her voice to a whisper. "Killed your friends!"

"Friends, Bethany? Really? Colleagues at best. But yes, Bethany. Of course. If you act without purpose, then why act at all?"

"But people died!"

"Joseph and Hyrum Smith died," Amanda said. "Consider it blood atonement for my people, delayed by too many years."

"Seriously, Amanda? You can't truly believe that!"

Amanda waved a dismissive hand at Bethany's words, then continued. "My people fled west from Illinois. They ended up in the Salt Lake valley because they were escaping persecution and the American government. Zion could not happen under the yoke of American capitalism; do you understand that? When they got here, the area was still part of Mexican territory. So, there was hope. But even that didn't last long. After the Mexican-American war, Mexico ceded much of its territory to the United States in 1848. Utah was part of the deal, but also most of what we now call Arizona, New Mexico, Colorado, Wyoming, and California. It didn't look good, but Brigham Young saw an opportunity. He was the new leader of the Mormon faithful. He knew that state governments had lots of power. And he recognized that controlling a new state in the American west would give Mormons the power they wanted."

Bethany fought the rising fog of inebriation, trying to put sense to Amanda's words. "What you're saying is that all those Western states you mentioned didn't exist yet?" she asked.

"Nope, not yet. Brigham Young went big, I'll give him that. He sent representatives to Congress in 1849. His proposal was the creation of the state of Deseret."

Bethany blinked her eyes heavily. "Deseret? You mean desert?"

"No, Deseret," Amanda said. "It's a word from the Book of Mormon. It means honeybee. That proposed state would have covered a huge territory. On modern maps, we're talking all of Utah, most of Nevada, and large parts of Colorado, Wyoming, and Idaho. I think even San Diego was in the mix. Brigham Young was smart. He probably wanted his proposed state to have access to the sea."

Bethany pictured a map of the United States. In her mind's eye, it was dotted with all the breweries she planned to visit someday. "That would have been a big state," she said. "Sounds more like a country."

"That's right," Amanda said. "Brigham Young probably had that in the back of his mind. Anyway, it didn't work out as planned. Congress shrunk the proposed state and named it Utah Territory. President Millard Fillmore named Brigham Young as territorial governor. And the rest, they say, is history."

CHAPTER 16

MILLARD FILLMORE

Bethany lifted her heavy eyelids, astonishment on her face. "Did you say Millard Fillmore?" she asked.

"President Fillmore, yes," Amanda said, pausing to think. She counted on her fingers. "Let's see if I can remember this from school. Washington, Adams, Jefferson, Madison, Monroe, Adams, Jackson, Van Buren..., oh, come on now! Ah, yes, Harrison, Tyler, Polk, Taylor, Fillmore! What was that? Thirteen? Yes, it sure was! Fillmore was the 13th president." She smiled at her own success.

"The funny thing," Bethany said, "is that I actually know about Millard Fillmore."

"The friend of the Mormons?" Amanda asked, astonished. "The forgotten president? He only served in office for two years, and that was because President Taylor died."

"Oddly enough, yes, I do know his history," Bethany said, brightening as she took another drink of beer. "I don't remember much from school, but Fillmore stuck in my head for some reason. He was from upstate New York. Grew up in poverty. Rose to prominence in Buffalo as an attorney and a politician. Actually, the Millard Fillmore house is in the Village of East Aurora. It's about a twenty-minute drive from Buffalo. He started his law practice there. Not much to it, just a tiny one-and-half story house."

"Amazing," Amanda said, listening raptly with her chin cupped in her hands. "I've never met anyone outside of Utah who even knows the name Millard Fillmore. Did you know that Brigham Young tried his best to get cozy with the president? He wanted to build strong relations."

Bethany shrugged, draining her beer. Her thoughts were swimming and the urge for a different flavor than Pilsner was bubbling across her palate. "Seems reasonable," she said, waving to the waiter. He quickly rushed over. "Is there something different I can try? Another Utah beer?"

"I might recommend the Kellerbier," he said. "It's a Salt Lake favorite."

"You have my attention," Bethany said.

"The brewery is downtown if you'd want to plan a visit," the waiter said, reciting the facts he knew. "The Kellerbier won a bronze medal at the Great American Beer Festival in Denver."

"Did it now?" Bethany asked, her voice suddenly animated. "You've piqued my interest. Bring me two of those. I'll drink one cold and let the other one warm up a tad." She noticed the waiter's curious look at that last comment and took a moment to explain further. "The warmth opens up the flavors a bit."

The waiter gave a brief nod, turned on his heels, and departed. Amanda chuckled. "Looks like you fell in love with German beer. You know Kellerbier is a German word, right?"

"Oh, sure. Kellerbier. Cellar beer. That's about my extent of German," Bethany said. She felt a touch of sadness as she spoke those words, remembering the encouragement she had received from Herta Stocker to learn the language. She swallowed the memory, returning her focus to Amanda. "The style is an easy transition from a Pilsner, too. But if it won the bronze medal at the GABF, I definitely have to try it."

"GABF?"

"Great American Beer Festival. Held in Denver each year, like the waiter said. It's a nationwide brewing competition. Huge. Been around for decades."

"There's another downside to being Mormon, I suppose," Amanda said. "We miss out on many aspects of American culture. But I am pleased that there's something you know about, and yet I'm absolutely clueless."

"Don't take that one personally," Bethany said. "It's a perk of being a beer expert." She smiled wide as the waiter placed her two beers on the table. Bethany poured the first glass carefully, this time limiting the foam to a thin head. "Kellerbier is one of those styles you don't hear about too often. In America, many breweries call it Zwickelbier. There's a brewery in St. Louis that brought Zwickelbier to the U.S. market as far as I'm concerned. Made it a household name. But whether you're talking Zwickelbier or Kellerbier, both styles tend to be like immature Bavarian Helles. More yeast character. Some fermentation byproducts like diacetyl might be present. Traditionally they'd be served straight from the barrel, straight from the lager cellar. Hence the name."

"Amazing," Amanda said, this time laughing out loud. "Who would think there's as much history behind beer as there is behind Mormonism!"

"Or Millard Fillmore!" Bethany said, raising her glass for a toast. She drank deeply, enjoying the rich flavor and anticipating the light push of more alcohol into her bloodstream. She raised the glass to the light. "Nice straw color. Clearer than I'd expect, but that's because I poured it softly. The malt layers are delicious. Well-balanced. Just a bit weak on the alcohol content."

"Oh, don't blame the brewery for that! It's Utah law!"

"That's right, that's right," Bethany said. "I heard about that at the Utah Oktoberfest. Strange law."

"Anyway, Bethany, can we go back to Millard Fillmore for a second?" Amanda asked. "There's more to what I was saying. Check this out. Utah has a county called Millard. And a city in that county called Fillmore. And the city of Fillmore was the first capital of the Utah territory."

Bethany whistled between her teeth, lifted her glass, and this time drank deeply. "Seems like Brigham Young was doing some old-fashioned brown-nosing," she said.

"Maybe, yeah. But as you know, President Fillmore only lasted a couple years in office. After he was gone, before long the capital moved to Salt Lake. But the county and city remain."

Bethany enjoyed another long pull of her Kellerbier. "You know, between Millard Fillmore and that hill—what's it called?"

"Hill Cumorah?"

"Right, that one. Between those two, I'm starting to sense this weird connection between my hometown and the Mormons."

"Sense it? Bethany, my dear, it's real. Exists as plainly as that beer in your hands. Perhaps it's for that reason that the universe—God—has drawn us together."

Bethany leaned forward, tension rippling through her body. She squeezed the beer glass, fearful for a moment that it might shatter in her grip. She hated the idea of coincidences and knew beyond certainty there was no risk of it playing a role here, but she had not considered the possibility that God or destiny might have created these current events.

"Hardly," Bethany said. "And you know it. Your postcard was a signal. An invitation. And then that murder happened in

Jackson Hole. I only had to look at a map to become curious enough to wonder."

"Wonder what?" Amanda asked, an expectant crease crossing her forehead.

"Whether you had played a role in his death. Edward Roth. The economist."

Amanda smiled, sitting back with a relaxed gleam in her eye. "Now a beer sounds really good," she said. "The conversation just got interesting."

"All this backstory," Bethany said, "and all this history about the Mormon church. You've been talking nonstop and acting like I'm supposed to care."

"Ah, but you should!" Amanda exclaimed. "It's all connected, like you and I are connected. Don't you see? The story weaves together. Can't you see the threads?"

Bethany shook her head. "No, I don't," she said, forcing sharpness into her tone. "What threads? Please, I'm dying to know."

Amanda reached across the table, grabbing Bethany's left hand. "They had their chances. All the history I just shared with you, back to the beginning of Mormonism. Think about it. They were on the right path. Zion was achievable. But then they fell into this disastrous succession of men leading the FLDS. Satan, the enemy of all righteousness, infiltrated our Church. And nearly destroyed it."

"Yeah, of course," Bethany said. "People are bound to do that. Men especially."

Something flickered across Amanda's face, a sudden and emotional recognition of the truth behind Bethany's words, and she squeezed Bethany's hand with enough force to make Bethany wince. "People are wicked, Bee! But those who seek to follow God can see when Satan is trying to tempt them. He wants us to be as miserable as him, cut off from the Heavenly

Father. And so, he leads us away from righteousness. Sadly, we've had a string of false prophets. Men who succumbed to Satan's temptations."

"The guys you mentioned," Bethany said.

Amanda nodded. "Read about them sometime. Even just a little. If you want to know what Satan's work looks like, think first of the perfect world that the Mormons call Zion, where everyone is pure of heart. And then learn about the awful things these false prophets managed to achieve on Satan's behalf. They undermined everything."

Bethany pulled her hand back, giving it a brief shake. She flexed her fingers several times, studying their movement as she worked away the stiffness that had developed in the ligaments and joints. "But the people let it happen," she said. "The followers. You can't just blame their leaders."

"Their leaders?" Amanda asked. "Hmm, see, they are called prophets. A word with more weight, don't you think? And if you adhere to the faith, then who are you to doubt a prophet?"

"Perhaps that's true," Bethany said, testing her hand with a lift of her beer glass. She was pleased to find everything in working order and took another sip, relishing the spritzy bite of carbonation on her tongue. There was something about the way it cut through the dryness in her throat that gave her a different appreciation for the virtues of beer drinking. She wasn't used to this much chatter.

Amanda seemed to read Bethany's thoughts. She sighed, dropping her hands heavily on the table. "This is too much for you, perhaps. It's a lot of information, especially for someone with such little education. But let me finish with this. The other end of the thread. You mentioned Edward Roth. His murder. You were right to be suspicious. Perhaps you even felt fear. You have a strong intuition, so I would expect nothing less. That murder was the new prophet proclaiming himself. The order was given as a signal of his ascension. His followers knew it. They understood what the headlines meant. The prophet was forging a path of power, taking a page from our greatest leaders. Joseph Smith. Brigham Young. Using the system that America makes available to us. Using the vote. And then building Zion."

Amanda paused, a dark shroud falling across her face. She took several moments to look around the restaurant, seeming to realize she might be overheard. She covered her face with her hands, breathing deeply several times, settling her nerves. When Amanda spoke again, her voice was steady and hushed.

"But we don't need to worry about that anymore, do we? I smite the enemies of my people, Bethany. And of me. No more false prophets. The path to Zion is clear. We were nearly there many years ago. Satan took us off course. I am guiding us back."

Bethany sat back, drunk enough to wonder if she had just misheard Amanda's words. She took another slug of Kellerbier, forgetting to ask the question.

"But enough of this talk," Amanda said. "The sheep will soon learn their shepherd is gone. And the flock will equate this to the love of Christ. To John 10:11."

Bethany cleared her throat. Bible references were like poison to her ears. Although she had some religious education, she had always rebelled against committing any of it to memory or giving it any thought beyond the weekly one-hour confirmation classes she had endured as a child. Now she felt some guilt for her lack of caring. Was she sorry? Between the bubbles that rose in her beer glass, maybe there was an answer to that question.

Amanda looked intently at Bethany, seemingly captivated by her own words as she continued speaking. "But John 10:11 is a heavenly promise. The earthly instincts of the flock will draw them to their new, true prophet. The one who will finally achieve what has been promised here on Earth. Make no mistake about it, Bethany. Mormons have been commissioned in this world to usher in the second coming of Christ. We will build a society from which He can rule the world. That achievement is now closer at hand."

Amanda rose, signaling the waiter to bring them the check. "But enough of this already. Drink up, buttercup. It's a nice day outside. Let's take a walk to clear our minds."

"I'll need a few minutes to use the bathroom," Bethany said. She stood, slightly unsteady on her feet, and shuffled toward the front door where she descended stairs to the cellar. The bathroom was located down a narrow hallway. Finding an open stall, Bethany relieved her bladder, puzzling over the words Amanda had spoken to her. As the stream of urine ebbed, then stopped, she found her thoughts suddenly blurred once more behind the images in her mind of the man assassinated at the Rock Pile House, and the dirty work they had done to hide the evidence. Bethany's face flushed, knowing now with certainty that she had again witnessed Amanda's ruthless handiwork. The whiskey and the impromptu beer tasting upstairs had deadened the shock, but in the moments that she wiped front to back, she let the reality of the day rush in with full force. A guttural sob erupted in her throat, then broke through her lips. A tear hung in the corner of her eye before tracing a path down her cheek and past her left nostril, finally coming to rest on Bethany's upper lip. She wiped it away before using her index fingers to dry both eyes, silently cursing the last several beers for her outburst of emotion. *Never blame the beer!* She smiled at the thought, etching it in her memory as a mantra for future use. She pulled some fresh toilet paper off the roll and finished with a quick pat between her legs to ensure she was dry.

Outside the restroom, Bethany stopped at the bottom of the stairs to admire the grain storage and mashing equipment housed in the building's basement. She took several long minutes to study the scene, feeling serenity creep back into her bones. Someday she might begin exploring the intricacies of craft distilling, but right now she wanted to keep her mind on beer. It felt like the surest way to prevent a descent into panic.

Upstairs, Bethany exited with Amanda onto the sidewalk. The sun was bright and the temperature crisp, sure signs of fall and the impending arrival of the season's first snow. Soon, these streets would be bustling with cars and pedestrians, many still wearing ski gear from an exhausting day on the mountain. Others would be shopping at the dozens of expensive art galleries, dressed in stylish clothes to reflect the wealthy trappings of those that participate in snow sports.

They continued up Park Street, walking in silence until Amanda finally spoke. "We'll turn up here on Fourth Street. I want to show you Park City's famous concert venue. Can you believe the band Iron Butterfly played there?"

"Iron Butterfly? I feel like I know that name."

"In-A-Gadda-Da-Vida?" Amanda asked. She tried her best to sing the opening lyrics and hum a few of the most recognizable notes. "You know that tune? From the late 60's? Hippy era, pot smoking song? The original album version of the track was more than seventeen minutes long. I wonder if they played it here."

"Hippy era?" Bethany asked. "Pot smoking? Honestly, Amanda, when you talk like that, I have a hard time believing you're a Mormon."

Amanda laughed. "Right? Don't forget that I went deep undercover in Germany. I know things well outside of my foundational beliefs."

They stopped to admire the venue's large marquee. "It lights up beautifully at night," Amanda said, her voice filled with admiration. "The place has quite the history. It opened in the late 1800's but a record snowfall collapsed the roof a couple decades later. They rebuilt and it's been around, what, at least a century now? Anyway, the place has needed plenty of preservation over the years. If you're ever interested in making a tax-deductible donation, this place could use your help."

"Is that a brewery up the road?" Bethany asked, pointing.

Amanda stepped to the side to follow Bethany's gaze, finding after a moment what Bethany had seen. "Imagine that! Now that you point it out, you're right. I should have thought of looking for a brewery in the first place!"

They were at the brewpub's front door when the sound of running feet approached them from behind. Bethany wheeled around, wobbling on legs made unsteady by her earlier drinks. She clenched her fists instinctively, a bit surprised that she was still tense after a whiskey tasting and several beers. Bethany did not know what level of blood alcohol she needed to calm her nerves, but she hoped to reach it soon.

She blinked, bringing her blurred vision into focus. The running men were quickly approaching and appeared familiar, but her brain struggled to compute the information. There were just two of them. She had the feeling there should be a third but did not know why.

Noah sprinted to a stop in front of them, barely out of breath despite his fast pace and the high altitude. Aaron lumbered up behind, obviously more distressed by the exertion.

"He's gone!" Noah chirped.

"Who's gone?" asked Amanda.

"The other one we brought with us!" Noah exclaimed, pointing his clawed finger at Bethany. "The one she was with at the Oktoberfest."

Amanda looked at Bethany and smiled. "Oh, not to worry," she said. "He was a fly that got caught in the web but managed somehow to escape. The real prize is right here, still with us.

Let's not trouble ourselves with what was lost. Come inside. I bet great things have been said about this little brewery, and our lovely Beer Judge would like to see if the hype is justified!"

CHAPTER 17

GRANDPA BOB

"Can a person even get drunk on Utah beer?"

Maybe it was the drinks at the distillery doing the talking, but that was the question Bethany had asked the bartender when she first walked into the brewery with Amanda, Noah, and Aaron. It had seemed a valid question, given what she had learned thus far in this land of Mormon rules. He had only laughed, saying the laws had changed a bit, beers had gotten stronger, and just to be careful. Something about the altitude and the alcohol catching up with you. Bethany had heard that story repeatedly during her trip and scoffed at his words. She would believe it when it happened. And besides, after seeing a guy get his head shot off and listening to the endless ramblings of Amanda Lang, a little voice inside her head kept whispering that she had earned a good buzz.

When the bartender had placed the first draft in front of her, Bethany remembered her career goal to tour the country as a beer expert, discovering and critiquing craft beers in every one of the United States. By her count, Utah was one of the fifty. As were Wyoming and Idaho. When it was all said and done, she was glad to be getting this part of America out of the way. Check the box and never come back. Maybe.

She had to admit, though, that all the beers had tasted damn good. Even if she had been drinking alone.

Bethany realized suddenly that she was half-asleep, only now awakening from a deep slumber. Her eyes remained closed. Her mind was relaxed and peaceful. She pushed into that feeling, embracing it, sensing the wish to envelope herself with a defense against the images that danced on the periphery of consciousness. As wakefulness beckoned, she felt the urge to be horrified. She resisted, restoring her calm. For some reason, she felt little anguish at the memory of Senator Young dying before her eyes.

Bethany decided at that moment that she had been wrong about Utah beer. She had gone toe-to-toe, not fearing the outcome, and had done it again. Quaffed a few too many. Swallowed herself into a state of inebriated unconsciousness and voided her sleep of dreams.

It was only then, on the creeping edge of returning sobriety, that her brain clicked on again, beginning the laborious work of categorizing her experiences, filing them into their appropriate spots, and playing like a movie in her mind. She wondered what the soundtrack of the film might be, stopping when *'Oops...I did it again!'* began churning as an endless loop in the recesses of her thoughts. Bethany saw moments in her life flash against the imaginary beat of the music, a ceaseless litany of tragic events that would not stop even when the song ended. She knew the lyrics conveyed a loss of innocence, but of what kind? The only kinds that Bethany knew were heartbreaking. She breathed into the fear and sorrow, trying to recapture the emotional equilibrium she had experienced just moments before. She refused to let the bad memories back into her life. She was a beer expert now.

Bethany heard a sound, followed faintly by another. She edged closer to wakefulness, urged forward by the nagging voice of her long-deceased Grandpa Bob. *"You have to do something, Bethany,"* he whispered from somewhere in the deep caverns of her mind. *"You can't just go around drinking beer and doing nothing. Nobody gets in a car and drives without a direction in mind. Accomplish something, for Christ's sake!"*

His imaginary voice raised the specter of a chuckle in Bethany's subconscious, but she suppressed it. This was no time for laughter, she sensed. Things were deadly serious.

But the vapor of her grandfather's words reminded Bethany of his curmudgeonly opinions and endless kindness. Bordering almost seven feet in height, he had been the epitome of a gentle giant, a towering figure to the young Bethany. She remembered his neatly trimmed, white beard. He had kept it short, but still reminiscent of Santa Claus. His older friends had preferred to compare him to Earnest Hemingway. He had smelled of sweet pipe tobacco most of the time, and thick cigar smoke the rest. She could still remember his legendary woodworking skills and his single car garage filled with tools that lined three walls and covered the floor. She had never learned what any of them did, but Bethany's bedroom had consisted of furniture that Grandpa Bob had built. Each night she had felt wrapped in his love.

When she was old enough by his calculations, meaning the day after her fifteenth birthday, Grandpa Bob became the first person with whom Bethany tasted a beer. Her parents had surprised Bethany with a family camping trip in western Maryland, promising her the fun of lake swimming and forest roaming. But it had been one week of miserable heat and humidity, so bad that she had sweltered at night inside her old canvas tent, never climbing into her clumpy sleeping bag, electing mosquito bites over bathing in her own sweat.

Despite the heat or maybe because of it, Grandpa Bob had built an evening campfire each night, stacking the wood high and letting the flames dance up above their heads. "Keeps the bugs away," he had claimed, winking at her as he had lit the wooden match and tossed it onto the stack of kindling.

He had taught her the trick of starting the perfect fire. "A secret," he had said in the most serious of voices, "taught to me by the ancient Indians." Bethany had gasped in awe at his words, and he had laughed, finally admitting he had learned the trick from her great-grandfather.

"It's an honor to pass the knowledge down the family line," he had said. "It all starts with building a teepee out of kindling. Dry, small wood that lights fast. And once it starts, slowly add slightly bigger pieces to the teepee. Be patient! Let the small wood become the base for the larger fire. It will never fail you."

One of those nights, after her parents had argued and disappeared to their tent, Grandpa Bob had sat in the firelight, a frown across his lips and his head shaking slowly back and forth. He had remained that way for many long minutes, lost in his thoughts and saying nothing. Bethany had known that was not unusual for him, that he often disappeared into his woodworking or his pipe or his cigar and just spent the time alone, the words inside his head keeping him company. But there was something different about that night. Almost as if his soul was connecting to the fire.

When he had finally moved again, it was purposeful. Bethany had heard the drink cooler creak open on old hinges, then the sound of Grandpa Bob's hand sinking into the ice-filled water, followed by the telltale sound of him fishing around inside the frigid liquid. Bethany had smiled and sat upright, anticipating that a sugar-filled soda might come her way. Like all the kids her age, there was endless pleasure in a late-night rush.

Bethany remembered hearing carbonation fizz, followed by a sudden snap, and then the sight of Grandpa Bob raising a can to his lips, drawing a deep gulp. Belching, he had stood and circled the fire, looking down at Bethany until he stood directly beside her. She had stared up at his face and then beyond, seeing through the canopy of trees and, despite the firelight, the twinkling lights of the universe. It was, in that moment, as if he was looking down from the heavens, sending a message from above.

"Try it," he had said, handing her the can. "My favorite beer. Brewed in Pittsburgh. My hometown."

Bethany had put the can to her nose, cautiously testing the aroma. The drink had smelled skunky and stale, but oddly inviting. Hazarding a sip, she had allowed a little of the cold fluid to creep across her lips and onto her tongue. Her nose had shriveled, and she had grimaced.

"What do you think?" Grandpa Bob had asked, perhaps wanting her opinion but not caring either way.

"Disgusting!" Bethany had said, handing the can back to her grandfather.

Grandpa Bob had laughed. "A cold beer on a hot summer night! Not the smartest thing to give my granddaughter, but certainly the kindest! You'll love it someday, I bet. There's something about an honest day's work and a good can of any Pittsburgh beer. You'll understand what I mean when you're older, Bethany. Trust me on that. And the brewery that makes this is a damn big deal. It's still around, and that's no small feat."

He had paused to put the can to his lips, this time enjoying several long gulps until the beer ran dry. "If we were to drive down the highway," he continued, "about ten miles from here, that's Cumberland, Maryland. They had a strong brewing scene once. Queen City Brewing. Cumberland Brewing. And some good beers. But only the strong survive. Yes, only the strong survive."

His voice tapered away into her subconscious, leaving an eerie glow of regret and want. There was no returning to that special evening, perhaps the night when her course toward becoming a beer expert had been sealed into her soul. The journey had been long and painful, beset with a broken marriage and an unexceptional law enforcement career, but somehow Grandpa Bob's lightly planted seed had grown like the tiny teepee that built the large fire. Bethany was exactly where she was meant to be.

Bethany's mind tugged at her to wake, sending a sudden jolt of anxiety that coursed to the tips of her fingers and toes. She suppressed it, sinking again into relaxation and the tail end of a drunken slumber, quietly reciting through parched lips a slice of Pittsburgh history that she had memorized in honor of her Grandpa Bob.

"Pittsburgh had one of the first American breweries that produced a lager," she whispered. Her dry tongue tried to pass saliva to her lips, failing. She was terribly thirsty. Thinking about beer was not helping the situation. It seemed to Bethany that Pittsburgh's brewing scene would be far different today than the sip she had suffered through so long ago. For a beer expert, that sounded like an invitation. Perhaps a trip to Grandpa Bob's hometown would be next on her list.

Bethany jerked awake. Her senses were muddled but fighting towards full alert. She knew that sound. A pistol shot. In all her years as a cop, she had heard it far too many times. Maybe even suffered some hearing loss as a result. But what mattered now was that the person firing off the round had been ominously close. Or perhaps it was just the remnant of a dream, another drifting thought connecting somewhere to her past. Sleep was funny that way, especially after drinking too much.

What seemed eternal was only a few brief moments. Bethany knew why. She was suspended in light sleep, trapped in the soft glow of relaxation. What had her therapist told her? The one the court had ordered her to visit after she saw that young boy jump from a Buffalo rooftop? Something about theta waves being most active in the sacred space between sleep and wake. This was the brain activity that helped process information, connecting with creativity and intuition. They were the holding cell of memories, emotions, and sensations, and were strongest during times of internal focus. If she were honest with herself, she doubted she was internally focused now. Probably just still drunk.

A second gunshot barked. Bethany's eyes popped open. The fog of sleep was gone. She stared into blackness and remained rigid, not moving an inch, realizing now that the shooter was distinctively close. Then she heard a voice that was impossible not to place. Despite the fear and panic in his words, a certain chirpiness peeped from his vocal cords. It was Noah.

"No, Malachi!" he pleaded. "She has it all wrong! I am loyal. I swear to it!"

"She is never wrong," a male responded.

Bethany could only guess it was Malachi doing the talking, and that he was on the trigger side of the gun. She could hear in his inflection that he was moving as he spoke, like he had turned toward Noah and taken a couple steps in his direction.

"You heard her," Malachi said. "She explained everything in the car. This should come as no surprise."

"It was him! It was him!" Noah screeched, panicked. "He wanted to meet at the Oktoberfest. He was the one doubting that she is the true prophet. He wanted to plan a way out. I only went to learn his motives! To report back to you!"

"Then justice was served. He was the first to die."

"And Aaron can be the last, please!" Noah cried. "I beg of you!"

"You seem to forget," Malachi said, "that even listening to false claims is heresy. It is treason. Today we wipe the slate clean. Senator Young wanted to expand *his* power. He wanted to feed off her glory and make it *his*. Gain power and claim the role of prophet for *himself*. But believe in *her*? Not once. Never. He demeaned that she is a woman, incapable of the role that God has bestowed upon her. He ridiculed her behind closed doors. He chose disgusting moral conduct over the glory of marriage and the sacred powers of procreation. He was as broken as every false prophet that preceded him. And so, we ended that before it began, just as we are now removing the bad apples before they spoil the bunch."

"Malachi—"

A single gunshot rang out from several feet away, followed a few long moments by a second. Bethany flinched both times. She guessed that Malachi had put the first round into Noah's chest. And, likely next, Malachi had leveled his pistol for the center of the forehead and squeezed off the second round. A capable assassin, most certainly.

Near to her, Bethany heard a muffled shuffling sound and realized that Malachi was not alone. She held her breath, listening for a voice or a clue about this other person's identity, attempting to control the surge of adrenaline that made her want to take some kind of action. Grandpa Bob would want that now, wouldn't he? That she finally did something?

A few seconds later, Bethany heard more. Footsteps on dirt and rock. The unmistakable sound of a car door opening. The sensation and sound of a person climbing into the vehicle. The car door slamming shut. The jingle of keys and the engine starting. Her mind raced at what this deluge of information was telling her but refused to acknowledge the obvious answer.

"It is done," Malachi said, his voice morose but matter of fact.

Bethany stiffened when Amanda Lang responded.

"It needed to be done," Amanda said. "Remember that. Have faith. '*For the one who doubts is like a wave of the sea that is driven and tossed by the wind.*'"

Tentatively, Bethany raised a hand into the blackness. She extended it an inch. Then another. Slowly, she reached out with low hopes and high despair in her heart. At somewhere less than eight inches her hand touched cold metal. And then Bethany realized the truth. She was in the trunk of the car.

CHAPTER 18

ROAD NOISE

Bethany listened, expecting more conversation to erupt between Amanda and Malachi. They refused to cooperate. Silence permeated the vehicle, only interrupted by the idling engine that slowly heated the car. Trapped in the trunk, Bethany stretched her hands toward the seat back that she could not see, trying to grab some warmth for herself. She shivered briefly, touching her pants, then her shirt. She was not dressed for cold temperatures, especially the type that could sneak up in America's Mountain West. Bethany thought about winter back in Buffalo, and the way plunging temperatures and lake effect storms often caught the homeless off guard, gripping them in hypothermia. First came the cold, then the sensation of burning heat that would cause the victims to tear off their clothes in the last throes before death. Bethany had found far too many frozen corpses that way. It had always seemed like a lonely, ignominious death to her. She hoped not to join those ranks.

There was no real sense of time, just the odd sensation of the car humming against her body and the haunting question about what the murder of Aaron and Noah meant for her future. She thought back to the Utah Oktoberfest, to the interrogation in the hotel room, and then to the debacle at the Rock Pile House. As far as Bethany was concerned, it had been a random series of events. But had it? Even tipsy, it had not been lost on Bethany what Amanda had said when Noah and Aaron had found them standing outside that brewery in Park City. Something about Ivan having escaped the web. That the real prize was Bethany. What the hell did Amanda mean?

She thought about Amanda and Malachi sitting in silence together, perhaps meditating in prayer. Or maybe breaking Mormon rules and having a drink of whisky to calm their nerves. The thought lifted Bethany's mood and she sniffed the air, trying to discern the sweet aroma of distilled spirits through the smell of exhaust. Bethany appreciated her own effort but soon flagged. The exercise was senseless. Despite Amanda's drinking while on assignment in Munich, these were devout Mormons. They would not allow alcohol to cross their lips.

Bethany rubbed her hands together, generating some heat. She pressed her palms against her cheeks, then repeated the exercise several times. It was a trick her dad had taught her for deer hunting, a kind of last-ditch effort on the cold and miserable days when he wanted to stay in the woods longer than Bethany could tolerate.

"You can also put your hands down there," he had said, pointing, "in your crotch, between your thighs. They taught us that when I played football. Warmest place on the body, at least that's what they said, probably so we wouldn't feel stupid touching our balls with all those people in the stands."

Even in the trunk of a car, his suggestion seemed too uncouth. Bethany cupped her hands over her mouth instead, exhaling, collecting the warmth before moving her hands to her ears.

The car continued to idle, and the silence between Amanda and Malachi dragged for an eternity. Bethany's mind whirled, every possible idea flashing in her imagination, playing out the potential scenarios. This could go a lot of ways, the least desirable version being when they dragged Bethany out of the trunk, made her kneel on the ground, and put a bullet through the back of her head. Bethany shuddered at that thought, then shivered deeply against the dropping temperature that continued to burrow into her skin. A moment later, when Amanda cleared her throat and spoke, adrenaline pounded back into Bethany's veins, chasing away the chill.

"Amen," Amanda said, solemnly. "You've done your sacred duty. They were covenant breakers. This was blood atonement."

"As was Senator Young," Malachi said.

"Yes. He was an adulterer. Just as these two were apostates. They had all fallen into the snares of the evil one. We mustn't forget that. Our path will be challenging, and many will be culled along the way. There is never joy in that—in taking the life of another person. But when you remember that their souls have been not only soured but truly trapped by Satan—that they have fallen for the temptations of the evil one and now are representations of him—then the performance of this task will no longer be about killing people. It will be about vanquishing Satan from our ranks so that Zion may be achieved."

"Thank you," Malachi said. "Your teachings bring me comfort."

"We teach each other," Amanda said. "Your courage. Your loyalty. I see in you the model against which all must be compared. Yes, and before you say anything, I know everyone can't be the same. But we can uphold a certain ideal, can't we? Something toward which our people must strive?"

"As you speak...I see in my mind...Angel Moroni," Malachi said, thoughtfully choosing his words.

"Yes, precisely! We're reminded to strive toward heaven when we see his statue! On Hill Cumorah. On our places of worship. He is our beacon to God's grace. Here in our earthly realm, where lives are so fleeting, but time is often eternal, people lose sight in the moment. They forget how to be obedient, godly humans. They fall into Satan's trap. They become like Senator Young. Or like the two out there. They want pleasure or, perhaps, glory for themselves. They have no sense of the wondrous thing that resides in you, in each of us, and propels us toward what God has promised."

Bethany heard a long, deep sigh followed by the drumming of fingers. It was a resonant sound, most likely Malachi's hands upon the top of the steering wheel. There was little doubt to her that Malachi was struggling with the emotions of the moment. She found some solace thinking that. Perhaps he did not have the stomach for so much killing. Maybe he would ask Amanda for a reprieve, even be so bold as to tell her that there was no reason to end Bethany's life. Or, Bethany feared, Malachi's finger drumming would end with sudden resolve, with his hands striking the steering wheel and the car door re-opening, and then Malachi yanking her from the trunk.

"Has she moved at all?" he asked, with a sudden change of subject.

Amanda laughed lightly. "No, nothing. Beer expert notwithstanding, she failed to understand the effects of altitude on her body. I daresay she was warned, but she's committed to her new career. Get her started and it is rather impossible to have her stop. I certainly admire her aspirations. There is much to explore now, beer-wise, in this country. And it wasn't always that way. It used to be that Europe was the only place to go for good beer. She and I met in Munich, but of course you know that already. She had other choices—England and Belgium, for example—but she wanted to try Munich's Oktoberfest and other Bavarian beers. Serendipity, don't you think, that we would meet in such a way?"

"She's in the trunk," Malachi said. "Do you think she would find meeting you to be serendipitous?"

"I mean the full arc of the story, Malachi!" Amanda exclaimed. "I've already given you one portion of it—we are surrounded by darkness and evil, like being inside a cave. The apostates like the ones you vanquished today—they are the air inside that cave. And once you understand that, once you realize the treacherous work we are undertaking, you will see that we need a canary in the coal mine."

"A canary in the coal mine?" Malachi asked.

"Are you not familiar with this phrase?" Amanda asked.

"I am not," Malachi said.

"Young people today," Amanda said, slightly exasperated. "Knowledgeable about so many things, yet ignorant at the same time. The phrase is an allusion to the caged birds that miners would take with them into mines. If the gases got bad—carbon monoxide and the like—it would kill the canary first. It was an early warning system to tell the miners to get out immediately. Speaking of that, start driving."

Bethany heard Malachi pull the gear lever into drive. A moment later the car eased forward, the wheels crunching on the dirt and gravel. Bethany's body swayed in the trunk as the vehicle bounced through light potholes, over larger rocks, and across a wide ditch. She did her best to remain relaxed despite her head bouncing several times against the trunk's interior. An unconscious, near lifeless body, Bethany figured, would have a distinctive sound to the driver and his passenger.

After several minutes they were on the pavement. Malachi accelerated, now putting distance between themselves and their latest victims. "As I was saying," Amanda began, "we need to be vigilant for the poisoned air. The apostates, do you understand? And so, we need the canary to keep us safe."

"The one in the trunk?"

"Precisely! I'll let you think about that for a while. I know how better you do when you have time to process things. Just keep on driving. Interstate 80 is, what, at least 30 minutes from here? My, how the Utah desert just goes forever, doesn't it? A good place for bodies never to be found, but so desolate for the living. I wonder sometimes if our people were ever happy to call it home. I do doubt it, you know. Just a temporary step to survive and thrive until we could finally return to our kingdom. To claim what was ours from the beginning. I'll close my eyes now and rest. Just take 80 to Rock Springs. You'll leave me there to continue my journey east."

"And her?" Malachi asked.

"The canary? You mean Bethany? She's in her cage now, isn't she? I wonder what that will tell us."

"Certainly, her fortitude to survive," Malachi said. "But then what?"

"Then," Amanda said, and before Bethany could hear another word, the cabin filled with music. One of them had turned on the radio, drowning out their voices. Bethany strained to hear, eager to learn the fate that awaited her. One song changed to the next, and occasionally the station would fade or crackle, and Malachi, presumably, would switch to a stronger signal. After what felt like thirty minutes, Bethany felt the car rising slightly and accelerating further. By her guess it was a highway on-ramp, verified as their speed picked up even more and they were soon going fast, far faster than the first leg of this journey, likely heading toward the destination that Amanda had plotted for herself, and then to Bethany's unknown conclusion. She fought to stay alert and focused, but the monotonous hum of the car's tires soon crept behind her eyes, reminding Bethany that she was still sluggish from sampling far too many beers. Sleeping really would not matter at this time, she decided. Maybe just a little bit of rest would sharpen her mind and prepare her for what was to come.

*

Bethany had learned to hate long distance drives. She blamed her ex-husband for that. He had always behaved as though driving from one side of Buffalo to the other was like making the three-hour journey to Cleveland, or equivalent to the 150-mile trip down the Thruway to Syracuse.

"Jesus," Bethany had found herself snapping at him throughout their failed marriage, "what else are we going to do with our time? Wouldn't it be nice to visit another city? Maybe even cross the Peace Bridge for once and go to Toronto?"

But her ex-husband had been against it, adamantly preferring provincial myopia to expanding his cultural horizons. Her married life had been relegated to a job she hated during the week, and to weekends spent investing her heart and soul into one failed Buffalo Bills football season after another.

"Sundays are about football," her ex-husband liked to say. "Not church." And throughout their marriage Bethany had stuffed her Sundays full with one-dollar pints of mass-produced American lager, overcooked chicken wings, and sports on TV. The kind of things her ex-husband loved.

Until one day it all ended.

Bethany did not regret walking out on him. Not once. The bastard had deserved the end of their relationship. Had it really been a relationship, anyway? No, not at all. Not after he had stopped worrying about her at work and started spending most of her paycheck on the beer that kept him at his favorite Cheektowaga watering hole all day long and most of each night.

And certainly not after the remainder of those paychecks had gone into stockpiling more cheap beer in the used refrigerators that he kept buying at neighborhood garage sales. Bethany had counted six full-sized fridges in the garage on the day she had finally called it quits, each packed with mass-produced American and Canadian beers.

She remembered her own long nights, though, when she had helped cut through that inventory, sitting with her head propped against her right hand, rubbing the bridge of her nose with her middle finger, wondering exactly what the fuck she had gotten herself into. The beers her ex-husband had preferred were not to her preference but, to be honest, she was never the type of beer snob to call them garbage, even to this day. She appreciated American Lagers for what they were. Now, especially as a beer expert, she understood their purpose and place in history.

But before she had learned the intricacies of beer and brewing, before she had embarked on the path to becoming a certified beer expert, she had always confessed that too many of her ex-husband's beers gave her a raging hangover that went far beyond the typical *I drank too much* complaint the following morning. No, those hangovers had been of an epic proportion, her body polluted, pain raging through her skull, begging Bethany to pop acetaminophen and suck down caffeine. That had been about the only medicinal combination that slogged her through those morning-after days.

And then everything changed with her discovery of America's craft beers. She had been a reluctant student at first, only wanting to separate from the repetition of her life's daily grind. *Could drinking beer become a profession?* It was a question that had come to her mind one night, out of the blue, when her ex-husband was already snoring, unconscious in his puke-colored, upholstered recliner. She had been sitting at the kitchen table, staring at the label of some locally brewed beer she had never heard of before, contemplating the first sip.

And then she had tipped the bottle against her lips, relishing the texture and bite of the carbonation, followed by the opening of malt complexity, and ending with crisp hop dryness that made her crave the next taste. The beer was not great, but it sure was good. And it had become the first step toward becoming the beer expert she was today. Just thinking about that moment made being locked in a car trunk all the worse.

Bethany snapped her mind to the present. She had slept much of the trip, perhaps woozy from remnant alcohol and carbon monoxide mixing in her veins. She could tell from her stiff limbs that this had been an agonizingly long car ride, and a cold one at that. She had slid once into wakefulness when they stopped—presumably in Rock Springs—and Bethany had listened to some quick words of farewell from Amanda to Malachi.

"Do as I instructed," Amanda had said. "No deviation. You understand?"

Malachi had said nothing in response, leaving Bethany to wonder if he had signaled compliance with some type of nodding of the head. And, if he had, whether his compliance meant a favorable outcome for her.

They had stopped for five minutes at most. Probably far less. Time had become amorphous in the dark trunk, with moments blending into moments, each punctuated by some sound or sensation that had no connection to her visual sense. However long they had been parked, they were back on the road soon enough and speeding in some unknown direction. Malachi had turned the music up louder. Bethany presumed he was alone, feeling freer without Amanda riding shotgun. Even more likely, he was probably unconcerned whether his trunk-bound passenger had awakened from her drunken slumber and approved of his music selection.

The trip, Bethany soon learned, was about to become much longer.

CHAPTER 19

BUFFALOED

Bethany could not figure it out. She knew it had been hours since Amanda had exited the car, not because she had any sense of time in the darkness of the car's trunk, but because she was practically dying of thirst. And, on top of that, she needed to take a leak. Bad.

Training her bladder to hold massive volumes of urine had been a trick Bethany had mastered even before becoming a beer expert. She had needed it as a cop while cruising nights through the nastiest parts of Buffalo, and even more while drinking down the brews her husband had stocked in the garage refrigerators. There was no pride in dropping her trousers to tinkle every time the urge struck. No, it had only incurred ridicule.

"Look at the little girl needing to pee again," her husband would say.

After a while, when her husband had decided he needed to become a bigger asshole, he had implemented a hall pass system. The rule was simple. Bethany had to ask for the pass before he would let her scurry off to the bathroom. She hated it and him for it. But, looking back on the whole thing, she had to admit that the practice had helped. Now she could tolerate the discomfort, hold back the little trickles that wanted to leak from her urethra, and just focus on drinking more beer. Or, as was the case today, just focus on surviving.

There had been many twists and turns on this endless highway, plus a quick stop for gas along the way at a station where, it seemed, little other traffic stopped to refuel. Bethany had remained silent while Malachi unscrewed the gas cap, inserted the nozzle, and started the pump, half expecting him to strike up some strange sort of one-sided conversation with his hidden passenger. Maybe words of warning or an indication of what was to come. Even better, concern for her well-being. But he gave her nothing. Malachi had just whistled as the gasoline flowed into the tank beneath her, acting as though his day was no different than any other patron at the pump.

Unfortunately for Bethany, she knew that was not exactly the case.

They were back on the road quickly. With so many miles behind them and her occasional bumping around inside the trunk, Bethany guessed that Malachi knew she was awake, and she took it as purposeful when he drove straight through a pothole as they left the gas station parking lot. Bethany's body slammed up and down with the impact. She whimpered lightly in pain but did not complain, hoping he would smooth out the ride a little. Her body could use the respite. But he showed little regard for her well-being, barely touching the brakes on the tightest of turns, seemingly relishing the sound of her head striking against metal.

Bethany cursed her dependence on GPS, knowing that if she had just studied a map before leaving Buffalo for this trip, she might be able to guess where they were at that very moment. Or at least be able to create a few possibilities using the cardinal points, beginning with Rock Springs, where Amanda had exited the vehicle.

If Rock Springs had been the actual location, Bethany reminded herself. There was no reason to trust what Amanda had said to Malachi. It may have been the truth, or it might have been some kind of code.

Either way, it didn't matter. All these ponderings were just ideas to tumble around inside her mind, something to toy with and fantasize about. They were nothing more than a way to pass what was becoming an endless, frigid grind.

I'll never again own a car with a trunk, Bethany thought. And, as if on cue, another voice inside her head reminded her of the obvious.

If you ever own a car again.

Bethany pushed away the ominous foreboding, focusing instead on the fact that the car had started gaining elevation, and then continued, and then continued some more. Her body slid slowly to the rear of the trunk, gravity pushing her against the cold metal that seemed to chill another several degrees in the thinning air. She could hear the engine straining a bit and felt the tight curves of the road. They were sharp enough to force Malachi to brake, mercifully, to avoid driving off the road.

There was an odd familiarity to the way this all felt, a harkening back to a dream or a blur or a drunken haze that Bethany had experienced somewhere in her life's pathway. She felt embraced in the methodical sway, back and forth, as if rocking in her mother's arms. But it was nothing of the sort. The sad truth was that Malachi was simply using highway switchbacks to his advantage so that he could gain elevation. Bethany knew that, at the top of the rise, the cradle would finally stop.

Is that my end of the road?

No sooner had she thought that, fearing the worst, when suddenly the engine ceased its incessant straining. There was a bend in the road to the right, and then they were descending. Malachi let the car run wide open, barely touching the brakes, appearing to relish the Law of Gravity. He raced around all the curves that followed, Bethany's body paying the price, but her mind barely cared. She felt as if she had driven this road before. It all seemed so familiar.

Bethany reached into the fog that was her past. There was little against which she could compare this driving adventure, and that had nothing to do with being stuffed inside a trunk. She could think of four occasions in her life when she had driven up or down mountain roads. The first had been somewhere in the outskirts of Munich. Her head was covered with a sack during that misadventure. The second had been driving with Heather to and from Table Mountain, crossing over Teton Pass each time. The third had been driving up to visit the Utah Oktoberfest. And the last one was on the way down from the beer festival to watch a man get murdered.

Eliminating the first experience from her limited choices was easy. There was no way Malachi had magically transported her to the Alps. As for the Utah Oktoberfest, yes. That was a possibility. She did not have the map in her mind but, undoubtedly, they could have dropped Amanda in Rock Springs —*wherever the fuck that was*—and returned post haste to Salt Lake City. Then it was just a quick drive up that canyon, whatever it was called, to where they had held the beer festival.

Maybe he's helping me retrieve my rental car.

She laughed silently at the preposterous thought and felt a pang of worry at the same moment. If she survived this ordeal, there would be hell to pay explaining this to the car rental company.

Hi, yes, my name is Bethany Judge. Umm...I rented a car in Jackson, Wyoming and drove it to Salt Lake City. No, no, not to go skiing. They had an Oktoberfest celebration going on. What's that? Yes, they drink beer in Utah. And it's pretty good beer, at that. Stronger than you think...the altitude will get you; I can promise you that. Ha! Anyway, I got kidnapped and...yes, I said kidnapped. Listen, as far as I know, the car is still in Salt Lake somewhere. What do we need to do to square this all away?

Malachi rounded another turn, this time a little too fast, forcing him to quickly hit the brakes. Bethany lurched forward under the force. She thumped her head against the trunk's interior, stars illuminating behind her eyes. Pain seared down her neck and into her cramped limbs. She forced it away, still thinking through the possibilities of where Malachi was taking her.

The Utah Oktoberfest was in a canyon, that was the thing. Up to the mountain. And then back down. A single road. Nothing you would drive up and over. Nothing with a bunch of switchbacks. She couldn't say for sure, but she vaguely remembered zooming out the GPS map and noting the canyon road extended a bit beyond where the beer festival was held and dead-ended by some ski area. *What had it been called?* Bethany rolled possibilities through her mind, guessing the detail might matter, but surrendered the effort after a long minute. There were so many ski resorts in the Salt Lake City area, it was hard to tell one from the other.

But, if she were correct, an up-and-back canyon drive would not feel like the trip she was taking right now.

Bethany whistled quietly between her teeth, confident this felt more like the drive over Teton Pass. The one she took with Heather.

Admittedly, Bethany guessed that there were plenty of other road choices and mountain passes sprinkled across the Rocky Mountains. And that any of those highways and byways might bear similarities to those she had traveled. But there was just something so familiar about the way the car moved, something that was connected to the beers she had consumed at that brewery in Jackson Hole the first night with Heather. It all rose to the surface now, like the hint of hop aroma in a perfect Pilsner.

The twisting and turning highway finally straightened. The engine surged under the enthusiasm of sudden acceleration. Bethany took a moment to rub the back of her head. Fortunately, there was no lump from the multiple times she had smacked it against the car's cold metal. She exhaled a sigh of relief knowing that, were it not for the trunk's cold darkness, she could have seen her breath.

Several more minutes passed before they again slowed, turning right off the highway. They drove a short distance, turned left, and then quickly left again. And then they stopped.

Malachi killed the engine. Bethany's heart raced at the sound of the driver's door opening, then closing, and then footsteps making their way to the rear of the car.

"We're here," Malachi said. "Are you awake?"

"Yes," Bethany responded, her voice both scratchy and feeble. She hated knowing that she was coming across as weak and defeated but could not really blame herself. From whatever moment they had placed her in this trunk, Bethany had not had a single drop to drink. Not water. And especially not a beer. Yes, even just one brew would have taken some of the edge off the tension and helped shave away the final edge of her still-lingering hangover.

"I'm going to open the trunk now," Malachi said. "You aren't going to do anything stupid, understand? No screaming. No fighting. No running. Just climb out and keep it cool."

"Okay," Bethany croaked, almost wanting to laugh as the sound broke from her throat. She doubted there was any strength in her body to resist. And, if she tried, she would move with the speed and dexterity of a tin man.

The trunk popped open. Instinctively Bethany squinted, expecting sunshine to pierce her dilated pupils. Instead, she was greeted with more darkness. The night was clear and bitterly cold. Stars filled the sky overhead. Her mind fought for orientation, not understanding how she had failed to realize the day had faded away to evening. Sunlight had squeezed its way into the trunk during the drive, albeit barely, but Bethany had not taken much solace from it, nor noted its absence. Her brain, she decided, had been focused on other ways to survive this mess.

"Come on, get out," Malachi said. "Be quick about it."

Bethany unwound her cramped body. Sitting up was painful. Her lower back screamed at the movement. Her hamstrings resisted Bethany's request to straighten. She debated asking Malachi for a helping hand but decided against it. She did not want any assistance from this asshole, despite whatever discomfort she was feeling now.

Bethany's feet felt good on solid ground. This place seemed oddly familiar and, looking about, she realized they were not alone. Several cars were parked nearby. A sound of laughter rose in the darkness, followed by some loud voices. Bethany bristled at first, clenching her fists in fear of Malachi's reinforcements, but another round of laughter erupted. And then some more. She turned to face a well-lit building. The noise was coming from inside.

"Recognize where we are?" Malachi asked.

The towering grain silo beside the building told Bethany one thing—they were at a brewery. Saliva surfaced in Bethany's mouth. Maybe Malachi was kind, or maybe this was another form of torture. One way or another, he had caught Bethany's attention.

"Inside, let's go," Malachi said.

The building's warmth was a godsend. Bethany's skin prickled as her circulation improved. She knew she looked like shit but, looking around the place, realized she was in good company. The other patrons wore frumpy, seasonally appropriate outdoor clothes. Most looked like they hadn't showered in a day or ten. Even better, nobody gave Bethany a second glance.

Except for one person that was waving at them from the corner, a smile lighting her face. Bethany looked across the bar, holding the stare until it eclipsed the moment of curiosity and switched to rudeness. The face was familiar, but the whole situation was surreal. She was slow to put the dots together. And then, suddenly, the light bulb clicked on.

"Heather?" she whispered.

Malachi grabbed Bethany's elbow and walked her across the room. As they approached, Heather held up her half-full beer glass and gestured to the bartender, indicating two more of the same.

"Welcome back to Victor, Idaho!" Heather exclaimed. "I thought you might enjoy a friendlier environment."

"H..Heather?" Bethany stammered. "What the fuck?" She fought for comprehension, her memories traveling back to the day she arrived in Jackson Hole, to all those beers that first night, to the hike to Table Mountain, to the beers she had enjoyed at this brewery. Salt Lake City and the Utah Oktoberfest happened because of Heather's recommendations, and now they were back here, sharing a table with Malachi. None of it made any sense.

The bartender placed two full pints of beer on the table. Judging from the color, Bethany guessed they were the same Brown Ale as last time and was grateful for the selection. At least Heather had been enough of a friend to take note of the beers Bethany enjoyed most from her previous visit. Of course, under the circumstances, a stronger beer sounded even better. Bethany glanced toward the bar, wondering if the Imperial Stout was still on tap.

"Cheers," Heather said, raising her glass. "To your success."

Bethany realized that Malachi had a glass in hand, also raised. She pressed her palm against her own cold glass, slowly allowing her fingers to curl around, securing her grip. "Cheers," she said, the word coming out equal part statement, equal part question.

They all took a drink. Bethany swallowed a slow sip, allowing the rich flavors to cascade across her palate. She eyeballed Heather, who succeeded with a tepid effort of taking the glass from half-full to half-empty. Malachi, on the other hand, drained a good portion of his glass with three hearty swallows, followed by a stifled belch. Encouraged, Bethany returned to her beer for a deeper influx of the energy and alcohol she needed coursing through her veins right now.

"Ok, to start," Heather said. "That's your car out there. Your rental car. Just to set your mind at ease about that in case you were worried."

"My rental car, what?"

"I retrieved it from the Oktoberfest," Malachi said. "Heather thought it best."

"It would be messy, you understand," Heather said. "You'd have to make some phone calls to resolve the issue. Maybe start explaining a crazy story. Maybe attract some attention to everything that has happened. I wanted to keep it clean. Get you back home with no loose ends."

Bethany took a longer drink this time, holding up her left hand and extending her index finger. She watched Heather look at the bartender and nod, signaling a full round. Bethany drained her glass.

"Don't be troubled by the whole thing," Heather said. "There's no way you could have known any of it. Prepared for it. You should be honored, really. Mormons go on mission trips to spread the word of God and seek converts. But we are seldom successful. It is more about building the character of our missionaries, more about shaping the future leaders of our people. But for Amanda to devote so many resources to you, she must feel strongly about your prospects."

"Prospects?" Bethany asked, turning to take her beer directly from the bartender's hand. He placed the other two on the table in front of her.

"Cheers again," Heather said, smiling. They all drank in unison.

"Look," Bethany said. "Okay, I'm confused. None of this makes any sense. I mean, what the fuck? You just referred to yourself as a Mormon. And I know he is. It's Malachi, right? And yet you're sitting here pounding beers with me?"

"Did I already tell you that joke?" Heather said. "You know the one? Mormons came to Idaho because God can't see over the Tetons. We take some liberties in this part of Deseret, I'm sure you understand. There's an implied understanding among the faithful."

"Deseret?" Bethany asked. "You mean the Mormon state? The one that Brigham Young tried to create?

Heather beamed from across the table, raising her beer glass with enthusiastic acknowledgment. "Ah, you have learned some things, haven't you! Now I understand what Amanda sees in you. You're far less the neophyte than when we first met."

"I'm not so sure I've had much of a choice," Bethany said. "I've been getting a history lesson from a firehose this entire trip."

"It's the essence of education, isn't it? Ten thousand hours at anything and you become an expert! Like your love of beer. Have you put that much time into your expertise?"

Bethany paused before drinking, remembering the endless hours after work and on weekends, spent either at dingy Buffalo bars or raiding her ex-husband's beer-filled refrigerators. Did those years and beers count toward becoming an expert? She supposed so but decided on the spot to hold herself to higher standards.

"Theoretically no," she said, finding a way to hedge her words. "But there is no other test that compares to what is required to become a certified beer expert. My success completing that program underscores my potential, but I'm still a work in progress. That's why I travel. That's why I grab a beer at every brewery I find. I'll pick up those ten thousand hours before too long."

Amanda pulled out her phone and opened her calculator. "Let's think about this for a second. You can probably drink two beers in an hour, right? Pretty easily? So, that's twenty thousand beers to get to your ten thousand hours. At an average of sixteen ounces per beer, that's three hundred twenty thousand ounces of beer. How many ounces are in a gallon?"

"One hundred twenty-eight," Bethany said.

"That's two thousand five hundred gallons of beer," Heather said, shaking her head.

Bethany nodded in agreement. She hadn't thought about it like that. "There are thirty-one gallons in a barrel," she said. "A full-sized keg, like the kind you see in bars, is fifteen-and-a-half gallons. So, there are two of those in one barrel."

"Let's see if I can do the math right," Heather said, again punching numbers into her calculator. "Two thousand five hundred gallons of beer divided by thirty-one gallons in a barrel means that by the time you have hit ten thousand hours you will have consumed something close to eighty barrels of beer. Is that right?" She looked over at Malachi, beaming. "Being an apostate is starting to sound like fun, isn't it?"

Malachi eyed his near-empty glass. "Enjoyable, but it muddles the mind. And if you are always drinking, eventually you become dependent on the stuff."

"We're all dependent on something," Bethany said, finishing her second glass and reaching for her third. "Marriage. A job. Religion. This is just another alternative."

"Chemical dependency," Malachi said. "That's a far different thing."

With those somber words, Heather pushed her beer glass aside. She fixed her eyes on Bethany, a shadow of pity falling across her face. She simply stared for several long moments, as if contemplating the image of the person across from her. Bethany wanted to believe Heather was seeing a priceless piece of art, but knew the opposite was true. Gross and disheveled from the long ride in the car's trunk, and now with some beer down her gullet, Bethany knew she probably looked more like the unfortunate homeless. Heather finally spoke again, her tone stern.

"Drink all you want, Bethany. And please, have no worries. Malachi will take care of you. Your flight home is tomorrow. We have arranged all of that for you. When you have had your fill, Malachi will take you back across the pass into Jackson Hole. You can sleep it off in the car and find a place to get cleaned up in the morning. Your flight to Buffalo leaves just after noon."

"You got me a flight home?" Bethany asked.

Heather smiled. "Amanda insisted. She said that you should wait for further instructions. That you would know what that means."

"Further instructions?"

Heather merely shrugged. "Or perhaps you don't. Maybe that is part of the mystery. A continuation of the intrigue." She paused, tapping her middle finger on the table. "It started with that; did you know? Just a light tapping on his door at first. I was nervous, you understand? I didn't want to draw any attention from down the hallway. I finally had to knock, of course, and he eventually did answer."

Bethany's mind swam through the sudden shift in the story line, trying to align her thinking with Heather's words. "Knocking? I don't—"

"Please don't act naive," Heather said, interrupting. "It was the genesis of this whole thing. The reason you came to Jackson Hole. She knew you would. I don't know how Amanda would have known, but she did. She might have guessed a high-profile death in the heart of Mormon country would catch your attention. And so, when Senator Young gave the order, I did the work assigned to me. And after that, she told me what you looked like. I didn't understand at the time, but it was a near perfect description, her memory of you was so keen. She said with certainty that your devotion to beer would land you at that brewery. Lo and behold, exactly as she prophesied, there you were."

"And here we are today," Bethany said. As soon as the words emptied from her mouth, she filled the space with more beer. She swallowed hard, tasting the hop bitterness more than anything else.

"I worried that I said too much the first time we met," Heather said, leaning forward across the table. "The beer made my tongue loose. I feared you had discerned my allegiances. But God chose to muddy your understanding. He wanted you to experience what Amanda had in store for you. And you're right. Here we are today. By tomorrow night, you'll be safely home in Buffalo. Be patient. I know it will be difficult, but just wait. She will provide instructions in the manner she chooses."

"But what about the others?" Bethany asked. "Will and Genevieve, I mean. Were they part of this, too? Did they know what you were up to?"

Heather smiled. "I've known Genevieve and Will for so many years. That is true. They are good friends of mine. But they know nothing of my true convictions, of the things to which I have committed myself. Still, a person never knows when pawns may be needed in a game of chess. It is useful to have some always on the table, as was the case when you came to town. They were easy and believable fluff to get you where we needed to be. Not here, I mean, but down in Utah instead. They are a lovely couple, I must say that, and your story certainly re-ignited their tireless passion to solve this mystery. Even now they are somewhere in the backcountry, hiking and overnighting, trying to answer the questions you brought to their minds."

Bethany said nothing more. She raised her right hand, index finger extended, and waited for the bartender to bring the next beer. And the next. And the next, until the barroom faded to blackness.

CHAPTER 20

SPICY FINISH

Winters in Buffalo are long and brutal. From January through March, daytime temperatures average in the low thirties. Steel gray skies rule the heavens for the better part of six months. Lake effect snow blows off Lake Erie, piling up by the foot throughout the region, sometimes coming in so heavily that house roofs risk collapse. For homeowners, there are two winter rules—rake your roof clear of snow and prevent ice dams in your gutters. Bethany knew she should be working on those two projects today, but drinking beer sounded like a better idea.

Everything in Buffalo is twenty minutes away was Bethany's famous line. Today might be different. She had hopped in her car and driven to the city of North Tonawanda, ignoring the fresh snow that was clogging the roadways. The city's snowplows were out in force and were doing an admirable job, but the snow was coming down too fast to keep up. She would be tipsy on the way home and the roads would be in bad shape. Bethany figured that drive might take a bit longer than twenty minutes but did not care.

Bethany took a seat at the bar of one of North Tonawanda's popular brewpubs, her mind swirling around the history of a famous building she had passed along the way—the old Wurlitzer Building, a beautiful and historic facility that began its existence as the North Tonawanda Barrel Organ Factory. At its peak, it was the largest maker of musical instruments in the world, and after World War Two had a stint producing radios, electronic organs, and jukeboxes. But fortunes faded and, like so many other industries in Buffalo, the Wurlitzer plant eventually closed.

Bethany pulled out her phone and typed in an image search that produced an array of historical photographs from the heyday of the Wurlitzer Company. She found herself pondering what it must have been like to work in that place at the height of its success. The black-and-white images captured a certain essence of the manual labor required for the job, but what did the people who lived back then think at the time? Did they wish for something more? Something less demanding on their bodies and their souls? Or were they satisfied with the opportunities afforded to them? Was it enough just to provide for their families and survive through the relentless Buffalo winters, like Bethany was attempting to accomplish today?

If this were a warm and sunny summer day, Bethany knew she would have been sipping on one of the brewpub's lightest beers. Something at around five percent alcohol by volume, and hopefully a beer she would consider to be an acceptable version of an American Light Lager. Bready and approachable came to Bethany's mind, with an easy spiciness of hops that slipped through to the palate. Two or maybe three pints would be a great way to get the day started, then grab a four-pack of cans, find a friend with a boat, and get out on Lake Erie.

But this wasn't a summer day. And it was far from a day she planned to enjoy. No, Buffalo was in the deepest throes of a winter storm, several more inches of snow were still expected to come down, and Bethany had some thinking to do.

"I'll take your Christmas Ale," she said when the bartender approached.

She pulled a postcard from her coat pocket and turned it over in her hand, first studying the image on the front side, then flipping it over to read the handwritten text on the back.

"Lovely seeing you again, Beer Judge," it read. "You came so far, I'm sure you have many questions! There is much more to learn, and plenty of beer for the journey. Interested? I look forward to your visit in the summer! Amanda."

The handwriting was most certainly Amanda Lang's. Bethany had compared that to the previous postcard Amanda had sent, the one she had received after returning from Munich showing the image of the Mormon Tabernacle Church in Salt Lake City. It had been the catalyst of so many things. Lives lost. Stories shared. Beers sampled.

Yes, lots of beers sampled.

The bartender placed the pint of Christmas Ale in front of her. Bethany set the postcard down, staring intently at the image, wondering what the hell Amanda was telegraphing to her. Was there a reason behind using the postal service? A logic to the picture postcards? A bigger message behind just the words Amanda had written? Bethany lifted the pint, shifting her focus to the beer. She loved this beer. It was a perfect reflection of the style, and even more exemplary because it was brewed in the Buffalo region. The chestnut color made the words from a famous holiday song drift through her mind.

Chestnuts roasting on an open fire...

Bethany took the cue from the lyrics, raised the glass, and allowed the aroma of cinnamon, ginger, nutmeg, and allspice to alert her olfactory system to the party that was about to begin. She reminded herself that, at 7.2 percent alcohol by volume, this

Christmas Ale would pack a punch. She took a delicate sip before setting the glass back on the bar.

"What are you up to, Amanda?" Bethany whispered under her breath. "What's your fascination with me?"

She thought again about the Wurlitzer building, once more looking down at her phone to take in the photos her search had discovered. Normally when out sampling locally brewed beers she would sit, fascinated by the brewhouse and the fermenters, working through tastings as she pondered the brewer's particular skills and techniques. That might still happen in the next several minutes, she guessed, but right now she felt drawn to reveling in Buffalo's history. Those people in the pictures. They had been the backbone to the greatness of the Queen City, as Buffalo had been nicknamed, having earned the moniker for being the largest city on the Great Lakes. Did anyone today even know that Buffalo had once been the nation's second largest port after New York City? Was anyone aware that the Erie Canal used to pass through North Tonawanda, carving a route to Lake Erie? Did anyone care that the demise of the Erie Canal had also signaled the beginning of Buffalo's decline?

Bethany again lifted the glass of Christmas Ale, this time being less shy about the amount of beer she allowed across her lips. She lamented the lost stories of the people in those photographs, sensing the oft-spoken truth that history is written by the victors. The winning cities today were scattered to different corners of the United States. East Coast. Florida. Texas. California. But certainly not Buffalo.

"Why would anyone even move to Buffalo these days?" Bethany said aloud, the question redundant. The bartender glanced her way, grinning. He pointed out the window.

"The beautiful weather," he said. "Oh, and of course the low taxes."

"Yeah, right," Bethany said, stifling a laugh. She decided the Christmas Ale was too good to sip and that nursing it was not going to unravel the mystery of Amanda's postcard. Maybe, in fact, the opposite effort would produce better results. She drained the glass with expert precision, not allowing a drop of beer to slip from the corners of her mouth. She motioned to the bartender for a refill.

Aside from Bethany, the bar and restaurant were empty. She shrugged her shoulders, not giving a damn. *Who the hell besides a beer expert would venture out in a storm like this?* The bartender poured the beer quickly and served it with a friendly smile.

"I'm sure you're thirsty," he said. "Probably spent the morning shoveling snow, right? Just be careful. Too much beer and driving in this kind of weather doesn't make a good combination."

Bethany heard the words but refused to acknowledge them. She turned the postcard one-hundred-eighty degrees to face the bartender and tapped the image with her left index finger.

"Do you recognize this?"

The bartender leaned toward the postcard, clicking his tongue between his teeth. "Not at all," he said, shaking his head. "It's an island? Looks nice, but pretty desolate."

Bethany turned the photo back around and took another long look, then lifted the postcard and flipped it over. "It says here that the island is called Beaver Island," she said. "It's on Lake Michigan, apparently."

"Hmmm, never heard of it," the bartender said. "I went to Put-in-Bay in Ohio with my friends for our high school graduation party. That's on South Bass Island in Lake Erie. Heard of it? Over near Sandusky and Toledo. Lots of great drinking on that trip. And plenty of fun with our girlfriends."

Bethany rolled her eyes, not wanting to imagine the sort of relationships her bartender had enjoyed at the ripe age of eighteen. Drinking adventures? Sure, she could get behind that. But teenage sex stories were not her thing. She had seen far too many bad versions of how that played out on the streets of Buffalo.

"Why the hell would Amanda send me this?" she asked, rhetorically. The bartender reached over anyway and took the postcard, this time reading what was written on the back.

"My mom studied in Europe when she was in college," he said. "She tells stories about how she would just send random postcards to her parents and friends. Pictures that had nothing to do with where she was, or what she was doing. And then she'd write some sort of nonsense on the back. I guess it was her way of having a laugh at their expense."

"I appreciate the thought," Bethany said, "but I know the person who wrote this. I don't think there's much of a chuckle factor going on here."

"Just a thought," the bartender said. "Tell you what, when I don't have the answer for something, I usually find that I can discover it with a little quiet contemplation over a glass of beer. Or two. Maybe even three."

"You said to be careful," Bethany said.

"And you should. The snow will keep coming. And then Buffalo will dig out. The city will return to normal and then the cycle will start again. Maybe you should do the same."

Bethany stared into her glass of Christmas Ale. The spicy scents of the holidays teased her nose, almost making her wish she were a child again, dressed in ill-fitted ski bibs, heavy boots, crappy gloves, a thick hat, and a down jacket. She could be rolling snowballs for a fight with friends, or pushing those balls of snow over and over, collecting more snow until they formed into the base of the body or the head of a perfect Buffalo snowman. And sometime later she would watch it melt, and she might cry, hoping for another snowstorm so that she might start the process all over again.

Bethany lifted the postcard once more and looked at the picture, this time letting her focus drift somewhere into the depths of the image. She spoke quietly, under her breath, saying, “Is that what this is, Amanda? The next snowstorm? Yes, I think it is. I really do. And you know I’ll come running, don’t you? An eager playmate. Beaver Island? What breweries can I visit on my way over there?”

Made in the USA
Monee, IL
16 July 2022